SEARCH AND DESTROY

A TOM ROLLINS THRILLER

PAUL HEATLEY

INKUBATOR
BOOKS

Published by Inkubator Books
www.inkubatorbooks.com

Copyright © 2023 by Paul Heatley

Paul Heatley has asserted his right to be identified as the author of this work.

ISBN (eBook): 978-1-83756-257-2
ISBN (Paperback): 978-1-83756-258-9

For Aidan

PROLOGUE

J orge Cruz sits in the back middle seat of the jeep, surrounded by men. *His* men, for now. *His* men, for the last few years. Perhaps not for much longer.

These men, truly, belong to Oscar Zavala. Oscar, however, is locked up. When he was free, Jorge was his right-hand man. In Oscar's absence, Jorge has been the caretaker of his organization.

The caretaker of his army.

There's another jeep ahead of them, and another behind. Both are filled with heavily armed men. They drive through Gracias a Dios, and while they are currently in a truce with the Colón Cartel, that doesn't mean they're to be trusted. Jorge is sure that if they think they can take a shot at him, they'll take it.

Jorge never intended to be the leader. This position fell upon him. He's always thought of himself as a follower, an advisor, but when the time came and he needed to step up, he rose to the occasion. He's proud of himself for this. He has kept the Zavala organization together despite how it almost fell apart when Oscar was captured and imprisoned.

His days of leadership may soon be coming to an end, however. Jorge is on his way to meet the American. The American has important information. Thus far, he always has. He's never let Jorge down yet. Of course, the American wants something. But that's fine. Nothing comes for free, and Jorge wouldn't expect it any other way.

The convoy of jeeps pulls off the road. They cross a field. The men surrounding Jorge keep their heads on swivels, surveying the area. The American always comes alone, but Jorge doesn't believe he's truly alone. He's too calm, too confident, to truly be alone. Jorge believes there must be a team nearby, ready to swoop in and extract him if he's ever in potential danger. Jorge doesn't know if this is true, though. It could be that the American just has huge balls. That he's fearless. He's clearly very confident in himself.

Case in point, Jorge can see him up ahead, standing alone in the center of the field, hands in pockets, waiting for the convoy to reach him.

The leading jeep and the following jeep circle around, approaching the American in a pincer maneuver. He doesn't flinch. The jeep containing Jorge comes to a halt in front of him. The men in front get out, their handguns raised as they approach. The American takes his hands out of his pockets and raises them, waiting. The driver is closest. He pats the American down, then backs off, satisfied. He turns and nods to Jorge that he's clean.

The men either side of Jorge get out of the jeep so Jorge can exit. Max Ross, the American, is smiling as Jorge approaches. There's that confidence. Max holds out his hand. "Good to see you again, Jorge," he says. "Keeping well?"

After they shake, Jorge places his hands on his hips and looks around. It's midday, and the sun is high, shining down on them. Max wears jeans with a T-shirt, a thin jacket, and sunglasses that hide his eyes. Jorge and the men surrounding them are wearing khaki. "Well enough," he says. "I received your message, Señor Ross. You led me to believe this would be a matter of some importance."

"And it is," Max says. "How's that helicopter I gave you, by the way? I hope your men are getting plenty of practice in it. It was decommissioned, but it's still a beaut, isn't it? Nothing wrong with it, so far as I could see."

"Is that relevant to what we're here to talk about?"

An eyebrow arches over the top of Max's sunglasses, and he grins. "It could be," he says. "It could be *very* relevant to the prison break of Oscar Zavala."

Jorge cocks his head. "I'm listening."

"We know where he's going to be," Max says, looking very pleased with himself.

"Then tell me."

"Why else would I bring you all the way out here?" Max flicks his eyes toward the armed men either side of Jorge. "I'm going to reach into my pocket. Don't get excited, boys."

Despite his alert, both men raise their guns a little higher as Max reaches into the inner pocket of his jacket. He pulls out a folded manila envelope and hands it over. Jorge takes it. He opens it and examines the papers. He speaks English, but he doesn't read it so well. There are others back at the house who can translate it for him.

"Everything you need to know is in there," Max says. "Oscar will be transferred to the new prison in a week. I'd say give it a few days longer than that, just so we can be sure they're not going to promptly move him again and this is all just a decoy, and then once we give you the nod, you can move in and take him out. And Jorge, I know this goes without saying, but make it look good."

Jorge looks up at him from the sheets of paper.

"We don't want any blowback," Max says.

Jorge nods, just once. "Of course." He slides the papers back into the envelope and then circles a finger in the air, motioning to the men to get back into their vehicles and prepare to go. The guards either side of him don't move. "Is there anything else?" Jorge says.

"I would've thought that was enough," Max says, still grinning, still confident.

Jorge can see himself nodding in the reflection from Max's sunglasses. "It is. I look forward to hearing from you again soon."

Max stays exactly where he is while the three jeeps circle around him and drive away. Jorge watches him in the mirror as they go, and as they get further and further away, and Max gets smaller and smaller in the distance behind them, there is no sign that he's leaving. Jorge believes that Max is situated in Honduras, and because of that, he's made it clear that Max Ross is under Zavala protection, but he doesn't know *where* Max stays. Jorge has sent men to follow him, but Max has always given them the slip.

It doesn't matter. Jorge looks down at the envelope in his lap, gripped with both hands. He smiles to himself. Soon, he won't have to lead anymore. Part of him is a little deflated at this thought, but he pushes it away. Pretends it never occurred.

Soon, Oscar will be free.

1

Oscar Zavala is being moved again. His wrists and ankles are shackled and chained, and there is a hood over his head. His body rocks with the motion of the armored truck that transports him, propped up by the two heavily armed and armored men either side of him.

Oscar doesn't keep track of his time in each prison. They move him around so frequently, all across Mexico, in an effort to prevent his men from tracking him down. The last one, he was there for six months. The one before that, only two. This one – who knows? Could be a month, could be a week, could be just a day. It's happened before. Just a stopover on the way to somewhere else, to keep his hounds off the scent. Oscar is flattered, really, that they keep him on the move, out of reach of his soldiers. It means they fear him.

They should.

No matter how often or how far they transport him, Oscar is confident his men will eventually find him. They'll free him. They'll take him from Mexico and return him to

his home in Honduras. Oscar has faith in Jorge. Jorge will
not let him down. Maybe this is the prison where they will
find him. Maybe this is where his incarceration finally ends.

Oscar doesn't try to keep track of the passing time. He
settles into the rhythm of the truck. Of the darkness of his
hood. He fades in and out of sleep until finally the truck
comes to a stop.

Oscar feels himself hauled upright. On shuffling feet,
he's led out of the back of the truck. Standing on the ground,
the hood is dragged from his head.

Oscar blinks against the light. He makes a point of
standing up straight, his eyes pained and narrowed. His hair
is long, and his beard is wild and unkempt, but it's clear to
anyone nearby, those who know him and those who do not,
that he emanates power and danger. It comes off him in
waves. His haggard appearance cannot diminish him.

The prison looms ahead of him. The yards are currently
empty of inmates. Oscar takes a deep breath, filling his
lungs, inspecting his new temporary home. The armed,
masked men surrounding him urge him forward, dragging
him through the barbed-wire-topped gate and toward the
main building itself. The pain eases from Oscar's eyes as he
enters the shadows. He's handed off to the guards inside, and
his armed entourage returns to their truck.

Processing does not take long. They were already
expecting him. While they fill in his scant paperwork, Oscar
looks down at his gray jumpsuit. "Do you have a new outfit
for me?" he says, winking.

The guard filling in his forms ignores him. A standing
desk separates them. Oscar leans on it. The guard gives him
a sour look. Another guard stands nearby. He looks friend-
lier than the other. "We have the same color here, Señor

Zavala," he says. He's respectful. Oscar likes this. He has a friendly, reverent face.

Oscar furnishes him with a smile, and the young guard brightens at this. It's clear he knows who Oscar is. Oscar can see that this guard will come in useful to him. It's always worth having a friend amongst the guards.

"*Señor* Zavala?" says the other guard, looking up. "Did I hear that correctly, Angel?"

The young guard – Angel – shifts his weight from foot to foot. "I just –"

"He's an inmate, Angel." This guard is older, sterner. He will not make for a good friend. It's clear that he believes he's seen it all, and nothing can faze him. He won't be impressed or intimidated by who Oscar is or what he has done. "If you're going to call him by his name rather than his number, you do *not* prefix it with a *señor*."

Angel avoids the older guard's eye. He lowers his face and nods a little and mumbles that he understands.

The older guard stares at Angel for longer than is necessary. "Take him to his cell," he says finally, dismissively, turning his head to something of more importance on his desk.

Oscar smiles at Angel, but he doesn't make any effort to move away, not just yet. He leans over the desk. "I assume my people called ahead, yes?" he says. "They booked me the executive suite, yes?"

The older guard slowly raises his head, forced to look at Oscar. He stares for a moment. Oscar grins back. "Are you trying to be funny?"

"Not at all," Oscar says. "My previous accommodations were not the most comfortable, and I would wake every morning with a pain in my back and a crick in my neck. As you can see, I'm not a young man – older than even *you*, I'd wager."

The guard snorts. "I'm not yet in my sixties, Zavala."

"And for me it's only been a few months. Could you imagine waking on your sixtieth birthday, with a pain in your back and a crick in your neck?"

The guard is silent a moment, staring. It's not that he has nothing to say – Oscar has no doubt that these prolonged, staring silences are nothing more than an intimidation technique. "Shut up and move," the guard says. "You're in solitary, as I'm sure you were in the prison before this and the one before that and so on. And I don't doubt that the mattresses here are just as thin as where you came from. If you're lucky, it might not smell of piss."

Oscar shrugs and lets out a big, exaggerated sigh. "Oh well. I had to ask, though, didn't I? Don't ask, don't get." He winks at the older guard and then allows Angel to lead him away.

They travel down into the bowels of the building. Another guard accompanies them, but he remains a couple of paces behind, a hand hovering near his sidearm like he expects Oscar to attempt something. It's always like this, at first. They hear so many stories about him that they're on edge for his arrival, thinking like he's going to attempt to take them all on single-handed and unarmed while still in shackles.

It's a long walk, and Oscar takes the opportunity to engage his new friend. "It's quiet here," he says. "The quietest prison I've been moved to yet."

"These levels were cleared for your arrival," Angel says. He keeps his voice low, presumably so the guard following won't hear him tell too much, and likely report back to the other guard with the bad attitude. "The warden didn't want the other prisoners to see you arrive. I think he worried you might spur them into a riot."

Oscar chuckles in the back of his throat. "If this were Honduras, perhaps."

"I'm sure you still have some influence in Mexico," Angel says.

"Maybe a little. But once I was captured, I think most of my influence leaked away, down through many borders and back to my homeland. Tell me, Angel" – he notices how Angel tenses at Oscar's use of his name – "the guard back at the desk, I sensed he had a problem with me?"

Angel clears his throat. "He has a problem with most people."

"That does not surprise me. He looks the kind of man who does not have many friends and persuades himself that he prefers it that way."

They reach the solitary confinement cells, and Oscar purposefully slows his pace. Angel slows with him. Unlike some other guards would, he does not attempt to drag him along or to force the pace.

"What's his name?" Oscar says.

Angel glances back at the other guard over his shoulder, then in the quietest voice he can, he says, "Mateo. Mateo Blanco."

"Am I going to have any problems with Mateo Blanco?" Oscar says.

"You might. Mateo, he likes to make points. He likes to prove that he doesn't fear anyone. I've seen him do it. Cartel members, cartel leaders, killers and cannibals, anyone fearsome who passes through this place, he makes a point of standing up to them. Of pushing them around. Be careful of him. Don't try to push him in turn. I've seen him become physical. He does not hold back."

Oscar nods at this. They reach his cell. His new temporary home. Oscar steps inside, and the door is closed. The room is bare. The walls are scarred with names, tallies, and curse words. There are stains that could be shit or blood, or both. There is a bucket in the corner for his toilet, and a thin mattress with no frame pressed up against the wall to his right. The mattress is stained and looks like it *will* smell of piss. A slot opens halfway down the door through which his meals will be transferred, but for now Oscar presents his wrists, and the cuffs are removed. Oscar kneels down and cranes his neck so he can look up at Angel through the slot.

"I appreciate our talk," he says, looking up into the young guard's face. "You have been good to me, and I never forget a kindness."

Angel nods. "I appreciate that, Señor Zavala."

"But you know, your friend, your boss, whatever he is – Mateo Blanco, you should tell him that *he* should be nicer to me," Oscar says. "I don't forget those who *aren't* so kind, either. And I won't be here forever." He winks as Angel closes the slot, and then turns, alone in his new cell, and he braces himself once again for the indiscernible stretch of time that lies before him. He closes his eyes and breathes deep and ignores the stink of the place. His men *will* be coming for him. His men *are* looking for him. This is what steels him. This is what gets him through. Eventually, they *will* find him.

2

It's been three months since Tom Rollins last saw his father, but he calls him often.

The bar where Tom works is quiet, so he takes this opportunity to place a call through. "Dad," he says when Jeffrey answers, "it's not too late, is it? I can call back in the morning."

"It's fine, it's fine," Jeffrey says. "I don't sleep too well these days anyway."

"From the treatments?"

"I reckon so. Or the cancer. Or both. Who knows?"

"How's Sylvia?"

"She's fine. She's sleeping right now. What are you doing? You with Hayley?"

"No, I'm at work. It's quiet, though, so I'm probably gonna close it down soon. I'll tell Hayley you said hello when I get home."

"Good, good, you do that."

They both lapse into silence. Before the sickness, they didn't make a habit of talking on the phone. They're not accustomed to it. When they're face-to-face, they don't say all that much to each other, either. Most of their communication is non-verbal. They understand each other well enough through looks and grunts.

"I'm going to go," Tom says. He knows this has been a very short call, but they don't have anything else to say to each other. He just wanted his father to know he was thinking of him and that he cares. "You should try to get some sleep. I just wanted to see how you were holding up."

"I'll do my best," Jeffrey says. "I always do."

"I'll call you again soon." Tom hangs up the phone and looks around the bar. There's only a couple of elderly regulars. The jukebox is playing ZZ Top. It looks like this may be the last of their selection, as they're getting up now, preparing to leave.

Tom watches them go. They exchange the standard good nights and the waves, and then Tom locks the door after them and cleans the place down. It doesn't take him long. He sends Hayley a message letting her know he's on his way home, and then heads out into the night.

The air is cool, and Tom breathes it in deep. He fills his lungs. His back is to the street while he locks the door after himself, and he feels the hairs on the back of his neck prickle. It's not from the cold. There are eyes on him. Tom is being watched, he's sure of it.

He stays loose, but he's on alert. He checks left and right out of his peripheral vision. His ears are open, and there's no one running up on him. He can't hear any car engines. The night is very still, very quiet, yet he still feels watched. Tom turns, casually, staying loose. He stays where he is on the sidewalk in front of the bar and looks around. Just a man enjoying the peace of the night. He continues to breathe deep, staying calm and focused. He scans the area, checking the windows of the buildings around him and looking into the cars parked up and down the road.

Bingo.

Opposite side of the road, five cars back at the end of the block. He spots two men sitting in the front of a dark green Camry. There could be more in the back, but it's too dark to see. The men in the front aren't looking directly at Tom. They occasionally glance his way, but only as they look over the street. They're busy talking to each other, their attention mostly on their conversation.

Tom goes to his own car and climbs inside. He starts the engine and signals as he pulls away. Keeps his eyes on the mirror as he goes, waiting and expecting the Camry to come to life and follow him. It doesn't happen right away, but he's not surprised. If they're professionals, they should leave some space.

All the way home, Tom watches his mirrors. The road remains clear behind him. The Camry does not follow. No one does.

Hayley is in the living room. "Hey," she says as Tom enters. The television is on. It's playing an old black-and-white movie. "How was work?"

"Quiet," Tom says. "How's your night been?"

"The same," Hayley says. "But that's what I was hoping for." She frowns, noticing how distracted Tom looks, the way he glances back toward the front door, watching for any lights that might strafe across the front of the house. They don't come. "What's wrong?"

Tom turns back to her. "Nothing," he says. He leans down and kisses Hayley. "Just tired."

"I was planning on going to bed soon. Come sit with me, watch the end of the movie, then we'll head up together."

Tom nods and sits beside her on the sofa. "When are you next on shift?"

Hayley is a nurse. "Day after tomorrow," she says, brushing a lock of hair behind her ear.

They settle onto the sofa and watch the end of the movie, but Tom can't focus on it. He listens beyond it, outside the house, to the road. Listens for any cars that could be approaching, pulling up, or idling out there. Listens for anyone approaching on foot, coming up the pathway to the front door.

He can't hear anyone coming. Part of him wonders if he's just being paranoid. If maybe the two men he saw in the car were there for an innocent reason. They could have been waiting for someone. The eyes he felt on him may have been when they were casting their eyes over the area, as he saw them do. Or else perhaps it was just his imagination.

Still, as the night wears on and the movie ends and he and Hayley prepare to go upstairs to bed, Tom can't shake the feeling. He was being watched. Those men were sitting in the Camry at close to eleven at night. There wasn't anyone else around so far as he could see.

As Hayley heads upstairs, Tom stays behind a moment. He turns off all the lights. He calls to Hayley, "I'll be up in a minute," and then he turns off the landing light. He moves through the darkened living room to the window, the drawn curtains, and he peers outside around the corner, careful not to twitch them. He stands very still, watching the front lawn and the road. He scans all the parked cars, and he freezes as he spots one in the distance. The house on the corner at the end of the block – the front end of a car pokes out, parked on the road running alongside it. It looks like a dark green Camry. Parked as far away as it can be while still able to see Tom and Hayley's home.

Tom stays where he is, glued to the spot, watching. His eyes dart left and right until he catches movement. A dark figure off to his right, moving across front lawns and sticking to the shadows, coming closer. He spots two forms, one following the other. Off to his left, he spots two more, moving in the same formation, darting forward.

Tom turns from the window and runs upstairs to the bedroom. Hayley is in the bathroom. She's finishing up brushing her teeth. Tom presses a hand to her waist and with his other gently covers her mouth. Hayley raises her eyebrows. Tom isn't worried about her making noise. She won't become hysterical, he knows this. He just needs her to listen to what he's about to say.

"Get in the bathtub and lie low," he says. "There are men coming toward the house, and they're probably armed."

Hayley's eyebrows rise higher still. Tom takes his hands away and backs off before she can say anything. He knows she'll do as he says. She'll get in the bathtub, and she'll stay there until he tells her otherwise.

Tom goes to the bottom of the closet, to his bag. The bag that holds his KA-BAR and his Beretta. He pulls them both out. The Beretta is unloaded. The bag also holds its magazines. Tom slides one in and hooks the KA-BAR's sheath to his belt. He kills the bedroom light and heads back out.

Two of the men will likely come to the front of the house, and two to the back. Tom heads to the back first. It's the least secured door. It's mostly made of glass, and easiest to break through. As he descends the stairs, he hears the door opening and light footsteps upon the linoleum. They didn't break the glass – they've picked the lock. Tom steps just as lightly toward the kitchen and conceals himself to the side of the closed door leading through to it. He pulls out the KA-BAR and holds both it and the Beretta raised and ready. At the front of the house, he can hear the men there also trying to pick the lock. It will take them longer. The front door has three locks – the main and two switch bolts.

Tom hears the two men in the kitchen coming closer. He's prepared. While he waits, he watches the front door. They're working at it, but they're not through yet.

The door to the kitchen slowly opens. A gun leads the way. Through the dark, Tom can see that it's a Hellcat. He doesn't let it come too far through the door. He brings the handle of his Beretta down hard on the wrist, causing it to drop the gun. He hauls the rest of the body through the door and turns it around, the man's back pressed to his front. He holds the man against himself like a shield, the KA-BAR pressed to his throat. Tom points his Beretta at the man behind, still in the kitchen. He's armed with a Hellcat, too. He doesn't lower it.

In the split second before he speaks, Tom looks the man over. Latino. Mid-twenties. His eyes are cold. Killer's eyes. His arms are steady. His gun does not falter. "What do you want?" Tom says.

The man against Tom's chest is the one to speak. He calls to the other in Spanish. Tom understands enough of what he says – *Do it! Shoot him!*

Tom pushes his human shield forward as the other man opens fire. His two shots thud into the shield's chest. Tom is following, Beretta raised. He fires three times, catching the other man in the right shoulder and the cheek under his right eye as the shield falls on top of him, and his third shot goes into the back of the shield's head. Both men down, Tom quickly checks that they're both dead.

Behind him, at the sound of the gunshots, the front door is kicked open. There's no further need for discretion. Tom, still in the kitchen, dives to the side as two more men come charging in. They spot his movement, and they open fire. Their bullets come from handguns. No automatic fire, luckily. Tom fires at them blindly around the doorframe, causing them to scatter. Tom feels his heart skip a beat as one of them runs for the stairs, like he's going straight for Hayley.

The other man is still present, keeping Tom pinned in place. The doorway is a no-go. Tom turns and heads out the back door. There's no time to waste. He runs down the side of the house and back to the front. The man covering the kitchen has not suspected this. He isn't firing, but his gun is raised, ready and waiting for movement at the kitchen doorway. He's watching the wrong doorway. From behind, Tom shoots him through the side of the head, dropping him instantly.

The other man, the one who ran for the stairs, he's still there. He wasn't running up to get to Hayley. He was gaining a vantage point. From there, he opens fire on Tom. Tom dives to the right as bullets tear into the door and the frame around him. He scurries out of view of the shooter's vantage point and takes cover behind a sofa. He hears the shooter come down a few stairs, where he can better see into the living room. He fires on the sofa. Tom presses himself low to the ground as bullets punch through the upholstery.

The bullets punch lower, the shooter covering as broad an area as he can, knowing that Tom has to be there somewhere. Tom feels a bullet whizz by just an inch above his back. The next shot will be as low as it needs to. It will hit his ribs. Tom needs to move. He prepares himself to dive forward. He'll be out of cover, wide open, but the movement should hopefully stall the shooter long enough for Tom to return fire.

But the shooter doesn't fire. The bullet doesn't puncture Tom's ribs. Instead of a gunshot, he hears a tumble, like the shooter has fallen and is rolling down the stairs.

Tom pushes himself up and looks toward the sound. Indeed, the shooter is tumbling. Hayley is halfway down the staircase. She crept up on the shooter, and she's pushed him.

It wasn't a long fall. The shooter will not be hurt. He will not be incapacitated. Tom moves fast. He wants to get to the shooter, to disarm him, to press his knife to his throat and question him – find out who he is, and what he's doing here. Find out who sent him – Tom has not recognized any of these men and doubts they came here after him of their own volition.

He won't get to question him, though. He won't reach him with the KA-BAR fast enough. The shooter has rolled onto his back, and he's raising his gun. He's pointing it toward Hayley.

Tom is faster. He opens fire and doesn't stop until the shooter has dropped his gun and is still.

As the shooting stops and the noise dies down, the house sounds incredibly quiet. Tom turns to Hayley, and she's looking right back at him. She's breathing hard. She knows as well as he does how close she just came to being shot. "Who were they?" she says.

Tom shakes his head. "I don't know."

3

It's morning, and the cops are finally leaving.

Before they arrived, Tom quickly patted down the bodies of the four men. None of them were carrying ID. He snapped pictures of their faces, and he's sent them to Cindy to see if she can find any leads on who they are and who might have sent them.

The cops kept asking the same questions, but Tom didn't have any answers. He didn't know who the men were. He didn't know what they wanted. If he *did* know, he still wouldn't have told the cops anything, but that's beside the point. He didn't tell them about the dark green Camry, either. He's been waiting to check that out for himself.

One of the cops was Duncan Mather. When Tom first came back to Hopper Creek over a year ago, Duncan Mather was working for the drug dealers who ran the town. After Tom had dealt with that situation, he had a sit-down conversation with Duncan. Made it clear it was in his interest to do his job properly going forward. So far as Tom can tell,

Duncan has done just that. He's kept his nose clean. Hasn't gotten himself involved with anyone he shouldn't.

He took Tom to one side and asked him in a lowered voice, "Look, I know you said you don't know who these men were or what they wanted, but what do you think happened here?"

Tom looked at him, picking up on Duncan's obsequious tone and his clear desperation for Tom to see that he's doing better now. He's doing the right thing. "I think it was a home invasion," Tom said. "And I think they picked the wrong house."

Duncan nodded at this. "Okay. Okay," he said. "I'll pass that on. Could be that they're part of a bigger gang still in operation. Not everyone has *you* in their home – we'd best let people know so they can be alert, double-lock their doors and windows."

"You do that," Tom said.

The coroners took away the dead bodies of the Latino men after forensics had photographed the scene. No one cleared up the blood, though. Hayley is already filling a bucket with water and bleach to scrub the stains away. Tom is outside, watching the cops leave, making sure none of them hangs around to watch the house. They don't spot the Camry, but there's no reason why they should.

The early morning is bright. The sky is clear. Birds are beginning to sing. The neighbors are not up yet. It's too early for them to head to work, or to take their kids to school. No doubt they were woken during the night by all the gunfire – one or more of them called the cops, after all. They were probably able to get back to sleep once everything had calmed down and the cops had turned up. Tom has not slept, but he doesn't feel tired. There's too much racing through his mind. Too many questions, and he won't be able to settle until he has answers.

When he's confident the cops are all gone, and they're not going to come back, he goes to the Camry. When he patted down the dead bodies, he wasn't able to find any of their IDs, but he was able to find the car keys. He uses them now to get inside, and slips into the passenger seat. He looks the interior of the car over, checking in the glove compartment, behind the sun visors, and in the door pockets. There's nothing to find except in the footwells of the backseat, where there are a couple of bottles that have been pissed into. Nothing else. Nothing of worth.

Tom drives the Camry out of town and dumps it at the side of the road. He returns to the house on foot. Returns to Hayley. She's on her knees in the kitchen, still scrubbing blood out of the linoleum. "Leave it," Tom says. "It's my mess. I'll clean it."

Hayley doesn't look up. "I just want it gone," she says. "Did you find anything in the car?" Last night when they heard the cops approaching, Tom told her about the Camry and about it being parked outside the bar when he locked up, the sight of which had made him so alert in the first place.

"No, nothing."

"Where did you take it?"

"Just outside of town. Let a wrecker truck take it away, or some kids strip it for scrap."

Hayley drops the scrubber into the bucket and looks up at him. Hair is slicked across her forehead from her exertions. She wipes her hands on her knees. She's wearing the shirt she sleeps in, and pulled on a pair of running shorts for the cops' coming. She looks tired. "Who were they, Tom?"

"I told you," Tom says. "I don't know."

"I know. I know you did," she says, and sighs. "What are you going to do?"

Tom holds his hand out to her. She takes it, and he pulls her to her feet. "You need to get out of here," he says. "Out of the house. Go and stay with your parents for a few days until I can find out who's coming after me. It'll be safer for you there. I don't think they're coming for you. They had the opportunity to go after you last night and they didn't take it."

"Tom, I –"

"It's better for both of us if you're safe," Tom says. "I made a lot of enemies while I was running operations for the CIA. Those men were Latino, and I spent a lot of time in Central and South America. Whoever sent them, I doubt he only has four men at his disposal."

"What are you saying?" Hayley says, cocking her head. "You think more are going to come?"

"They might. I need to be prepared in case they do."

Hayley hesitates. "If Cindy finds out who they are, who sent them, what will you do then?"

He looks at her. He doesn't need to say anything. She already knows the answer. He'll strike back. He'll go after them the way they've come after him. It's the only way they can be safe.

Hayley nods, understanding. "I'll go and pack a bag," she says.

"I'll drive you," Tom says. "I want to make sure no one follows and sees where you're going."

Hayley reaches out and squeezes his hand. "Are you going to thank me for saving you last night?" she says, managing to grin.

"Thank you for pushing a crazed gunman down the stairs."

"And thank *you* for shooting him before he could shoot me." She lets go of his hand. "These stains, though, you're gonna have them all cleaned up before I come back home, right? I get that the bullet holes might take a bit longer, but you'll get rid of the blood, won't you?"

"It'll be the first thing I do after I drop you off," Tom says, though as Hayley makes her way up the stairs and he watches her go, he thinks to himself how this isn't entirely true. There are a few other things he needs to do around town first, and things he needs to buy, in order to fortify the house in her absence.

But *then* he'll clean up the blood.

4

Naomi's parents live between Baton Rouge and New Orleans. Zeke has been driving for three and a half hours now, back to Shreveport, but they're almost home.

Naomi's parents have been married for forty-two years. It was their wedding anniversary yesterday. Zeke, Naomi, and the kids stayed over last night to help them celebrate, along with Naomi's older brother and his family. Zeke didn't drink much. He never does. But he also knew they were going to have an early start this morning to get home.

Naomi has been snoozing in the seat beside him. She wakes now, stretching and then rubbing her eyes. "Was I asleep?" she says.

Zeke grins. "Pretty much since we set off."

"Oh really?" She laughs and looks around. "Oh, yeah. We're almost home." She glances into the backseat and sees that their children are sleeping, too. Tamika, six, is resting her head on her older brother's shoulder. Tre is eight. He hasn't yet reached the age where he would shrug his sister off, but both Zeke and Naomi know it's likely coming soon. Neither of them is looking forward to it. Tre and Tamika still get along, there is no sibling rivalry between them, and both parents dread the inevitable breaking of this peace.

Naomi turns back, yawning. "Sorry to leave you all on your own, baby."

"That's all right, I didn't mind," Zeke says. "I just kept the music low and drove. It's been nice. The roads haven't been too busy."

Naomi listens to the music coming from the stereo. "Marvin Gaye?"

"You know it." Zeke smiles at her. 'How Sweet It Is' was the first dance at their wedding. He remembers holding her by the waist and lifting her over his head. She shrieked, but she was laughing, too. He put her back down, and they spun around the room together. "Something gentle while you all slept."

Naomi strokes his leg. They can see Shreveport coming up.

"Did you have a good time last night?" Naomi says.

"I did," he says.

"Do you think the kids did?"

"They always do. They love their grandparents. And they're always happy to see their cousins. They all kept each other entertained while their mothers and grandmother were up dancing on the table."

Naomi laughs. "Their grandmother did *not* dance on the table."

"That's true. She stayed on the ground. She wasn't drunk enough to try to get up there with you and your sister-in-law."

"*I* was not that drunk, either. I was just enjoying myself. We all were."

Zeke grins. "I know it. I'm just teasing. I think the only person who really got drunk was your father, on that bottle of Cutty Sark we got him."

"It was *supposed* to be for both of them."

"Yeah, but we knew it was for him, really. That's why we took the bottle of wine, too, for your mom."

"My dad's always been a funny drunk," Naomi says, shaking her head. "He tells a few jokes, busts a few moves, and then falls asleep with his chin on his chest. He's always been the same."

"We'll all take a fun drunk over an aggressive drunk any day of the week."

"That's true."

They reach Shreveport, and Zeke drives through the city to the outskirts. To home. The kids remain asleep in the back. They don't show any signs of waking any time soon. Naomi looks back at them, smiling at their peaceful faces.

Zeke turns onto their block and approaches their house. As he gets closer, things begin to feel off. He frowns, slowing the car and studying the front of the house, trying to put his finger on what is perturbing him. It's a minor thing, but it doesn't take him long to realize what it is. The curtains. They left the curtains drawn when they left the house the day before yesterday. They're still drawn now, but the one concealing the living room isn't all the way closed. There's a gap down the middle, like someone has peered out and hasn't bothered putting it all the way back where it was.

Zeke racks his brain, remembering. He closed the curtains in the living room. He wouldn't leave them with a gap like that.

Naomi starts to notice something is wrong. "What's up?" she says. "Why are you going so slow?"

"Just give me a minute," Zeke says, still watching the house. It's on their left, and he stays in the right lane as he pulls alongside it.

"What do you see?" Naomi says. She knows there must be a problem, or else Zeke would have pulled straight onto the driveway.

Zeke looks to the front door. It's closed, but it doesn't look right. Straining his eyes, he looks around the frame. He can see splintering. Low down on the door itself, there's the faint print of a boot. The door has been kicked open and then slotted back into place. Someone has been in the house.

"Stay here with the kids," Zeke says. "Someone's broke in. Pass me the handgun."

Naomi reaches for the Glock in the glove compartment, but before she can get it, something in the side mirror catches Zeke's eye. Behind him, off to his left, one of the parked cars there has started up. Zeke didn't see anyone get into it. Whoever is inside has been there since Zeke and his family reached the block. The car is rolling forward. It's coming slowly, getting closer to them. The passenger-side windows are rolling down, both front and back.

Zeke doesn't like what he's seeing. There's no time to wait for them to draw up. He slams his foot down on the accelerator, throwing Naomi back in her seat. "Zeke, what's happening?" she says, her hands drawn back from the glove compartment in the lurch.

Zeke doesn't answer. In the mirror, he sees the car speeding up, coming after them.

"They're still here," he says.

"Who?"

"Whoever broke into the house – they're right behind us."

Naomi looks back. Zeke can hear the kids waking at the sudden movements. "What's happening?" Tre says, his voice thick with sleep.

"Zeke, *gun!*" Naomi says.

Zeke swerves left and cuts across the lawn of the house at the end of the block. He turns the corner directly beyond this house. He can hear the gunshot behind them. It doesn't hit the car.

Naomi unbuckles herself and gets into the back of the car with the kids. She covers them both with her body, holding them close to her.

"Stay down!" Zeke calls back.

He puts his foot down, flooring it, taking another corner. The car behind pursues. It's falling back, but it's persistent. The roads here are quiet. There are only a couple of other cars. Zeke overtakes and weaves past them. He hears angry horns blare, but they're the least of his concern. He hears another gunshot, but again it doesn't hit the car. He takes a right turn, a tight one that causes them to skid across lanes. Zeke battles the steering wheel and manages to steady the car. He pushes on. He needs to shake their pursuers.

Zeke hits a long stretch of road in Midway. To the left and right are grassy verges, and beyond that are gated-off lots where now-demolished factories used to stand. The car behind accelerates close. Zeke's foot is pressed flat to the floor. It's not enough.

Up ahead, a truck approaches. There are two cars behind it. "Hold on!" Zeke calls. He goes into the oncoming lane. The truck and the cars panic. They flash lights and blare horns, but they need to get out of his way. They scatter. The truck and one of the cars swerve into the opposite lane. The remaining car turns right and mounts the grass at the side of the road. Zeke plows on, looking into the mirror, seeing how their pursuers have to slam on their brakes and manoeuvre to avoid a crash. It buys Zeke some time. He moves back into the proper lane and takes the next turn-off, to the right. Another long stretch, but there are buildings here. Still-standing factories. Zeke spots an automotive repair center. It has a large doorway, like on a fire station. He checks the mirrors. There's no sign of their pursuers. Zeke veers off the road and into the darkness through the repair center's open door. Inside the building, he tucks the car to the left, in the shadows and out of view of the opening. He grabs the Glock and tells his family to stay where they are.

The mechanics inside are all looking at him, wide-eyed. Zeke keeps the gun low so as not to alarm them. "Don't panic," he says, still in motion, heading toward the center's open door. "I'm CIA – just do what you were doing, and I'll explain in a moment."

He turns his back on them, hoping they'll do as he says, that they'll stay casual. There's no commotion behind him, and he takes this as a good sign. He reaches the door and conceals himself to the side of it, gun raised and held tight in both hands beside his head now, and he peers out, looking down the road. He sees the car coming. Their pursuers. It's coming fast. Zeke ducks back. He waits, watching the road. The car passes. It doesn't slow. Zeke peers out again, watching it go until it's all the way out of sight.

He pulls back from the door and wipes a hand down his face, blowing out air. He puts the gun away and looks to the car. Naomi and the kids are all looking out the rear window at him, watching. Zeke looks back at them, knowing they are going to want – to need – an explanation. The problem is, he doesn't know what to tell them. He doesn't know who those people were, or why they were coming after him and his family.

But he intends to find out.

5

It's early afternoon when Cindy gets back in touch with Tom.

"What have you got for me?" Tom says.

"Not a lot," Cindy says. "All four men were from Honduras. You been?"

"Honduras? Yeah, I've been. It doesn't narrow down who might have sent them."

"You've made a lot of enemies in Honduras?"

"I've made a lot of enemies all over. Was there anything else on them?"

"Just what you'd expect – criminal records and some time served in prison for a couple of them. You want their names, see if that jogs anything?"

"Might as well."

Cindy reels off four names that are unfamiliar to Tom. "That help?"

"Not particularly. Any known affiliations mentioned?"

"Nothing major, but if it's a big player, they could have been recruited recently, and those affiliations wouldn't be known yet. I've checked for bounties, too, see if anyone's put a price on you, but that didn't bring anything up either. But listen, I'll keep searching, see if I can find anything, anything at all that might help you out here."

"I appreciate it, Cindy."

"Don't mention it. I mean, it's hardly like I've found anything useful yet. Speaking of, until you have some kind of idea who's coming after you, what're you gonna do?"

Tom is sitting in the living room, staring at the bullet holes in the sofa he took cover behind last night. He's cleaned up the blood that was on the ground, but he can see where the stains all were. "I'm going to prepare," Tom says.

Cindy chuckles. "I guess I wouldn't expect anything else. Listen, you be careful, Tom. I'll be in touch. And you do the same, okay? Let me know you're all right."

"Will do." Tom hangs up. He sat down to answer Cindy's call, but now he stands. On the ground at his feet are bags. They contain security cameras. Tripwires. Tools. Nails.

Bear traps.

After he dropped Hayley at her parents' house, he drove around the town. He drove slowly, casually. He made himself visible. He kept his eyes peeled while he did so. Checking for any sign that the men who came after him have reinforcements in the town. Looking at cars parked at the bar again, or on the street where he lives. Nothing leapt out at him – neither people nor vehicles. He swung by the motels, too, and asked if anyone from Honduras had checked in recently. They hadn't. To cover all bases, he asked if anyone from south of the border had checked in. Again, no.

He got in contact with Duncan Mather. Told him to keep an eye on Hayley's parents' house. Told him to keep a patrol car parked on the street, as well as regular passes to make sure the place was clear. Same again at the hospital when Hayley is on shift.

"I'll see what I can do," Duncan said.

"I'm not asking," Tom said.

Duncan was silent at this. "Okay," he said finally. "I'll get right on it."

"I'll check, Duncan."

"I know you will. It'll be done. What about you? You want someone watching the house?"

"No," Tom said. "I can take care of myself."

Then, all this done, Tom went shopping. He bought the equipment that sits bagged at his feet. If anyone is in town, waiting to come after him again, he reckons they'll do it at night. And this time, they'll come heavy. They'll be more prepared after last time. They'll know he's expecting them.

It's still a while until it gets dark. Tom has plenty of time to fortify the house. Plenty of time to prepare. He gets to work.

6

Oscar isn't sure how many days have passed. In the past, while in solitary, he has measured time in the meals brought to him. This time, however, his meals are not regular. Sometimes, they don't come at all. The only days they have any kind of regularity is when Angel is the one bringing them. These are the days he's allowed outside, too, into the exercise yard. He goes out there alone, escorted by Angel and usually a couple of other guards, and he spends an hour pacing the yard in the fresh air.

Oscar doesn't think he's been here long. He doesn't think it's been a week. Four days, maybe.

Someone he sees a lot of, however, is Mateo Blanco. Oscar knows that when his meals don't come, that is Mateo's doing. The one time Mateo has taken Oscar for a shower, he dragged him so roughly that Oscar ended up with bruises on the inside of his arm and on his shins. Mateo pushed him into the freezing cold water. Oscar flinched, but he refused to step out from under the spray. He stood there, and he took it, holding Mateo's eye all the while. Mateo didn't like that. He struck Oscar with his baton, dropping him to his knees. Soaking wet and naked, Oscar was dragged back to his cell by his hair and thrown into it. Mateo left him naked and cold for endless hours, finally dropping his jumpsuit back through the door without a word.

Oscar refuses to be broken by Mateo. Instead, he keeps a mental log. He remembers all of these things Mateo does – all these slights and assaults, big and small. Remembers them all.

Today, though, he hasn't seen Mateo. He hasn't seen anyone until Angel comes to his door, opening the latch through which his meals are delivered. He slides him a tray of lunch.

"Senor Zavala," Angel says, crouching down to look through. "Senor Zavala?"

"I'm here, Angel," Oscar says, getting to his feet and then lowering himself so he and Angel are eye to eye.

Angel appears nervous, jumpy. His eyes flicker from side to side, and he checks back over his shoulder. He keeps his voice low. "Senor Zavala, I have a note for you." He lowers his eyes to the tray, and Oscar can see an envelope there in the center.

Oscar picks it up. He opens it. The message inside is short and to the point.

Today.

Oscar smiles. He slips the note back into the envelope and conceals it within his jumpsuit. "Was this handed to you directly, Angel?"

Angel nods. "I don't know how they knew me, or that I would bring you your meals –"

Oscar waves a hand in the air. "We always have our ways. Was anything else said to you?"

"No, Senor Zavala. I was just told to give you this note, today."

"Is Mateo here?"

"No, he's not. He's off."

"That is a shame. Angel, listen to me."

"I'm listening, Senor Zavala."

"I like you, Angel. You've been good to me while I've been here, so I'm going to give you some advice. Heed it if you want, but believe me when I say this is all in your best interest."

Angel looks pale. He doesn't say anything. He listens.

"First, I would recommend you unlock this door. Don't worry, I'm not going to do anything right now. Just unlock it, and walk away. No one will know you've done it. Secondly, when you leave my cell, go somewhere quiet. Somewhere out of the way. I don't know what direction they'll be coming from, so go somewhere no one has any reason to go to. Do you understand me, Angel?"

Angel manages to nod.

"Good. I hope you do. When the time comes, Angel, when all the noise begins, do not come running. Believe me when I say your life may well depend on it."

Angel swallows. Oscar can hear a dry click at the back of his throat.

"Unlock the door now, Angel," Oscar says.

Angel hesitates.

"It's for your own good," Oscar says. "If the door is open and I can make my own way out, they won't have to come so far looking for me. You don't want to run the risk of them coming across *you*, especially in that uniform." He holds Angel's eye for a long time until finally Angel nods. He looks around again, checking the area is clear, and then he unlocks the door. He leaves it closed. Oscar does not test the handle. He doesn't have anywhere to go just yet.

Angel leaves, and Oscar is alone again. He eats the food on his tray, taking his time. When he's done, he sits on his thin mattress with his back against the wall, and he waits. He thinks to himself how it's a shame Mateo Blanco is not here today. He's sure they'll catch up with each other again somewhere down the line.

Oscar begins to doze. He's not sure how long he's asleep for before the noise from outside wakes him. Gunfire and explosions, and he knows the time has come.

Oscar gets to his feet and pushes open the unlocked door. He makes his way through the prison, from the bowels of the building to the floor above. The noise from outside grows louder. He can hear men screaming, dying. In the cells around him, the inmates are going wild. It sounds like a riot is about to break out. The sounds all bring a smile to Oscar's face. He makes his way toward the yard. On the way, he sees Angel. He's cowering in a hallway, covering his head with his hands. He feels Oscar's eyes and looks up. Oscar grins at him.

"Stay there, Angel," he says, though everything is so loud he can't be sure if Angel hears him. It doesn't look like he has any intention of going anywhere. Oscar holds out his hand. "Give me your keys." Again, whether Angel hears or not, he understands. He gets to his feet and comes to Oscar, pulling a key from the loop. He holds it out.

"The way you're going, this is the key you need," Angel says.

Oscar holds up the key in thanks and then continues on his way. Angel backs off into the corridor, out of view.

Before he steps outside, Oscar pauses, remaining behind cover. He waits until things quieten. Until the shooting stops. When it's done, he unlocks the door and steps outside into the exercise yard. A glorious sight greets him.

Somehow, his men have acquired an American helicopter. Oscar recognizes the kind. Military. A Sikorsky UH-60 Black Hawk. He's impressed.

More impressive is the damage the helicopter has perpetrated. The guard towers above have been completely destroyed by missiles, and they are smouldering still. In the yard, eviscerated bodies of both guards and inmates alike lie in pieces. The damage is so severe, it's hard to tell where one body ends and another begins. A glance at the prison's walls to his left, and Oscar can see the damage the rounds from the helicopter's artillery have done to the concrete.

Eight of Oscar's men are in the yard, fully armed, sweeping the grounds with AKMs, covering the area. Two more remain inside the Black Hawk. The pilots. Oscar holds out both hands in the air. The men have already seen him. They recognize him. Two of them run to him, AKMs raised to the building beyond. Oscar strides through the carnage, through the destroyed bodies and the pools of blood, treading red footprints behind him, his two men sticking close to him, covering him all the way.

The man closest to the helicopter steps forward. The Black Hawk is still running. The man hands Oscar a headpiece. Oscar slips it on.

"It's good to see you again, Senor Zavala," the man says, helping him to climb inside. "Jorge sends his regards."

Oscar smiles, settling himself in the helicopter and strapping himself in. He smiles at the man talking to him, watching as the others fall back and climb in after him. "Take me home," he says.

7

Zeke has taken his family to a motel to hide out. He left his car at the repair center where they managed to give their pursuers the slip, and he persuaded the mechanics to rent him one of their courtesy vehicles. They did so – a silver Ford. Something the people looking for them won't recognize.

Zeke checks the windows regularly, front and back, alert for anything that looks like it could be out of place. The children are scared. They don't understand what is happening. Naomi does her best to comfort them. Zeke wishes he could help her. Wishes he could give his family all of his attention, but he needs to find out what's going on. He needs to find out who is coming after him.

He assumes the object of the attack was himself, as opposed to his wife or children. He can't imagine why anyone would be going after *them*. To be safe, though, as soon as they reached the motel, he got Naomi to call her parents and make sure they were okay. He told her not to let them know about the attack. They don't want to alarm them or bring them running to Shreveport, which would potentially put them in danger.

"Less they know, the safer they are," Zeke said.

Naomi nodded her agreement. Her parents were fine. No one had been by the house.

Zeke is calling the CIA. "I'll get them to send someone to keep an eye on your folks," he says, the phone dialing. He stays by the window, looking out. Naomi sits on the end of the bed with Tre and Tamika either side of her. She holds them close. The television is on, playing cartoons, but no one is watching it.

Zeke gets through to William Taylor, associate director for Operations, and tells him what has happened. Zeke has known William a few years now. They're in regular contact with each other, as William is Zeke's direct superior. The two men liaise on missions. They cooperate and coordinate together.

"Someone came after me, Will," Zeke says, finding it hard to keep his cool. "Someone came after my *family*. They were in my house, Will. I need to know who this was."

"Zeke, listen, I understand," William says. William is in his late fifties. He's spent all of his life in service to the government. It's been more than ten years since he was last in the field himself, but Zeke knows he remembers those days well. He keeps himself lean and in shape. He hasn't let himself go soft. His hair is graying and his mustache is equally salt and pepper, and Zeke can imagine him plucking at the edges of it while he speaks. "I understand what's happening, but you know you need to stay calm. That's our best way to work through this."

Zeke forces himself to take deep breaths. He steps out of the motel and into the cooler air. On the porch, he looks around, scanning the area. It's quiet. The parking lot is directly in front of him, enclosed on both sides by trees and bushes that have been left to grow wild. The silver Ford he's renting is parked in the corner off to his left. There are only three other vehicles in the lot. Beyond, he has a clear view of the main road and the cars that pass by, going in both directions. He doesn't see anyone pulling into the lot. "I'm as calm as I'm gonna get, Will."

"Let me look into anything that's been flagged that could relate back to you," William says. Zeke can hear him hitting keys on his computer. "Uh, Zeke, I'm gonna need you to bear with me. I've got an alert coming through – something big. I'll call you back – Zeke, listen, I'll call you back as soon as I can." William hangs up.

Zeke stares at the blank screen of his phone, gnawing the inside of his cheek. He slips the phone into his pocket and straightens up, looking around again. He tries to calm himself. Getting worked up isn't going to help anything. When William knows something, he'll get back in touch. Zeke has to be strong for his family. He has to show them that he's here for them, and everything will be all right. That no matter what is coming at them right now, he will deal with it.

He goes back inside. Naomi looks at him expectantly. Zeke shakes his head. "He's going to call me back."

He sees how his wife visibly deflates at this – that they don't have any answers yet – and it breaks his heart. Zeke doesn't let this show. He goes to where his family are sitting together at the end of the bed, and he crouches down in front of them. He takes Tre's hand, then one of Tamika's. "Hey," he says. "Hey, look at me."

They both do. Naomi strokes their hair and their cheeks,

doing her best to keep them soothed.

"I know what happened today was scary," Zeke says, looking each of his children in the eye. "But I promise, I will never let anyone hurt you. Okay? I will always keep you safe. Whatever happened today, whoever came after us, I'll find out who they were, and I'll make sure they can't come after us again."

"What are you going to do?" Tamika says. "Are you going to arrest them?"

Zeke and Naomi look at each other. Zeke takes a deep breath. "Yes," he says. "I'm going to arrest them."

"I thought you said you weren't a cop," Tre says.

"I said I wasn't *exactly* like a cop," Zeke says. It's eating him up inside, lying to his kids like this. He hates it, but he can't tell them the truth. Can't tell them that, depending on who's coming after them, he's likely going to put them in the ground. "But sometimes I'm allowed to arrest the really bad guys."

Tamika accepts this, but Zeke can see confusion and a little doubt in Tre's face. He's eight, he's still young, but he's getting older every day. It's clear he's not sure if he believes this story.

Zeke leans forward and wraps them all in his arms. He holds them as close and as tight as he can. He feels their little arms wrapping as far around him as they can. Naomi strokes the back of his neck. He holds them a long time until his phone finally begins to ring. He checks and sees that William is calling him.

"I'll be right back," he says, getting to his feet and heading back outside before he answers. "Will," he says, looking the outside area over again, remaining ever vigilant, "do you have anything for me?"

"I think I do, Zeke," William says. "I assume you remember Oscar Zavala?"

The name hits Zeke like a sledgehammer. He flashes back a few years, remembers when he and his old team moved in and extracted him from his hideout in Mexico. He remembers what Captain Robert Dale and his lackeys did that night, too, to Oscar Zavala's family.

"Zeke?" William says. "You still there? You got signal? I can't hear you."

Zeke grits his teeth, and he swallows. "Yeah," he says. "I remember Oscar Zavala. What's happened?"

"He's escaped."

"Goddammit," Zeke says, running his hand back over his head. "How'd it happen? I thought he was being moved around."

"He was," William says. "We don't know how his men tracked him down, but they did. Flew a helicopter right into the exercise yard, shot the place all to shit, and flew right back out of there with him."

"A helicopter? What kind?"

"One of ours – a Black Hawk."

"How the hell'd they get their hands on that? How'd they even afford it? I thought after we'd captured him, his organization was supposed to have fallen into disarray."

"Looks like someone was holding it together in his absence. But listen, Oscar Zavala is out, and there's a chance the people who came after you could be linked back to him."

"When'd he get free?"

"About an hour ago."

"If this *is* him, then that means he's had people watching me." Zeke pauses, thinking. "If that's the case, then that was presumably in anticipation of this, of his getting out. It sounds like he's been waiting, Will. Plotting and planning."

"We can't be sure that's the case," William says, "but whether it is or not, we need to get Oscar back in prison."

"An American one this time," Zeke says, grinding his teeth.

"Well, I can't guarantee that, but I'll see what I can do."

Zeke clenches his jaw. Try as he might, he can't calm down. And the truth is, he's not expecting to bring Oscar Zavala back in alive. If Oscar is behind the attack on his family, Zeke will end him.

William is talking. "We're following up on some intel – we're trailing Oscar, trying to find where he might be holing up. When we're more confident it's him and we have him pinned down, I'll let you know."

"I'm going after him."

"I figured as much. But like I said, we can't be sure this is him. The two things don't necessarily correlate."

"I know that," Zeke says. "But there's only one way to be sure, and I'm not going to wait around here sitting on my hands."

"I'll bring your team in."

"My family needs protection."

"Of course. We'll place them in a safe house."

"With bodyguards. And I need regular drive-bys on Naomi's parents. I promised her I'd make sure they're safe, too."

"I'm on it. Zeke, I'll call you back when we have something."

"Make it fast, Will. I want to get my family home as fast as possible."

"Got it." William hangs up.

8

I t's late. Tom sits in darkness. The house is fortified. It's
ready. It's waiting.

The front door is locked, but that's all. It's not
barricaded. There aren't planks of wood nailed across it. It's
the same at the back. He knows that if they come for him
tonight, they'll be as able to deal with the minor issue of the
locks as well as the men last night did.

Tom is not in complete darkness. He sits upstairs, in the
bedroom he and Hayley share. He's on the floor beside the
bed with his back against the wall, lit up with the glow from
a laptop that shows what the security cameras he's planted
outside see. The night is shown to him in greens and blacks.
His Beretta and KA-BAR are strapped to him, should anyone
who comes get past what is waiting for them downstairs.

There are cameras inside the house, too. They're downstairs. Tom isn't watching these yet. He doesn't need to. He
knows there's no one else in the house. Instead, he stares at
the outside. He blinks hard and rubs his tired eyes. They're
feeling the burn from watching the screen for so long.

Tom took a nap this evening while the last of the early evening light was still shining. He didn't expect anyone would try to come for him then, while it was still light out. Despite running on only a couple of hours' sleep for the last two days, he doesn't feel tired. He's alert. Primed. Waiting.

By two o'clock in the morning, Tom is still vigilant, but he's starting to feel like maybe no one's going to show up. Of course, if someone *is* coming, that's what they want him to think and feel. They'll know he'll be more alert after last night. They want him to grow lax and to stop paying as much attention as he should be.

Another hour passes. Tom sees movement in the darkness. He picks it up from the camera at the foot of the front lawn, concealed in the shrubs between the grass and the sidewalk. The movement is coming closer. It looks like one man, but then Tom sees what they're doing. They're coming in file formation. Because of this, Tom can't see how many of them there are. He won't know this until they're at the house. He catches blurs of bodies and heads in a line behind the man running point. He's armed with an assault rifle. It looks like an AKM, but it could be an AK-47.

As they reach the lawn, the man running point drops to a knee and raises the AKM, covering the house. Behind him, the file formation splits. Two of them head around the back. Two head to the front door. These four men are armed with handguns, like last night. Not Hellcats this time. A mix. Tom spots a Beretta and a Glock, but the other two are lost in the shadows.

They come to the door, and Tom can hear them. They're not picking the lock this time. They're coming in fast and hard. At the back, the kitchen door, they shoot out the lock. Things are about to get louder. Tom gets up on one knee, switching the cameras on the laptop to the interior view. Staying low, crouching, he moves to the window, pulling out his Beretta and raising it. His eyes don't leave the laptop screen. They flicker between what's happening inside and the man kneeling outside with his rifle raised.

The men at the back are already inside. The man taking lead comes through the door with his handgun raised. He doesn't get far. He hits a tripwire planted out of reach of the door's inward swing. An axe falls from the ceiling on a hinge and buries itself in the center of his face. It lodges so deep he doesn't go down. He hangs in place, his body drooping.

The man behind him sees what has happened. He's still advancing, but he's panicking, scanning the area for any sign of more traps. He searches for a light switch and frantically jabs at the one next to the rear door. Nothing happens. Tom removed the fuse.

At the front door, they're coming in now. There's another tripwire. The man at the back hears them enter, and he's shouting warnings to them in Spanish, telling them to be careful. They don't hear him. They've already hit the trip-wire. They set off a nail bomb Tom made this afternoon. Tom watches as the nails puncture their torsos and faces. They go down screaming. They're not dead, but they're badly wounded. His eyes flick to the guard outside. The guard's attention is drawn by all the noise. By the screams. Tom gets to his feet and pushes aside a curtain. He doesn't open the window. He shoots through the glass three times. Two of them hit the guard outside, knocking him onto his back. When he's down, and with the window already broken, he's an easier target. Tom puts two more bullets into him to keep him down. He turns back to the laptop.

The unharmed man in the kitchen hesitates, confused and scared. Tom can see him baring his teeth, psyching himself up, preparing to move in. He likely has a good idea he's the only one left. Tom waits to see what move he makes. If he gets beyond the kitchen, there's an unpleasant surprise waiting for him.

He moves on, and Tom gets to his feet, preparing to go downstairs. He keeps the Beretta in his hand, down by his side. He checks the outside cameras to make sure there is no sign of another wave coming. There's not, so far. All the noise, and the dead guard outside, would have drawn them out by now.

The man in the kitchen steps through, his handgun raised. He's being cautious. His eyes are scanning everything, checking the area ahead of him, up and down. His eyes will have adjusted to the dark, but Tom has planted the next trap in a darker spot, where even adjusted eyes will not pick up on it right away.

The man gets out of the kitchen and steps directly into the bear trap. He looses a shot from his gun as he goes down, crying out in surprise at the sudden pain of his shin snapping.

Tom makes his way downstairs, moving fast, Beretta raised. He can hear the victims of the nail bomb still screaming. Last he saw on the cameras, they were still on the ground. One of them has lost an eye.

The man in the bear trap is at the bottom of the stairs. His ankle and shin look all messed up. Tom kicks the gun out of his hand on his way past. He goes to the two who were nail-bombed and shoots them both, stilling and silencing them. He returns to the man in the trap, turning on a light as he comes. He crouches down next to him, out of reach, letting the Beretta dangle between his thighs.

"That looks like it hurts," Tom says.

The man curses at him in Spanish, spit flying from his gritted teeth.

"Quite a bit of blood, too. It's got a lot of clamping power, right? I mean, it's not built for humans. It's built for much bigger, more powerful legs than yours. This trap isn't actually legal, but if you know where to look and who to ask, you can always find one." Tom pauses deliberately and looks again at the man's leg. He's made sure he isn't carrying any more guns. He has a knife, but Tom is out of reach of it. The man hasn't made any effort to reach for it.

"Do you speak English?" he says. "I only know a little Spanish. I know the curse words, though, so don't worry, I get the gist of what you're saying."

The man spits to the side. "I speak English," he says. Tears are streaming down his face. Tom knows it's from the pain, same as the sweat that drips from his temples. Soon, he's going to go into shock.

"I'll make this quick," Tom says. "Who sent you? And don't fuck with me. Don't waste my time. I want an answer. If you're not forthcoming, well, I can make that trap hurt a whole lot worse. Don't try me."

The man grits his teeth and swallows. He looks into Tom's face, and he smirks. "He'll come for you," he says. "And he won't stop. He'll kill this whole town if he has to. He'll burn it to the ground."

"Uh-huh," Tom says. "And *who* is he?"

The man's smirk widens. "Oscar Zavala," he says. "And he's coming for you, Rollins. You can't stop what's coming next."

Tom grits his teeth. He remembers Oscar Zavala. His capture. What Robert Dale did. He remembers the kind of man Oscar Zavala was. How dangerous he was – and probably still is. He doubts prison has mellowed him, especially if he's sending his men out after his enemies.

"Oscar Zavala, huh?" Tom says. "I figure you're right – he won't stop. Sounds like I'm gonna have to meet him halfway. You've seen what I've done to your buddies here tonight and last night. He wants to come at me? I hope he's ready for what he's set in motion, because *he* can't stop what's coming next."

The man snarls. "He doesn't care. He wants you to come to him. He wants you to know. You think I'd be talking to you like this if I was told I couldn't?"

It's Tom's turn to smirk. "Tell me," he says. "Your boss – I'm guessing he's still partial to torture, right? He was always real big on the torture. His favorite pastime, seemed like. So here you are, sent after me, and you've failed, yet you're still alive. What do you think he's going to do to *you*?"

The man starts laughing. "I came here ready." He reaches for the knife, pulls it from its sheath. Tom is too far away to worry about it. The man doesn't make any attempt to swing for him. He drives it into the side of his own neck, his eyes locked with Tom while he does so. His eyes bulge. He makes a choked noise and sputters blood. With everything he has left, he pulls the knife out and sprays blood across the ground. He falls flat, bleeding out.

Tom straightens. He doesn't need to watch him die. The man would rather kill himself than face Oscar Zavala's wrath over his failure.

Tom hears sirens approaching. He doesn't plan to be here when they arrive. He doesn't have time to deal with cops again. He needs to get moving. He goes upstairs and grabs his bag, slinging it onto his back. He heads out to the car and drives away as blue and red light up the night sky, drawing nearer.

9

Max Ross rolls out of bed and makes himself coffee.

For the last year, he's lived in Honduras, on the outskirts of Gracias a Dios. It's not a safe place for him, especially as a white American, but Max knows how to take care of himself. He's also made himself very valuable to some very important people. Jorge Cruz, and by extension Oscar Zavala, is the biggest of those, but he's also paid off members of the Colón Cartel, from whom he rents this house. They make sure he's left alone. That no one tries to break in and rob him, to hold him for ransom. Jorge does not know about this arrangement. The first thing Max did when he reached this country, he made sure to cover his bases. He's not careless. He's not an idiot. About the only thing that matters to him is his own life, and he's determined to safeguard it.

Likewise, the Colón Cartel don't know about his dealings with the Zavala Cartel. The latter don't even know where he lives, or whether he stays in Honduras or travels back and forth from America when he needs to see them. He likes to keep it this way. The less both sides know about him, where he is and what he's doing, how he's operating, the better.

The house isn't big, but he doesn't mind. He doesn't plan on being here forever – maybe another year, two tops. It's one level, surrounded by trees, and just a twenty-minute walk from the beach, though he's been advised to only go there with cartel accompaniment. He's been advised not to go anywhere without cartel accompaniment. Max doesn't always heed this warning. Sometimes he doesn't mind taking the risk, such as if he's just running along to the local store to get in some groceries. He always makes sure to take a concealed gun with him, though, and some extra cash, just in case.

Standing in the kitchen, sipping from his coffee, he looks out the window through the trees. He's topless, nearly naked, wearing only the boxer shorts he sleeps in, but already he's sweating. It's always hot here, and the AC is not as reliable as he would like. With the back of his hand, he wipes the sweat from his brow before it can get into his eyes. Soon, he'll take a shower, and he'll stand there for a good half hour under the cold water.

As he finishes the coffee, his phone begins to ring. Max checks the number. The call is coming from America. He's been expecting this. Oscar got out of prison yesterday.

"Let me guess," Max says, answering. "You're calling to congratulate me on yet another operation running so smoothly?"

There's a pause at the other end. Max doesn't think it's a problem with the connection. The man on the other end has been caught off guard. He clears his throat. "I assume you're referring to Oscar Zavala's escape."

"Of course," Max says, dropping his coffee mug in the sink and heading through to the living room, lowering himself into a chair while still thinking of his forthcoming cold shower. "Isn't that why you're calling?"

"Have you seen him since he got out?"

"Not yet, but I imagine I will soon."

"They made a lot of noise in Mexico."

"I didn't expect them to be quiet, not after we supplied them with the Black Hawk. How did you think it was going to go?"

"They destroyed most of the prison. Killed a lot of guards and inmates alike."

Max makes a noise, blowing air through pursed lips. "And?"

"If this comes back on us –"

"It won't. That's why I'm out here full-time, to make sure of things like this. You need to relax. This is all in hand."

"Perhaps you need to tighten. Speaking of, Oscar is out – and he only *just* got out – so what's happening with this apparent vendetta of his?"

Max picks his teeth, frowning. "What do you mean?"

"He's going after the surviving members of the CIA team who brought him in – Ezekiel Greene and Tom Rollins. Ezekiel is still with the agency, but Tom Rollins left a long time ago."

"So? What are you getting at?"

"Attempts have been made on their lives, and they coincide with Oscar's escape. Sounds to me like his organization has been planning this for a while."

"That wouldn't surprise me. From what I've heard, Oscar isn't the type of man to let grudges go."

"You weren't aware of this?"

"I can't keep an eye on every little thing they're doing. I'm interested in the broad strokes. The bigger picture. That's what I'm here for."

"Uh-huh – if he continues to make so much noise, the bigger picture is going to fall apart. Everything we've been working towards won't matter anymore, and all because he couldn't let an old grudge lie."

"From what I understand, it's not a minor grudge," Max says. "I heard what happened when they brought him in."

"The men who did that are dead – under questionable circumstances, I hasten to add. It's my understanding Rollins and Greene had nothing to do with the darker aspects of Oscar's extraction. They reported it."

"And yet it seems like Oscar still holds them equally responsible."

The other man grunts. "He's a wild card. I've always said that. How can we trust him to do what we need him to do, when we're already starting out like this?" He sighs hard, clearly exasperated. "When Jorge refused to cooperate with us unless we found a way to return Oscar to him, we should have walked away right then and found someone else."

"Listen," Max says, "I'm out here in the field – I *know* there's no one else."

Max doesn't admit it, but he agrees with the other man. He thinks about Jorge and how he would have been an ideal candidate for what they have planned, but Jorge doubts himself too much. Max has been trying to persuade him otherwise, but it takes a delicate hand, and he doesn't want to reveal anything here, especially after the lengths they've gone to already to get Oscar out.

"Besides, they have an army, and if we weren't the ones putting them in this position, then the chances are they were just going to take it themselves eventually anyway. It's better we put them there, and they know we can take it away from them just as easily. But down here, no one can match up to them. Only the Colón Cartel come close, but they're not as well organized or as strong."

"They're currently in a truce with each other, isn't that right?"

"It is. The Zavala Cartel are bigger and have more power, but they couldn't crush the Colón Cartel as easily as they like, and both sides know it. If they went to war, it would be long and costly, and the Zavala Cartel would *lose* a lot of that strength they have."

"Is this something we should be concerned about?"

Max laughs. "Once we put them where we want them, they'll outnumber the Colón Cartel a hell of a lot more than they do now. They won't have to worry so much about a war. It won't affect them as much as it could now. By then, it'll be too late for the Colóns to do anything about it."

"Of course, all of this is a moot point if you can't get Oscar under control."

Max grins to himself. He's not concerned. "Things will go as they're supposed to. Like I said, you need to relax. Trust in me. When have I ever let you down before?"

"There's a first time for anything."

Max bristles a little at this, but he bites his lips and prevents himself from saying something he shouldn't. "What do you want me to do?"

"I want you to answer this – did you know he was going to go after Rollins and Greene?"

"I had an inkling."

"Uh-huh. I assume you told them the whereabouts of Rollins and Greene?"

"Only Zeke. I didn't know where Tom was. Oscar's men must have found him themselves."

"Mm. Now what I want is for you to talk to Oscar and Jorge and get them to either hold off on this vengeance of theirs, or else speed it up and keep it neat. What's happening right now, all the noise and mess it's causing, it's no good. We can't have it, Max."

Max licks sweat from his top lip. He wants that shower. He's growing desperate for it now. "Sure," he says, wanting to be done with this conversation. "I'll talk to them."

10

N ow that Tom knows who's coming after him, he knows what he needs to do.

He's on the road, heading to Louisiana. To Shreveport. He still has a long, long way to go. The first thing he needs to do, before he goes after Oscar Zavala, is to warn Zeke. He's tried calling ahead already, on a burner phone, but there was no answer. This is concerning, but Tom is trying not to fear the worst. It'll slow him down. Instead, he tells himself how Zeke is a busy man. He still works for the CIA – he's most likely out on an operation. Except Tom also tried calling the home number, the landline, and there was no answer from Naomi, either. So Tom tells himself they could be on vacation. A family vacation. It doesn't need to be the worst-case scenario. He *hopes* it's not the worst-case scenario.

Before he set off from Hopper Creek, after he'd slipped away before the police had a chance to reach the house, once again drawn by all the gunfire and the screams, Tom called

Hayley to let her know that he was all right, and that he was heading out of town and he wasn't sure for how long.

"Tom, what happened?" she asked, worried but doing her best to stay calm.

"They came to the house again," Tom said. "And they're going to keep coming until I deal with this thing head-on. Listen, stay with your parents while I'm gone. You're safe there and at the hospital. I've got the cops watching both places, but you still need to be careful, okay? If I'm out of town, I think they'll leave, too, once they know I'm not there. But they're not beneath coming after families, do you understand? These are the kinds of people I'm dealing with here."

"Jesus Christ, Tom, what's going on?"

"Trouble from my past. I'm dealing with it. Just stay away from the house, okay? I don't want anyone to see you there. And it's a mess – I'll fix it all when I get back, I promise."

"Tom, I don't care about the mess. I care about *you*."

"I'll be all right." He didn't know how true this statement was. He still doesn't. Oscar used to have an army. It seems like he still could.

Tom drives, hoping that Zeke and his family are all right. That Oscar's men haven't been able to find them. He's curious how they were able to find *him*. Tom has been careful. He always is.

His phone rings. It's Cindy. He answers. "I know who's coming after you," she says.

"So do I," Tom says, and tells her about last night.

"I've heard from Zeke," Cindy says when he's finished.

"You have?" Tom feels a fist he didn't realize was clamped inside his chest loosen. "How is he?"

"Worried about *you*," Cindy says. "He sent me an encrypted message – he didn't want Oscar to be able to track you down. He said he's been compromised, couldn't run the risk that maybe they were into his phone lines. They came after him and his family. He wanted me to get in touch with you, let you know about Oscar Zavala – which you obviously do. Are you driving right now?"

"I'm heading to Zeke's."

"To tell him about Oscar?"

"You got it."

"So what now? That he already knows, I mean."

"I'm still going. Strength in numbers. We can help each other and do a better job of looking out for his family together."

"Well, maybe you should let me tell you the rest of Zeke's message. He says they have intel, and he and his team are going after him. They should have this whole thing wrapped up soon."

Tom is silent. When he finally makes a sound, it's, "Hmm."

"You sound doubtful."

"It sounds too neat and easy. I'm gonna stay the course, go to Shreveport."

"If you think that's best."

"I do."

"Where you at now?"

"Funnily enough, I'm in Texas." Cindy lives in Texas.

"Oh yeah? You want some company? If Zeke and his team aren't able to wrap things up, you could need my help."

Now that he knows Zeke and his family are safe, Tom doesn't feel such a need to rush. He can afford to turn off the I-10 and make his way north to Lubbock, especially to get help. And it's been a few months since he last saw Cindy, since he dropped her off on their way back from Chicago.

"We could," he says. "And if Zeke is heading out on an operation, I have time enough for a detour."

"Do you remember the way?"

"Roughly. Send me directions to be safe."

"I'll do that now. Where are you, exactly?"

Tom tells her he's near Pecos.

"Then I've got a few hours. I'll pack a bag, and I'll see you then."

Cindy hangs up, and Tom waits for her message to come through with directions to her apartment. He doesn't have to wait long. He pulls to the side of the road to reroute his journey on the GPS, and then sets off to get Cindy.

11

Z eke and his family spent the night in the motel. Come the morning, Zeke woke to details of the safe house from William. He bundles his family into the car while it's still early. Tre and Tamika yawn, and Tamika is quick to fall back asleep.

Zeke drives his family to the safe house. Naomi is awake all the way, but she's quiet. Zeke is quiet, too. They're both lost in their own thoughts. Zeke is desperate to get on the move, to meet up with his team and get in the air and head to wherever Oscar is holing himself up. William has promised him the intel will be verified soon, and they'll get the green light to move in.

While he drives, he watches the mirrors, making sure they're not being followed. Naomi is watching the window on her side, too, her face propped up on her hand with her elbow on the door's armrest.

They reach the safe house, but Zeke doesn't pull straight up to it. He circles the block a couple of times to be sure it's clear. Naomi doesn't question him. The kids don't notice what he's doing.

Zeke goes up to the house first. The Lincoln Navigator that belongs to the bodyguards is parked on the driveway. While Zeke rings the doorbell, he makes sure to keep his family in view.

Both of the men he's trusting to guard his family answer. One of them is white, with a shaved head and a red goatee. The other is black, clean-shaven, his hair cut short around the sides and back. Both men are equally as tall and broad, and they're dressed in slacks and white shirts.

"Mr. Greene?" says the white bodyguard, holding out a hand.

Zeke checks their IDs before he shakes each of their hands in turn. The white bodyguard is called Bill Flowers, and the black is Ben Coombs. Zeke goes back to his car to get his family. He carries Tamika, who's rubbing her eyes, waking up. He holds Tre's hand. Naomi walks beside him to the house. Bill and Ben step aside for them. Zeke sets Tamika down.

"You're not going to be here for long," Zeke says, looking both of his children over. "But it could be a couple of days, so why don't you go and find the room you like best for you to share while Mom and I talk to Bill and Ben here."

Tre and Tamika regard the two men warily.

"They're here to look after you all while I'm at work, okay?" Zeke says. He points out which is Bill and which is Ben. "You both do as they say while I'm gone. But most of all, listen to your mother." Zeke straightens and sends them off to find their preferred room. He wraps an arm around Naomi's waist and turns to Bill and Ben. "I don't know either of you, but Will has vouched for you both. I'm trusting you to look after my family."

Bill nods solemnly.

"We won't let you down," Ben says.

Zeke steers Naomi away so he can speak to her in private. "I'm not going to hang around."

Naomi nods, expecting this. She folds her arms and strokes them like she's cold.

"I'll say bye to the kids, and then I'll go," Zeke says. "I'll be as fast as I can. We'll be back in our home and our own beds before we know it."

"It's going to be hard going back there," Naomi says. "Knowing that someone broke in, looking to kill us."

Zeke nods. He knows this. They'll probably end up moving. It will be hard for him to continue living there knowing someone was able to track him down. He'll never be able to relax. Constantly checking the windows and the street, more than he already does. It won't feel like home anymore. "Just stay close to the kids at all times. Nothing should, but if anything happens and you need to run, you want to be able to grab them and *go*. You don't want to lose time looking for them."

"I know," Naomi says.

"Bill and Ben – I don't know them, but if Will sent them, they're good, though, I trust that. So just stay low and do as they say." He places his hands on her shoulders and squeezes, though knowing this is scant comfort. "This will all be over soon."

"I hope so."

"I won't be able to get in touch while I'm gone. You won't hear from me until we've dealt with Oscar."

"This isn't my first rodeo, Zeke. I know what it's like when you're on an operation. Just go."

Zeke leans in and kisses her on the forehead. She stops him as he draws away, placing a hand on the back of his neck and pulling him in for a longer, deeper kiss.

"I love you," Zeke says. "I love all of you so much."

"We know you do," Naomi says. She kisses him again, lighter this time, on the corner of the mouth. "Now go say goodbye to the kids."

12

O scar Zavala wakes, and it takes him a moment to register where he is. The unfamiliar surroundings. The deep, comfortable mattress. The sun streaming in through the window, splashing across his chest, warming him. This is no prison. In fact, this room is large enough to house six cells. He smiles and pushes himself out of the bed. His bare feet touch down on cool tile.

He does not yawn or stretch as he crosses the room to the window. He's wide awake despite how late he stayed up last night. He feels better rested than he has in years of sleeping in filthy Mexican cells. He steps out onto the balcony, breathing deep the morning air and feeling the sun on his skin. He wears only the underwear he slept in, and he basks in the sun warming him.

The house is on the coast. It's a mansion, acquired in Oscar's absence. Yesterday, when they touched down after escaping Mexico, was Oscar's first time seeing it. Directly opposite him, about a mile or so away, he can see the sea. He stares at it for a long time, watching its gentle waves. One day, soon, he will go down onto the beach and put his bare feet into the sand and the sea. Not yet, though. There is too much that needs to be done just now. His beach visit will be his reward for accomplishing his vengeance. In the meantime, he'll admire it from afar.

He takes a sharp breath, thinking of Marie and of Edwin. His wife and his boy. Except, he wasn't a boy anymore. A man. He should be thirty now. He *should*. Instead, he is forever twenty-six.

Oscar grits his teeth. There is no time for mourning. No time for despair. Those days are done, fully indulged within solitary confinement. Angry thoughts of vengeance sustained him. He can't think of anything else. That's what matters now. It's all that matters.

Oscar tears his eyes from the sea, and his mind from the past. He looks down at the mansion's expansive grounds. There are other houses dotted around – or, more precisely, barracks – for the men. *His* men. *His* army. Some of them are on the grass below, running drills. He watches them for a moment, pleased that discipline has been maintained. The men look good – they look strong. They look *ready*.

To his left, beyond the rear corner of the house, sits the Black Hawk that brought Oscar home. It sits atop a landing pad that has been set upon the grass, a square slab of concrete.

Behind him, Oscar becomes aware of knocking on his bedroom door. He steps back inside. "Come in," he calls, crossing the room to the wardrobe near the foot of the bed and pulling out a pair of slacks and a loose shirt. He's pulling them on as Jorge enters the room. He's smiling.

"Oscar," he says. Jorge was there to greet him off the helicopter upon his return last night. They embraced for a long time, and then Jorge ushered him into the house, for a night of eating and drinking – as well as the company of the finest prostitutes in Gracias a Dios – to truly welcome Oscar home. "I wasn't sure if you'd be awake yet. We all had a late night."

Oscar grins, stepping forward and shaking Jorge's hand. "Indeed we did," he says. "But I always wake early when there are things to do." He buttons up the shirt. "I didn't get much of a chance to admire the area last night. I'm pleased to see that you've been running a tight ship in my absence."

"I did the best I could," Jorge says. "We never lost faith we would get you back, and we wanted to make sure you had an organization you would be proud to return to."

Oscar claps his hands together. "What can I do for you, Jorge?"

Jorge wears a pair of khaki trousers and a khaki T-shirt tucked into them. He stands with his legs slightly spread and his arms clasped behind his back, standing at ease. Oscar has always run his organization like an army, and Jorge remains the loyal lieutenant. "I came to invite you down for breakfast," he says. "And while we're there, I thought I could give you an overview of our current operations."

"Do we have Rollins and Greene yet?"

Jorge clears his throat and shifts his weight. "Not yet," he says. "But I assure you, we're working on it. I have men looking for them, and with the assistance of our new American friends –"

Oscar waves a hand in the air, and Jorge looks surprised by this dismissive gesture. "I've waited a long time to get my revenge," Oscar says. "I can wait a little longer. I'm not concerned. I'll get them both soon, one way or another. Either my men will bring them in, or they will come here of their own accord. I'm sure that neither man will run away, or go to ground and hope we'll pass them by." He chuckles and adds, "If they do, then I have sorely overestimated them all this time."

Jorge clenches his jaw and looks like he has information he doesn't want to share.

Oscar picks up on it. "What is it? Spit it out."

"I don't think Rollins will hide, at least," he says. "He's killed nine of our men."

Oscar raises an eyebrow. "*Nine?*" He can't deny that he's impressed by this number. "Is that so?"

"Over two nights. They attacked in two separate waves. I'd hoped to have both him and Greene here for your return, but unfortunately it was not to be."

Oscar nods, then pats him on the arm. "I appreciate the thought. But I am patient, Jorge. I've had to be. I don't plan on breaking that new habit now."

Jorge grins suddenly. "I do have a surprise coming for you, though. One I think you will be very pleased with and will tide you over until we have Rollins and Greene."

"A surprise?" Oscar raises an eyebrow. "What kind of surprise?"

"Do you remember much of what we talked about last night?"

Oscar frowns, trying to recall. It's all a hazy, drunken blur. "All I remember is talking of prison," he says.

There's a gleam in Jorge's eye. "And maybe that was all we talked of. Who can say? I don't want to ruin the surprise."

Oscar regards him, wondering what Jorge could be talking about, still trying to remember anything else they may have spoken of last night.

Jorge changes the subject. "Would you like to come down to breakfast?"

"No, I don't think I will," Oscar says, crossing the room and taking a seat by the window. "I'm not hungry."

"Would you like me to update you on our various businesses now?"

Oscar waves his dismissive hand, and again Jorge looks surprised. "I'm sure I can guess at them all," Oscar says. "Drugs, guns, and women, yes?" Oscar isn't interested in business. He has one interest. *Vengeance.* This is all that concerns him. It consumes him. Jorge has run their illicit activities for this long, Oscar is sure he can continue to trust them in his hands. "I'm sure they're all doing well."

"Uh, yes. Yes, they are."

"Good. That's all I need to know. Keep on top of them, Jorge. Keep things running smoothly. Do you know what I *do* want this morning?"

"What?" Jorge says.

Oscar tugs at his beard and at his long hair. "A shave," he says. "And a haircut. You can get someone for me, yes?"

"Of course. I'll get someone now." Jorge makes to leave the room.

Oscar stops him. "Good," he says. "And Jorge? There is *one* thing I'm interested in hearing more about."

Jorge raises an eyebrow.

"The Americans," Oscar says. "While my hair is being cut, you can tell me exactly what it is the Americans want from me."

13

"You really like driving in silence, don't you?" Cindy says.

They've been driving for an hour since Tom picked her up. She jumped into his arms like she was excited to see him, despite the circumstances. Tom didn't mind. He squeezed her in return, keeping her lifted off her feet with ease. Tom put her bag in the trunk, and they set straight off.

Cindy has helped Tom out many times over the last few years, since he first met her. They've helped each other out. She's good with computers. So far as Tom is concerned, she's the best. She can get into any system. Because of this, she can usually find anyone via security footage and online trails. If Zeke isn't able to wrap things up and capture Oscar soon, Cindy might be able to help them out.

"Only when I'm thinking," Tom says. "I listen to music when I don't have things on my mind. We just always happen to be traveling together when I have things on my mind."

"And when you're not thinking, it's usually Springsteen, right?" She grins at him.

"Usually," Tom says. "But I do have a very broad musical palate, you know."

"I'm sure. I've just never been around while you've explored it, is all."

"That's unfortunate for you."

"How's Hayley?" Cindy says. "You never said otherwise, so I assume she hasn't been hurt."

"No, she wasn't. Thankfully. She's with her parents right now."

Cindy nods. "I'm glad she's all right. I'm sure she's worried about you."

"She'll feel a lot better once I let her know you're here to take care of me."

Cindy laughs. "Of course. Big strong Cindy to the rescue." She looks out the window. They still have a far way to go across Texas.

"Was this all a subtle way of you asking if you could put on some music?" Tom says.

Cindy laughs. "I was just pointing it out."

"Uh-huh. Last time I let you pick the music, it was Throbbing Gristle. I didn't hate it, but I'm not sure I want to listen to that again."

"If you want silence, I'm happy with silence. Just you, me, and the engine. *But* before that, I do have a question – *what* are you thinking about?"

"Oscar Zavala."

Cindy nods. "I figured." She waits a beat, then says, "Are you going to tell me about him? Why he's coming after you?"

Tom nods. "I was planning on it. I just wanted to give us a chance to catch up first before we got down to business."

"I know you have your doubts, but if we're lucky and Zeke is successful, we won't have to get down to business at all, and this will just be a peaceful Tom-and-Cindy road trip for a change. For the first time ever, in fact."

"It was peaceful on the way back from Chicago."

"Yeah – on the way *back*." Cindy laughs. "You can take your time with the Oscar stuff. We've got plenty of road left to go."

Tom doesn't need to take his time. He has the story set in his mind already. He remembers it well. It's all he's thought about since he heard the man in the bear trap say Oscar Zavala's name. "It was a few years ago, thereabouts," Tom says. "Not long before we first met – maybe a year. It was the second-last operation I ran with the CIA, before the final one in Afghanistan that forced me out of the agency."

"Why do I get the feeling Robert Dale is going to fit into this?"

Tom nods. "Robert Dale, Simon Collins, and Nathan Sapolsky. The trifecta. I'm sure you remember them."

"I remember them well."

"Well, it was the same kind of thing. They went into business for themselves. But I'm getting ahead of myself. Oscar Zavala is Honduran, but he must have thought he'd outgrown his homeland. He was operating out of Mexico at that time, growing his army, growing his power and his influence. There were indicators he might attempt to overthrow the Mexican government. I've been told the CIA was keeping an eye on him – he'd already moved north from Honduras to Mexico, and they were worried he might move more northerly still, into America.

"He never got a chance to get that far. Oscar started targeting Mexican government officials. He was torturing and killing them. That's a big thing for him, by the way – the torture. And he didn't have a preferred method. He liked to experiment. He'd flay and burn and bludgeon. He'd break bones and eviscerate and filet. I've seen pictures of his work. He was a real butcher. How well do you know your Mexican presidents?"

"I don't know them too well at all."

"Not even the current president?"

"I'm not enjoying this judgment, Tom."

Tom laughs. "All right, okay. So you don't know the name Luis López? He was the president of Mexico before the current one. Oscar had his younger brother kidnapped, and held him ransom. To show he was serious, he started sending fingers back to Luis. Luis raised his brother. Their parents died when they were both young. Luis was seven years older than his brother, and he had to grow up very fast. It's not hard to imagine he saw his younger brother almost as a son, even though both men were now middle-aged. It's easy to believe that Oscar was aware of this. Most people were. It was well documented."

He glances at Cindy. She's listening intently, and it's clear from the look on her face that she can guess how this story culminates.

"Luis paid the ransom. And then he waited. And he waited. And eventually, Luis's body was found, his eyes gouged out and his intestines cut loose and wrapped around his neck. Luis was distraught, naturally. He wasn't good for much after that, but members of his cabinet started to worry about what Oscar might do next. He'd already been targeting them, and what he'd done to Luis's brother felt like a warning for what was to come next. It seemed like he could be about to make big moves. Overthrow the government.

Install himself as dictator, perhaps. So his cabinet reached out to the States and asked for help.

"Like I said, the CIA had already been watching Oscar, with growing concern. They didn't want to be seen to be interfering in an official capacity, so they sent us. Luis wanted Oscar captured. He planned on burying him *under* prison, to never see the light of day again. Nothing was said about his family, though, and Robert and his boys took advantage of that. While Zeke and I were extracting Oscar, Robert, Simon, and Nathan were running wild through his hideout, putting bullets in everyone they could find. Oscar's wife and adult son were the first two to bite it."

"Holy shit," Cindy says. "Why?"

Tom shakes his head. "Same reason they usually went off course – they were looting the place."

"And now Oscar is coming for the only two members of the team still surviving."

Tom nods. "Yeah, and I doubt he's going to care that we killed Robert and Nathan and Simon, that we were the ones who put the men who killed his family in the ground. He's not going to listen to reason."

"And he's got an army?"

"He *did*. Seems like he's still got a lot of men under his command. I won't know much more for sure until we can speak to Zeke."

They drive in silence while Cindy absorbs all this.

Tom turns on the stereo. "I think I'm ready for some music now."

The music starts, and Cindy cocks her head, listening. "Tom Petty?"

"See?" Tom says. "I'm full of surprises."

14

Zeke's team are silent on the chopper flight. Ordinarily, they would make small talk. They would joke around. They'd grow quiet only as they neared their objective. Not this time. They know this is personal for their commander. They're all business.

They fly low, soon to land, following up on the intel secured by the CIA. Zeke holds the collar of his body armor in both hands, feeling the bulk of his M4 strapped across his chest. He squeezes the vest. He closes his eyes and grits his teeth. He thinks of his family. It's not long until they land. Zeke has been watching the time on his watch the whole flight, willing the minutes to go faster. Once they have Oscar, they can mop up the rest of his organization. Then Zeke can go home. Then they'll be safe.

A niggling thought sticks with him that maybe it's not Oscar. He and William discussed this briefly on the phone. They could go to all this effort, eradicate Oscar and his organization, just to find he's not the original attacker. Oscar fits the bill, and the timing of his escape can't be a mere coincidence, but they don't have any proof Oscar is responsible.

Zeke pushes this thought down. If it's not Oscar, then this is all *too much* of a coincidence.

He opens his eyes and looks around. None of his team are looking back at him. They check their equipment or else stare at the ground, no doubt putting themselves in his shoes and imagining what they would do if the lives of their children had been put in danger, and how they would react.

To Zeke's immediate left is Guy Roberts. Guy is white. He sits with his eyes closed, but he's not sleeping. His breath is regular and controlled. He's preparing mentally, perhaps even meditating, as he readies himself for their mission. Guy thinks of himself as a spiritual person. He meditates daily. He fasts. He does breath work. He's told Zeke he thinks he could be a Buddhist, but he feels like he can't truly convert until he's left the CIA. "There's too great a dichotomy between what we do and how I want to be as a person, for me to fully convert just yet," he said.

While Guy fills his lungs and calms his mind, Zeke looks beyond him, further left, to Shaun Andrews. Shaun is black. His eyes are wide open. He inspects his weapons, one after the other, a perpetual cycle. This is how he calms himself. How he prepares. Zeke notices he almost fumbles handling his Glock 19, almost drops it, but he quickly rights himself. He stops and holds steady, checking that his hands have stopped trembling. Zeke is surprised by this. He's never seen Shaun fumble. Before he joined the CIA, he was a professional football player. His hands needed to be ready, and his grip needed to be strong. A knee injury cut his career short, but there's never been anything wrong with his hands.

Shaun stares at his hands until he's confident they are still, and then resumes his cycle.

Zeke looks directly opposite. Selena Gutierrez and Daniel Alonso. Both are of Latin descent – Selena Mexican and Daniel is Guatemalan. Daniel stares at the ground, his hands clasped, lost in thought. Daniel used to be a cop in Arizona. Selena was in the Army. She feels Zeke watching her and looks back at him. Their eyes lock, and she nods once, her expression sympathetic.

Zeke checks the time. "All right," he says, speaking into his mic, hearing his voice come back tinny in his ears. "Get ready. We touch down soon. We move in, and we get this motherfucker out."

The others respond in the affirmative. Guy opens his eyes and pounds Zeke on the arm with the side of his fist. They get ready. They feel the chopper begin its descent.

They land in a clearing surrounded by trees. They dismount and start moving. The pilots remain behind, waiting for them. It's still light, so they landed far out from their target. They have ten miles to cover. They didn't want to land too close. Oscar will be vigilant, especially so soon after his escape. The sight or sound of anything alarming, he'll flee.

There's a van waiting for them on the other side of the trees. The team file in the back, and the driver sets off. They stay low in the back. There's nothing separating them from the driver, a local asset who stares straight ahead. He's good. He's calm. Zeke has seen assets who are sweaty and jittery, too talkative. This guy is the opposite. He winds down his window and smokes a cigarette. Zeke stares out from the gap between the seats, watching the road ahead, waiting for the house to come into view.

When they're almost there, the driver turns his head a little, says, "One mile."

They're on a dirt road, bumping and jostling them. There are trees on either side. Zeke hasn't seen a single other car on the way here. The place is isolated.

He can see a roof up ahead, poking through a gap in the trees. Orange tiles, some of them cracked, some of them missing. The driver rolls to a stop. Without turning, he nods.

"Out," Zeke says to his team. "Let's go."

He takes point, ducking low and running toward the trees. They move through, using the trunks as cover. They scan the area, searching for armed guards, anyone on patrol. As they get closer to the house, Zeke watches the windows. He can't see anyone in them.

They communicate in hand signals. Zeke tells them he's going in first. He wants Selena and Shaun with him, pincer formation. Guy is to cover the front of the house, and Daniel the rear. They spread out and move in.

A rusted gate creaks, caught in a breeze. Surrounding the property is a chain-link fence, also rusted. The house looks still. Quiet. Zeke hasn't seen any signs of life yet. They cut through the fence and encircle the house. Zeke looks through a window. It's clear inside. He sees dirt and branches on the floor from where a window has been smashed and the outside has blown in.

Zeke regroups with Selena and Shaun. "I think it's empty," Shaun says.

"No signs of life," Selena says.

Zeke has seen this too, but he doesn't want to believe it. He needs to believe that Oscar is here, inside. He *needs* him to be. This has to end here.

"We're going in," he says, thinking that perhaps there is a

basement, or they could be hiding behind corners in anticipation of this raid, just out of view. "You checked for traps?"

They both nod. Zeke alerts Guy and Daniel that they're
moving in.

Zeke tries the door. It's unlocked. He knows this isn't a
good sign. He steps inside, M4 raised. There are no tripwires.
No traps. He moves through the downstairs rooms, followed
by Selena and Shaun. There is no one else present, but
Selena finds signs of recent life.

"The hearth is still warm," she says. "They've been using
it for cooking."

Zeke joins her in the living room. There are emptied tins
of beans strewn across the floor, along with a bottle of wine
with cigarette butts dropped into the bottom of it, swimming
in the dregs.

"Goddamnit," Zeke says, storming out of the room and
out of the house. He gets on the radio back to the chopper.
"He's gone," he says. "We're on our way back. Get in touch
with William Taylor – tell him it looks like Oscar hasn't been
gone long. He can't have gotten far. Tell him to find his trail
and send it to me – *now*, while it's still hot."

Zeke looks around, at the trees that surround this house.
It pains him to know that Oscar was here, and he missed
him. He gets back on the radio. "I'm not leaving Guatemala
until we have him."

15

Oscar has had a haircut and a shave, though he's kept a neatly trimmed mustache. He's had a shower, and he's put on fresh clothes. He wears black trousers and a white shirt, the top three buttons undone. Checking his reflection in the mirror, he sees that he finally looks like himself again.

He takes a walk around the house and the grounds. His men nod to him, bow to him. Respectfully. Reverently. They don't look him in the eye. They barely speak to him except to say *Señor Zavala*. It isn't last night anymore. It's not his return. It's not a party. They're down to business. He's glad to see that they know the difference.

In the kitchen, he makes himself a sandwich, enjoying the freedom of feeding himself what he wants when he wants. There are half a dozen women present, preparing meals and snacks for the men. They offer to make Oscar's sandwich for him, but he insists on doing it himself. He carries it upstairs, taking bites from it while he looks through the rooms. There's an office, clearly Jorge's. Oscar goes to the desk, runs a fingertip over its highly varnished wood, and takes a seat. He gets breadcrumbs on the desk. He doesn't bother to wipe them away. He gets up and leaves. The office does not interest him. The room directly opposite has a small cinema screen inside. Oscar frowns, looking this room over. He wonders if the cinema was an installation of the previous owner. He can't imagine why they would need to have one here. He returns to his room.

When Jorge comes to find him, he's beaming from ear to ear. "Oscar," he says.

"I found a cinema room," Oscar says.

Jorge's smile falters. "Pardon?"

"Opposite your office. Does it get much use?"

"Sometimes," Jorge says, looking confused.

"You may be overly fraternizing with the men."

"I rarely use it," Jorge says. "I leave it for them. As a reward, when things have gone well."

Oscar grunts. "What did you come here for?"

Jorge's smile returns. "I have your surprise."

"That was fast," Oscar says.

"I put things in motion last night," Jorge says. "As soon as you told me about him."

Oscar cocks his head. "Him?" he says.

Jorge waves him to follow. "Come and see."

Oscar follows Jorge out of the room, down the stairs and through the house. He notices how Jorge is grinning to himself all the way, like a child eager to gift a parent a present they know they'll love. They reach the kitchen. The women all stop what they're doing, almost standing to attention. They look far different from how they did earlier, when

Oscar was in making himself a sandwich. A couple of them have blanched.

"How long ago did this gift arrive?" Oscar says as Jorge leads him toward a door at the rear of the kitchen. Oscar does not know where this door goes. "I was in here less than an hour ago. Did I just miss its delivery, or was it already here, perhaps?"

Jorge turns to him before he opens the door, still grinning. "A matter of minutes," he says. "I came straight to get you after he had arrived."

Jorge opens the door. A set of stairs leads down into a basement. Jorge goes down first, and Oscar follows. He's cautious. He doubts that Jorge would be leading him into a trap. It would make no sense, especially after he's gone to such effort to break him free. But Oscar has always been paranoid. It's gotten him far, and it's kept him alive. Right now, just to be safe, he wishes he had a gun on him, or a knife. So long as this isn't a trap, he makes a mental note to rectify this. These are his men, his army, and he should feel safe, but he can't forget the lessons he has learnt in prison – no one is *ever* safe.

They reach the basement, and Jorge steps aside for Oscar to see. Oscar blinks against the harsh glare of an unshielded light bulb to see a familiar face opposite him, chained to the wall at ankles and wrists. His being here is so unexpected, so out of context, it takes Oscar a moment to realize who he is.

Mateo Blanco.

"To tide you over," Jorge says, "until the main course arrives."

Oscar smiles. He crosses the basement, closer to Mateo. There's a lump on the side of his head above his right eye, presumably how he was persuaded to come all the way to

Honduras. He's been stripped naked, and already the skin at his wrists and ankles has been chafed raw by his pulling at his bonds. There is a gag in his mouth. His jaw is set, his eyes narrowed. He wants to stand strong, to appear resolute. To show no fear.

"Mateo," Oscar says, smiling as he takes the gag from his mouth. "What a pleasant surprise. I thought I might not see you again, and what a shame that would be." He looks around, seeing a low table to his right. The top of it is covered with tools and weapons – hammers, screwdrivers, nails, and a variety of knives and scalpels.

"Oh my," Oscar says. "I'm sure you've seen all of these, Mateo." Oscar laces his fingers and pops his knuckles. "It's been a while. Jorge, you can leave us. Mateo and I are looking forward to getting reacquainted."

"Of course," Jorge says, and leaves. Oscar hears the door leading into the kitchen close behind him. He imagines the women working there are still frozen, listening, waiting.

Mateo has not made a noise since the gag was removed. He knows there's no point in shouting.

"Do you know why I removed your gag, Mateo?"

He doesn't answer. His eyes burn holes through Oscar.

They don't affect Oscar. He laughs the glare off. "Quite simply, there's no need for it. You can make as much noise as you like. Everyone can hear, and no one will care." Oscar steps closer, his hands clasped behind his back. His face is inches from Mateo's. "You're going to scream. You will, I promise you that."

Mateo gulps. It's clear he doesn't want to. The action is involuntary.

Oscar takes a step back, looking down at the table again. He takes his time, allowing the anticipation to build. "Your downfall, Mateo, has arrived due to your insistence on being such a hard-ass. You understand that, don't you?" He straightens and turns back to Mateo. "Truth be told, this is all so unexpected. I had no idea Jorge would have you wrapped and trussed and brought to me like this. I only mentioned you in passing, while drunk. When you weren't there for my escape, I shrugged it off. I thought to myself *Oh well. Maybe one day.* And to think that day is *now*, so soon. Well, it's a surprise. A pleasant one."

Mateo almost speaks, but he stops himself.

Oscar cocks his head. "You don't have to be shy."

Mateo is silent.

Oscar shrugs. "Suit yourself. You know, Mateo, I don't even resent you that much for how you treated me in the short time we were together in Mexico. I still have some bruises from your rough handling, and I'm still a few pounds lighter than I would normally be when not eating to your arbitrary schedule. But, honestly, I've dealt with worse. You were just the most recent. Here's the thing, though." He pauses, stepping in front of Mateo again and folding his arm, stroking the corner of his mustache. "Now that you're here, it's not like I can just let you go, is it? What kind of example would that set? You've seen the men I have here, under my command. They're a rough and ready sort, aren't they? How could they ever respect me, or do as I say, if I didn't prove to them that I'm just like them – that I'm worse, in fact? Truly, I've found the only way to control terrible men is to be more terrible than they could dream. So I *am* going to hurt you, Mateo. I'm going to do awful things to you that you could not conceive of. And you are going to scream, and everyone here, every single man and woman, will hear you."

Mateo is trembling. His face remains the same, impassive, but his body betrays him.

"And, truth be told, it's been a while since I last did this kind of thing," Oscar says. "What with my years spent on the floors of your country's filthy cells. I could have grown rusty, though we won't know until we get started. But you see, I have some old friends coming this way, and I want to be sharp for them. You will be my practice canvas before I paint my true masterpiece."

Oscar looks at the tools again. He's going to start with the hammer. A wonderful, blunt instrument with which to begin, and to tenderize Mateo's tense body. And then? Well, then, the world is his oyster. The flat-headed screwdriver is smiling at him, however. He's sure he can put it to good use.

"Before we begin," Oscar says, "is there anything you'd like to say?"

Mateo swallows. "Just get this over with," he says, the first thing he's said, and possibly the last. After this, there will be screaming, and crying, and incoherent babbling while he begs for mercy.

"Oh, Mateo," Oscar says, shaking his head and smiling patronizingly. "You will regret saying that." He picks up the hammer, and without further warning, he swings it at the inside of Mateo's right knee. The patella twists to the side, almost all the way around to the back of the leg. Mateo's first scream escapes him, and it's a loud one. His leg bends at a bad angle, and only the clasps on his wrists keep him upright. They bite hard into his already raw flesh, and blood runs down his forearms.

Oscar laughs. "Oh, that felt *magnificent*, Mateo!" He laughs louder, harder. He hopes the people inside and outside the house hear *this*, too. He uses the head of the hammer to lift Mateo's chin, so they can look into each other's eyes. "Age and imprisonment have not mellowed me, I'm afraid."

He lets the man's head drop back down. "I hope you have so many more screams, Mateo. I really do. They're like music to my ears, and we're only just getting started."

16

Tom and Cindy are tired by the time they finally reach Shreveport, but the first thing they do isn't to find somewhere to spend the night and rest up. No, first they go by Zeke's house.

They know Zeke won't be there, and neither will his family. Tom wants to see it for himself, to check the area. Just because Oscar is not in the country does not mean all of his men have left. If this is the case, Tom wants to know where they are. If Zeke is successful in recapturing Oscar, that doesn't mean they're just going to go home. He was still imprisoned when they first made their moves, coming after both Tom and Zeke. He's not sure what he's hoping to find here, but it's worth looking. There could be some clue, something tiny and seemingly insignificant, that could let him know where they're hiding out.

It's early evening and still light. Tom takes his time driving down Zeke's block. "What should I be looking out for?" Cindy says.

"Something like that," Tom says, nodding toward the end of the block. There's a cop car parked on the corner.

"Zeke said his family are at a safe house," Cindy says. "Maybe cops were sent by to keep an eye on his home in case the guys after him and his family come back?"

Tom grunts. "Sitting there in a cruiser, for everyone to see? If they're wanting to capture anyone, it's hardly subtle."

"What are you suggesting? That those cops – what? That they're crooked? That they're not watching the house, that they're waiting for Zeke to come home?"

"I'm not saying that exactly," Tom says. "But I'm not ruling it out."

Cindy stares at the cruiser. "I suppose it's not like we haven't seen cops accept a pay-off before."

"Oscar certainly had the funds to spare in the past. From what I've seen so far, it seems like he still does." Tom cruises past Zeke's house, looking toward the front door. He spots the damage it has suffered. "I'm going to go around the back. Eyes forward. Don't look at the cops. If they *are* waiting for Zeke, they might have been told about me. We don't want to draw attention and have them see my face."

"You know I can appreciate the paranoia," Cindy says.

They get to the end of the block, and Tom turns left, past the police cruiser. A way down the road, Tom checks the rearview. The cops haven't moved. He takes the next left and finds a place to park on the street. He scans the left side, the houses that are behind Zeke's. Searches for the ones that don't have any cars outside or on driveways.

Tom spots one. It's to the left of Zeke's backyard. "That one looks empty."

"You're sure?" Cindy says.

"No cars. Curtains are open, presumably since they left

this morning. Haven't been back since then. Chances are they're still at work, or else they've gone out to dinner. You stay here, keep an eye out. Anything happens, anyone comes, you call me."

"Got it."

Tom gets out of the car and goes to the empty house. He walks with purpose, like he belongs here. Like he knows the people who own the house. He walks straight down the side of it and glances inside the windows as he goes. As he suspected, there's no one inside.

He watches the windows at the back of Zeke's house as he approaches the fence separating the backyards. The curtains are drawn. They don't twitch. No one peers out.

Tom climbs over the fence and approaches Zeke's house, hand on his Beretta. He goes to the back door and finds that it's been unlocked. When they came here looking for Zeke and his family, they likely came in the front and back, like they did at Tom's. Tom steps inside and takes a moment to listen to the house. There's no one here. He takes a look around. It's been tossed, top and bottom. Tom imagines that when the men came looking for Zeke and found his home empty, they searched it for any evidence of where he might have been, much like Tom is doing now, to find anything that might reveal where *they* are. He comes up empty. There's nothing here that doesn't look like it belongs to the Greene family.

Upstairs, Tom looks down toward the cop car. He peers around the edge of the curtain. It's pointing down the road, so the two cops inside have a clear view of the house. One of them sips from a takeout coffee cup. The other leans with his elbow resting on the open window frame, looking bored. He yawns wide, not bothering to cover his mouth. Tom looks at the other cars parked on the road. They're all empty. He looks to the other houses, too, checking the windows. No one is watching the house. Just the cops.

Tom gives the house another sweep, then leaves, climbing the fence again and returning to Cindy.

"Find anything?"

Tom shakes his head. "Nothing."

"A bust?"

Tom thinks. "Not completely. Those cops are bugging me."

"You'll have to tell Zeke."

"I plan to."

Cindy nods. "Motel?"

"Yeah. One way or the other, our next steps are dictated by Zeke. We might as well rest up while we wait to hear back from him."

17

Max contacts Jorge and says he'd like to talk. Jorge says he's busy, but invites him to the house.

Max has been to the house only once before. He prefers to meet away from it, in secluded areas. The last time he came was only his and Jorge's second meeting. Jorge insisted. They'd met once on Max's terms, now it was time to meet on his. Begrudgingly, Max went. He feared the worst. A trap. It turned out, nothing happened. It was fine. They talked. They made plans and arrangements. Max was not in any danger. Afterward, it became clear to him why he'd been summoned to the house. Jorge wanted to see what kind of nerve he had. How big his balls were. Max never faltered. He never showed fear. He made out like he always does – like at any point, a team could swoop in and extract him and kill everyone present who isn't him, the second a threat is made upon his life.

Max goes to the house, steeling his nerve. At the checkpoint leading into the grounds, he's all smiles, his eyes hidden behind his aviators. "Jorge's expecting me," he tells the guards, who look him over through the open window of his car, fingers hovering near the triggers of their AKMs. One of them backs off and gets on the radio. A couple of minutes pass. Max stares straight ahead, appearing calm and relax, drumming his fingers on the steering wheel like he doesn't have a care in the world. Finally, the other guard returns and gives the nod. The barricade blocking the road is moved, and Max is ushered through.

Jorge is waiting for him outside the house, hands locked behind his back, puffing on a cigarette. Max gets out of the car. He keeps his smile slapped across his face. It's his defense. His best form of confidence. "Jorge," he says, wiping sweat from his brow, "hot today, ain't it?"

"Usually is," Jorge says. "What can I do for you?"

"Well, first off, we could go inside and find a nice, quiet, cool room that we can speak in. Oh, and a glass of water wouldn't go amiss. With ice."

Jorge grins, then turns and heads into the house. He flicks his cigarette.

Max follows. "How's Oscar?" he says.

"Oscar is well," Jorge says. "He's busy right now."

Max hears something. It sounds like a scream. It's weak and forced, like the person giving it barely has the energy left to make any sounds. Max doesn't question it. He knows better.

They go to a room at the rear of the house. A sitting room, with a sofa and two chairs. There's a bar in the corner loaded with hard liquor, and there are paintings of fields on the walls. On the way, Jorge tells someone to bring them two beers, ice cold.

"Beer is better," Max says.

"I thought you would approve," Jorge says, lowering himself onto the sofa. Max takes the chair nearest him. "What do you want, Max?"

"Charming," Max says. "I feel unwanted, and that's painful, considering the recent aid I've brought to you and Oscar."

"It's not that I'm not unhappy to entertain you," Jorge says. "But as I told you on the phone, I'm busy right now. We're all very busy."

"I was hoping Oscar would be present," Max says. "I haven't met him yet. I'm interested to meet the man in person, especially after hearing so much about him."

"Soon, I'm sure. Right now, though, I wouldn't dare disturb him."

Max remembers the feeble scream. He's heard stories about how Oscar used to operate. The tortures. The mass executions.

There's a knock on the sitting room door, and Max and Jorge are brought beers. Max presses the cool bottle to his forehead and temples, then gratefully takes a long drink. "Y'know, it's nice and cool in the car, with the AC, and the windows down, but the second I step outside, I feel so swampy."

Jorge regards him, sipping from his own bottle.

Max clears his throat. "I've been asked to relay a message," he says. "Primarily it's for Oscar, but I'm sure I can leave this in your capable hands."

"What's the message?"

"Rollins and Greene," Max says. "Speed it up and quieten it down."

"We're not purposefully taking our time."

"I'm sure you're not, but there's been a lot of noise so far, and a lot of mess. Who do you think has to tidy all that mess up?"

Jorge crosses one leg over the other. He doesn't say anything for a while. He doesn't look at Max, either. He stares off into the distance, thinking. He takes another drink, longer this time.

Max doesn't press him. He waits.

Jorge finally speaks. He raises his head. "Oscar wants his vengeance," he says. "He will take it. No one will get in his way, and that includes you, Max, *and* the people you represent." He pauses, then adds, "And I feel it would be wise not to say this to Oscar."

Max sits back. He strokes his chin. He gauges the room. He gauges Jorge. He considers his next words carefully. He takes a deep breath and then looks around, as if he's seeing through the walls and his eyes are encompassing the whole house. He whistles low. "Y'know, I'd almost forgotten how big this house is. And that ocean view? Nice. You picked this place out, isn't that right, Jorge? While Oscar was locked up. He'd never seen it before until yesterday."

Jorge looks at him. It's clear he knows the point Max is going to make. "That's right," he says.

"You're quite a leader, Jorge."

"You've told me that before."

"Because it's true."

Jorge lowers his leg and sits forward. "Max, I have told you before. I am not the leader here. I never have been. I am the caretaker. *Oscar* is the leader. The only leader. He is the one the people here follow, and if not for Oscar, then the people do not follow me."

"Now, see, I think you're selling yourself short."

"I'm a realist."

"Uh-huh. How many of the men here were part of this organization *before* Oscar was arrested? How many of them had ever set eyes on him before yesterday? From what I hear, this whole cartel was in disarray. It was *you* who built it back up."

"They joined because of his name. Because of who he is, and the belief he would return to us. Which he has."

Max laughs. "You're making him sound like Jesus."

"To some of the men here, he may as well be."

Max cocks his head, doubtful. "Again, all I hear is you selling yourself short." Max has been dropping hints into Jorge's ear – sometimes subtle, sometimes more overt – while they've been working together. Hints that *he* could lead this organization. Jorge has never taken the bait. He's remained loyal to Oscar.

But now Oscar is back. Max thinks on this. He thinks about all that he has said to Jorge already. A lot of the men on these grounds have never served under Oscar. Only Jorge. Perhaps Max's entreaties won't fall on such deaf ears for much longer.

"You led for years, Jorge, all while Oscar was locked up. The people here willfully followed you during that period of time, no matter what you might believe."

Jorge frowns. Max thinks he might be getting through. Max only ever needed Jorge. Jorge has been easy to work with. Already, with all the mess he's caused and his insistency on following through on his revenge, Oscar is proving himself to be a problem. He needs Jorge to see this for himself.

As Jorge opens his mouth, the door into the sitting room opens. There's a brief knocking as the door swings wide, and then, for the first time outside of a photograph, Max lays eyes upon Oscar Zavala. He's shorter than Max was expecting, and thinner, but this last is likely due to his years in prison. Oscar looks the two men over, and he smiles. He comes forward, rubbing his hands together.

"I heard you were entertaining a guest," Oscar says, in Spanish, as Jorge and Max stand. He stops in front of Max. "I understand you're the man I owe my gratitude to for being free."

"One of them," Max says, responding in Spanish.

Oscar holds out a hand, and they shake. Max notices that Oscar's hands have been recently washed, but they are not fully clean. There are marks upon them. Red stains around his fingertips and under the nails. Max is confident that this is blood.

Oscar notices where his eyes have gone. "I missed a spot," he says, grinning.

Oscar takes a seat and motions for them both to do the same. He's in the chair opposite Max. He picks dried blood from under his thumbnail and then looks up and smiles at Max. "I understand we are to see a lot more of each other," he says. "And that we're going to be working together."

"I look forward to it," Max says.

Oscar looks between the two of them. "What is the purpose of this visit?" He asks the question looking at Jorge. It's clear he wants *him* to be the one to answer it.

"I believe Max was hoping to meet you for the first time," Jorge says. His lie brings Max some hope that they're on the same page, but then he adds, after a hesitation, "Also, he was asked to pass on our new allies' request we quieten down on your quest for vengeance."

But then Max thinks maybe his saying this is a good sign. Earlier, he cautioned against mentioning any of this to

Oscar. And yet, he's the one to say it. Max glances toward Jorge, looking for some kind of giveaway as to his swaying loyalties, but his face is unreadable.

Oscar's eyes narrow momentarily. "To stop?"

"Not to stop," Jorge says. "They wouldn't be foolish enough to dare make such a request. No, they worry about the level of noise and mess that has been made so far. Unsuccessfully."

Oscar shrugs and holds out his hands. "Sometimes you have to break a few eggs."

Max clears his throat. "We're just asking that you keep those eggs to a minimum," he says. "And maybe try to avoid how far the shells are scattering."

Oscar laughs. He tents his fingers, the bloodied tips of left and right pressing against each other. He watches Max over the top. He regards him, silently, for a long time. Max tries not to let his discomfort show. He sits still. Does not shift his weight or slouch in his seat.

Oscar lowers his hands, smoothing out the creases in his trousers. Max realizes for the first time that the blood is not just on his fingertips. There are splashes of it on his clothes, too. "Is Max short for anything?" he says. "Maxwell? Maximillian?"

Max doesn't understand. "No," he says. "Just Max."

Oscar smirks. "How boring. Max, allow me to make something clear, to both you and your paymasters. Tom Rollins and Ezekiel Greene are my priority and will remain my priority until they aren't. Do you understand me? What you and the rest of the Americans want is a far, far second to me. Right now, your wants are behind me. They are so far behind me, I can't see them if I were looking in a mirror."

Oscar is friendly, he's smiling, but Max can feel the implied threats.

Oscar sits back. "I appreciate you handing over their names. Tom Rollins and Ezekiel Greene. For a long time, I didn't know who I was looking for, and I have you to thank for that. But have you truly handed over everything?"

"What do you mean?" Max says.

Oscar waits a beat. He takes his time with his answers. "You gave us the names, and Jorge did the rest. But now you come here talking about noise and speed. I'm wondering if perhaps there is anything pertaining to Rollins and Greene more up to date that you have not deigned to share with us."

"I'm sure everything we have has been passed on to you."

Again, Oscar pauses. His eyes flicker toward Jorge and then back to Max. "*Everything?*" he says.

The appraisal causes Max to falter. "As – as far as I'm aware."

"Then perhaps you should make yourself more aware." Oscar shifts his weight and sits forward. "You're dealing with *me* now, Max. You will find that I am not as laid-back as Jorge can sometimes be."

Max notices that Jorge tries not to react to this, but he's struggling to keep his face straight. His brow furrows slightly. Max stores this information away for the future.

"I like *details*, Max," Oscar says. "And I want to make sure I always have *all* the details. Do you know what will happen if I'm not being provided with all the details, Max? Well, let's hope it doesn't come to that. I'm sure you'll do the best you can, and bring me everything I ask for. Because if you don't, I can become a big problem for you, Max. Do not forget that I have an army at my disposal. We won't be a *small* problem for you and your paymasters."

Max takes a deep breath before he responds. "We certainly wouldn't want it to ever come to that."

"I'm sure you wouldn't." Oscar sits back. "And?"

Max takes this as his cue to leave. He begins to stand. "I'll see what I can do," he says. "And I'll relay everything back to you as soon as possible." He glances at Jorge again, but Jorge avoids looking back at him.

Oscar smiles warmly, but there is a cold glint in his eyes. "I have every faith in you, Max. I look forward to seeing you again soon."

18

Cindy sits in the corner of the motel room. She's cross-legged in a chair, on her laptop, monitoring online chatter to see if there is any news on whether Zeke has managed to recapture Oscar. She combs through a lot of Central and South American notifications. She doesn't speak Spanish and needs to run the conversations through a translator. The translations aren't the cleanest, but she gets the idea. So far, there's nothing worth reporting.

"I don't think Zeke's going to try to capture Oscar," Tom says. He stands by the window. The curtains are open, and late afternoon light is streaming into the room, though the glass is covered by sheer netting. From outside, it makes it hard to see into the room. Tom stands to the side, looking out, watching the area around them. He pays particular attention to the road and notes the vehicles that pass by. "Not after he put his family in danger."

Cindy grunts, like she figured this out already. She has

music playing while she works. She says the background noise helps her concentrate.

"Is that Depeche Mode?" Tom says.

"You're just noticing?"

"I noticed as soon as you put it on," Tom says. "I just got distracted is all. It's not the kind of band I usually hear you listening to."

"I'm full of surprises, Tom. I too have a broad musical palate."

Tom doesn't look back, but he can imagine her grinning as she says this.

"What distracted you?" Cindy says.

Before Tom can answer, he feels his phone vibrating. It's Hayley. "I'll tell you after I've taken this," he says, stepping outside to answer the call.

"Hey," Hayley says.

"Hey," Tom says. Outside, he has a broader view of the area. There's not much to see left or right. Flat fields with dying grass. Down the road to his left is a truck stop, and beyond that he can see trees. A woodland.

"So, I haven't been by the house," Hayley says, "like you said. But the police have been around, and Duncan says it's a real mess. It's going to need a lot of work."

"Did they take the bodies away?"

"Yeah, they did. He was asking if I knew where you are."

"I assume you didn't tell him."

"I don't rightly *know*, Tom. Where are you, anyway?"

"I'm in Shreveport."

"Shreveport – where Zeke lives? Are you with him?"

"No. Zeke's trying to wrap this thing up. I'm waiting for him to get back, to be sure. I've got Cindy with me."

"Cindy?" Hayley says, and then she pauses. It's a long pause.

Tom notices it, but he's more distracted watching the road. A cop car goes by. He doesn't turn his head as it passes, though he knows the passenger will be looking his way. Tom pretends not to see it going by. Out of the corner of his eye, he reads the plates. He's seen this car a few times already, and not just here. Tom glances at his watch and notes the time of its passing.

Hayley takes a deep breath. Tom picks up on it. "Something wrong? Are you all right?"

"I'm just thinking..." She trails off.

"Thinking what?"

"I asked you once, not so long ago, if there's anything going on between you and Cindy."

Tom grits his teeth. "I remember."

"You said no."

"I remember that, too."

"And yet it feels like whenever you go off like this, you always seem to find an excuse to take her along."

"She's helping."

"I'm sure she is, Tom, but is that the only reason she's there?" Before Tom can make any kind of response, Hayley sighs. "Listen, I know this isn't the time to talk about something like this. But you know I'm not the kind of person where if you ask me if something's wrong, I'm going to lie and say I'm fine. I guess I just don't understand why you leave me behind and get me to hide out with my parents for my safety, but she's out there with you." She laughs, but it's humorless, then says, "I mean, should I take that as a compliment? Does it mean you care about me more, or does it just mean you think I can't take care of myself?"

"I want you to be safe."

There's a long silence. "Listen, Tom," Hayley finally says, "I shouldn't have said any of that. Not now. I was just caught off guard when you said she was there." She clears her throat. "Are you safe right now? Have you gotten into any trouble? Has anyone come after you again?"

"Nothing's happened," Tom says. "I'm fine."

"Okay. Well, I need to go on shift soon. Duncan has said cops are going to be stationed at the hospital to make sure no one comes after me there the way they came after our house."

"Good."

"Yeah. Be careful out there, Tom. I hope you get back soon."

"Me too."

Tom hangs up. He doesn't think too much on what Hayley has said. He can't. His thoughts need to be streamlined. They can't be cluttered, worrying or thinking about anything else. They need to be focused.

He steps back into the motel. Cindy looks up. "Anything important?"

"It was Hayley," he says.

"How's she doing? Is she okay?"

Tom nods. "She said to tell you hello."

"That's nice. I hope you told her I'd asked how she's doing."

"I'll have to tell her next time." Tom returns to the window. "I don't recognize this band," he says. The music is no longer Depeche Mode.

"They're not a new band, but they're pretty new to me," Cindy says. "They're called Lebanon Hanover."

"It sounds very eighties."

Cindy laughs. "Yeah, but they're not."

"Reminds me a little of New Order."

"You never told me what distracted you."

Tom nods. "That's right. Come over here."

Cindy puts her laptop to one side and joins him at the window. Tom checks the time. Five minutes have gone by since the cop car passed.

"We might have to wait a couple of minutes," he says.

"What are we looking for?" Cindy says. She stands close to him. Her head comes up to his chin. A strand of her hair tickles his jaw.

"Watch the road," Tom says.

They watch in silence for a moment, then Cindy says, "What was Hayley calling for?"

"Checking in," Tom says. He looks at the time again.

"That's nice of her. I'm sure she's worried about you."

Tom grunts.

"It's easy to worry about you," Cindy says. "You're always in trouble. Good thing I'm here to take care of you."

"Good thing," Tom says. "They should be coming soon. From the right."

Cindy turns her head.

A red Chevy Impala passes by. Cindy might not see on first glance, but Tom knows it's filled with Latin males. "Do you see them looking this way?" he says.

"No, but I'll take your word for it."

The red Chevy passes. Cindy makes to step back, but Tom places his hands on her shoulders and keeps her in place. "Keep watching," he says. "From the left, this time. It'll take a few more minutes."

"The people in the Chevy," Cindy says. "What do you think they were looking at? Us?"

"My car," Tom says. "And beyond it, our room. I've seen them pass a few times already. Every time, the passengers are looking this way."

"Should we be concerned?"

"Maybe when it gets dark."

"What am I watching for now? Are they going to come back?"

"Someone's going to. Someone who passed when I was on the phone." He points. "There they are."

It's the cop car. "They're looking this way," Cindy says.

"That's not all," Tom says. "Do you see the plates?"

"I see them, but they don't mean anything to me."

"It's the cruiser that was parked on Zeke's street."

"Oh. Shit."

"Yeah. I'm starting to think they may have seen my face when we passed them by, but they played it cool, and they sent the Chevy to follow us, knowing they'd be too obvious."

"Why do you think the Chevy has anything to do with them?"

"Both of them are passing by at regular intervals, like they're making sure we don't leave the motel. There's been plenty of other vehicles pass by on this road, but none more than once going one way or the other. They're the only two turning around and coming back over and over."

"So what do we do?" Cindy says.

"Nothing yet," Tom says. "But I'll deal with them soon."

19

Z eke and his team have remained in the field. William has sent out messages and called in favors. They've been attempting to track Oscar's movements since he fled the house where it looked like he'd been staying in Guatemala. They've picked up a lead and got back to Zeke. He and his team are back on the move. This time, they're going to El Salvador.

"He's heading south," Daniel says. They're in the air again and not so silent this time.

"Trying to make his way back to Honduras," Guy says.

Zeke nods.

"Does he have connections in these countries he's passing through?" Selena says. "Allies we should know about?"

"I've checked," Zeke says. "And not so far as we're aware."

"Sounds like his guys have kept busy while he's been locked up, though," Daniel says. "They could have cultivated relationships while he's been gone. Plotted this escape route for once they got him out."

"They broke him out in a Black Hawk, right?" Selena says. "Why wouldn't they just fly him straight back to Honduras? Sure, they might've had to stop to refuel on the way, but it would be a lot more straightforward than cutting through countries by land."

"Maybe to throw us off the scent," Shaun says.

"Yeah," Guy says, nodding, clearly having a thought. "And maybe they destroyed the Black Hawk as soon as they could so we wouldn't have a chance of finding out how they got it in the first place."

Daniel tilts his chin toward Zeke. "What do you think, chief?"

Zeke takes a deep breath. "Honestly? I don't really care. I just want to catch up to him and get this over with. These are all questions we can think about *after*."

"Uh-huh," Guy says, nodding.

"Get ready," Zeke says. "We're nearly there."

This house is even more secluded than the last in Guatemala. It's bigger, too. L-shaped. There will be more rooms to hide in.

It's concealed among the trees. It looks run-down again, and the trees are untended. Their canopies arch over the roof in various spots. It's getting dark. Zeke and the team take a van ride close to the house. The driver isn't as cool and calm this time. He's jittery. The kind Zeke likes least of all.

"Play it cool," he says, leaning close from the back. "What are you worried about? It's a clear road."

The driver swallows and nods. He grips the steering wheel in both hands, holds it tight.

The light is failing fast. It's practically dark when the team dismounts. They put on their night vision. Zeke takes point. He wants to run to the house, but he holds back. Does things properly. Selena and Guy are by his side. Daniel and Shaun go wide, to cover front and rear respectively. There's no fence or gate this time. Zeke covers the ground cautiously, expecting traps.

Through a window, Zeke spots movement at the end of a hall. A dark shadow hurrying into another room, out of view. Zeke signals to the others that he has eyes on someone. They move in. Selena and Guy stick on Zeke's six, following him down the hall. Zeke presses himself to the wall next to the door. He locks eyes with Selena and Guy, exchanges nods. They have him covered. The door is ajar. Zeke kicks it open and drops to a knee, M4 shouldered. He scans the room. It's empty. There's a door at the other side of the room, wide open.

"Spread out," Zeke says, keeping his voice low. "Stay in touch."

Selena and Guy both nod and separate, spreading out, searching the house. Zeke gets on the radio. "Check in," he says, awaiting their responses in his earpiece.

"Nothing out here," Shaun says.

"No signs," Daniel says.

"Call out if you see anything," Zeke says. He crosses the room, toward the other open door. He takes his time across the floor, testing each floorboard before he lowers his weight upon it. He peers into the darkness beyond. He reaches the corner and peers out. It's another hallway. Before Zeke can step down it, Daniel comes back on the radio.

"Gunshots," he says. "Distant. I think they're coming from the van."

"Copy that," Shaun says. "I have eyes on the gunfire. It's an ambush."

Gunshots erupt closer to Zeke, from the end of the hall,

concealed in the shadows. He dives back behind the door-frame. Out of the corner of his eye, he spots someone behind him raising a gun. A dark shadow in the first doorway he came through. It's not one of his team. Zeke doesn't hesitate. From down on his back, he opens fire, his bullets strafing across the wall and the chest of the other man. He falls back, squeezing off his automatic rifle, blasting a hole in the ceiling.

There's another shooter behind the one Zeke has just put down. He twists around the corner and lets off a blast. It tears a chunk out of the wall above where Zeke lies.

Zeke gets on the radio. "Gunshots inside," he says. "I'm pinned down."

He backs into the corner, staying low. The room is empty. No furniture. Nothing for him to take cover behind. He fires at both doorways to keep them back.

"Ambush!" Guy says over the radio. "They're all through the house! They're fucking everywhere!"

Zeke can hear gunfire echoing down the hallways. He needs to find another way out. The only other exit available to him is a window opposite, but it's in the crosshairs of the two doors. Zeke remains low, M4 at his shoulder, sweeping from door to door. The shooters fire blindly around the frame. Zeke scuttles to the right and to the left, not wanting them to catch a glimpse of him and pinpoint his position. He's not sure how many of them are at each door. He stares at the window. He's boxed in here. He needs to get out of this room or else eventually one of their stray bullets will find him, or they'll rush him and overwhelm him with their numbers. Taking a risk on the crossfire is the best option available to him.

Zeke braces himself. He fires at both doorways and then

at the window. It shatters. He's about to rise, to run, but then he hears gunfire outside the room, in the hall, from the direction he originally came. The potshots from that doorway cease.

Selena comes through on the radio. "Zeke, you in there? It's me. I'm coming through. Don't shoot!"

"Careful of the other door," Zeke tells her. "There's hostiles present."

Selena comes into view, M4 pointing at the other door. "We going after them?"

"Oscar could be there," Zeke says. "What's it like in the rest of the house?"

"Seemed like they were coming out of the woodwork. There were waiting for us, Zeke. They knew we were coming."

"Let's not keep them waiting." Zeke stands and heads to the doorway. Selena follows. They open fire down the hallway and clear it out. Zeke checks his magazine, changes it, and then presses on.

He can still hear gunfire throughout the rest of the house, but it's fading. Zeke and Selena move through the rooms and down the hallways. They come across two more attackers and promptly deal with them. "Guy, speak to us."

"I'm outside," Guy says. "I'm with Shaun and Daniel. The house is looking clear."

Zeke hasn't seen any sign of Oscar. He grits his teeth. "Is there anyone else out there?"

"No one living."

"Oscar?"

"We don't see him."

Zeke and Selena check the house. The attackers are all dead. They check the bodies. Zeke counts twelve. None of them are Oscar. He calls the others inside, apart from Daniel, who remains outside on guard.

"Tear this fucking house apart," Zeke says. "Look in every closet, under every floorboard, anywhere that could double as a hiding space – we're not leaving until we know there's no one else here."

They nod at him, and they get to work, and Zeke accompanies them, but he already knows this is hopeless. Searching the house is a last desperate act, and though he hopes otherwise, he feels the outcome is inevitable.

Oscar is not here.

20

As it gets late, Tom sneaks out the back of the motel. Cindy stays behind with his Beretta. He moves away from the motel in a straight line, across the field behind it, obscuring himself with the building should the cop car or the Chevy be passing by. Once he believes he's far enough away, he goes toward the truck stop and the woodland beyond. Passing through the trees, he pauses as he nears the road, and he waits. For the frequency with which the two vehicles pass by the motel, he doesn't think they can be going very far. He wants to see where they go. He wants to see if they stop anywhere nearby.

While watching from the motel window, he hasn't seen the cop car in a while. Only the Chevy. The cops may have been pulled away somewhere else. To do their actual job, perhaps. Last time he checked, it had been over ninety minutes since he'd last seen them. Hopefully they stay gone.

The red Chevy comes into view. Through the trees, Tom can see it off to his right, coming down the road. It's slowing as it nears the truck stop. It passes the stop, and then it passes Tom's hiding spot. His head turns with it, watching. It goes a little further down the road, then it stops. It turns around in the road and pulls to the side. It's off the road, on the grass near the treeline. Tom gets on the ground and crawls a little closer so he can see them better. There are four men inside. They're all looking down the road, watching the exit of the motel's parking lot. Tom wonders when they might be planning on making a move against the motel. It's getting late, and it's getting dark. If they're going to make a move at all, he reckons it will be soon. When the cops return, perhaps. Strength in numbers.

One of the passengers in the rear of the Chevy gets out of the car and moves closer to the trees. Tom lies very still. The man doesn't come far into the woods. He puts a tree between himself and the road, and then he takes a piss against it. He returns to the car. A couple of minutes pass, and then the Chevy rolls away, making its regular pass once again. Tom imagines they'll get down the road, beyond the motel, and find somewhere else out of view to sit for five or so minutes. Maybe take another toilet break if necessary.

Tom gets out of the woods, but he doesn't return to the motel. He goes to the truck stop and into the diner. Straight up to the counter, where he can see the drinks fridge behind it. He needs something in a bottle. A glass bottle.

The waitress comes to serve him. He asks for a beer left in the bottle, and after she hands it to him and he's paid, he leaves. He goes around the back of the truck stop and returns to the woods, pouring out the beer as he goes. He gets close to where the Chevy stopped last time, and he breaks the bottle against a tree. In the failing light, he crouches down and gathers up all of the shards, holding them close, keeping his hands loose around them so they don't cut him.

It's dark when the Chevy returns. Tom hides behind a tree as it turns and its headlights cut through the trees. Once they've parked and there's no sign of anyone getting out, Tom moves down through the woods, ducking low. He gets to the rear of the car and then crawls out on his stomach with the broken shards of glass held out ahead of him. He gets to the back of the car, holding his breath against the exhaust fumes. He stays away from the sides of the car, from the mirrors, and then deposits shards of glass in front of the two rear wheels. The largest shards he angles so they're pressing into the rubber in between the tire treads.

He backs away, re-entering the woods, and then he runs across the dark fields and back to the motel, climbing in through the same bathroom window he climbed out of.

Cindy is by the front window, Beretta down by her side. She gives a start when she realizes Tom has returned, then says, "They've passed a couple of times. No sign of the cops."

"Good," Tom says, grabbing their bags, which they've already packed and left by the door. "Let's go."

They exit the motel and get into Tom's car. He turns it around and pulls out of the parking lot, turning right. He watches the mirrors as they go. The road is quiet at this time of day. Behind, in the far distance, he sees the lights of the Chevy pull away from where they've parked.

"Did you find them?" Cindy says.

"Yeah."

"Do you see them now?"

"I can see them."

The lights are gaining, half a dozen car lengths behind them, and then suddenly they're pulling back, slowing. The rear tires have been punctured by the broken glass. They're bleeding air. No doubt the handling of the car is growing heavy and hard to control. Tom sees in the mirror as the Chevy is forced to pull to the side of the road to find out what is happening. He grins and continues on his way, putting his foot down on the accelerator and leaving the pursuing Chevy far behind.

21

Zeke is not happy.

They're back in America now. It's a couple of hours after midnight, and he's tired, but he can't sleep. They're in Shreveport, he and his team. Zeke wants to be close to his family, even if he can't go back to them just yet. He's made it clear to William Taylor that, after the ambush, they can't trust their intel. He wants solid confirmation of where Oscar is, and *then* they'll move in again.

This is one of the reasons Zeke is not happy. There are more. He's worried. No, *worried* isn't the right word – he's *suspicious*. He doesn't like being suspicious, especially when it's in regard to his own team.

They're lying low in a motel. Zeke insisted that they all share a room. He wants everyone together. Close. It's cramped, but he doesn't care. Guy sits on a chair in the corner, meditating. Selena is cross-legged at the top of the bed with Daniel lying next to her, flicking through the TV. Shaun is lying on the couch under the window, eyes closed and his hands laced behind his head. Zeke stands by the door, arms folded, sucking on his teeth and looking over the room. He tries not to stare at anyone for too long while he thinks.

He replays the ambush over and over in his mind. The men there had the drop on him. If it hadn't been for Selena, he'd likely be dead now. His family would be all alone. His children would be orphaned, and his wife a widow.

It raises the important question – how did the men there in El Salvador know they were coming? They were prepared. Selena said it was like they were coming out of the woodwork. They were ready for the team's arrival. They were in position to get the drop on them. They killed the asset who drove them to the house, despite his van being parked nowhere near the house. Who told them they were coming?

And this in turn raises the question – was it someone on his team? Did one of these four people here in this motel room with him betray him? Was it someone in the agency?

He knows where Selena was. Selena came back for him. Selena was *with* him. For that reason, Zeke is confident he can trust her. But the rest of them, he can't speak to where they were. Guy left the house. He went outside, with Shaun and Daniel. Outside, it would have been easy for any one of them to have stayed out of the way of the gunfight.

There were other dead bodies in and outside the house, gunned down, who had nothing to do with Zeke or Selena. Shot by either Daniel, Guy, or Shaun. If – *if* – there is a traitor in his team, it doesn't need to be all three of them, or two of them. There only needs to be one.

Of course, it could have nothing to do with anyone in his team. It could be someone in the CIA. A mole, feeding information back to Oscar Zavala, keeping him one step ahead of them and their pursuit.

Zeke feels sick. He pinches the bridge of his nose between his thumb and index finger and closes his eyes tight. He breathes deeply. He doesn't know who he can trust. He doesn't know if there's anyone here he *can* trust.

But then he pauses.

Tom.

By now, Cindy will have passed Zeke's message on to Tom. Zeke knows Tom well. Knows exactly what he would do after receiving that message. He'd come *here*. To Shreveport. And he'd wait to hear back.

"I'm stepping outside," Zeke says. "I need some fresh air."

He takes a moment, breathing deep, then pulls out his phone. He glances back at the door and at the room's window. He decides against making a phone call. He could send an encrypted message to Cindy again, to pass on to Tom, but there's not much point, especially if the CIA has been compromised. An encrypted message wouldn't make a difference at this point. Instead, he sends a text directly to Tom.

> I'm back in Shreveport. No Oscar. Potential compromise. Get in touch – don't call.

He stares at the screen. Tom doesn't respond straight away. Zeke knows he could be busy. He could be sleeping. It could be a while before he gets in touch. Zeke puts the phone away. He braces himself and then steps back into the room.

22

Max receives a call from America.

"Zeke Greene is stateside."

Max sucks his teeth. "Well, shit," he says. "El Salvador was a bust?"

"Clearly." There's a long, deep intake of breath on the line. "Rollins has been spotted in Shreveport."

"Ah." Max knows Zeke lives in Shreveport, and he knows Rollins has gone there to meet him.

"*Ah*. Zeke is going to meet up with Rollins, there's no doubt in my mind. Once they meet up, they'll eventually work out where Oscar is, and they'll make it to Honduras. We can't have that happen."

"Oscar has plenty of men here. They'll have an army to get through."

"He had plenty of men in El Salvador, and now they're all dead."

"They weren't his men. They were contacts. They weren't as well trained."

"Then maybe he should have sent some well-trained

men, and we wouldn't have any issues right now. He demanded information, and we gave it to him, and how does he use it? He sends in amateurs. Zeke is a professional, and so is his team. You told him that, didn't you?"

Max goes into his kitchen. "He knows," he says. He goes into the refrigerator and presses a cold soda can to his temple. "He was very grateful for the information."

"And *I'd* be grateful if he'd *done* something worthwhile with it. Instead, we still have both Zeke and Rollins coming after him. Max, you understand what's at stake here, don't you?"

Max closes the refrigerator and opens his soda can. He takes a drink. "Of course I do."

"The success – or the *failure* – of this operation is entirely upon your shoulders."

"I know that. But let's not forget you're carrying some of this weight, too."

The voice doesn't respond.

Max takes another drink and returns to the living room. He sits. "What else can you give me?"

"What do you mean?"

"For stopping Zeke and Rollins. For capturing them. Oscar said he wanted everything. What else can you give me?"

"I gave you enough."

"You need to give me it *all*."

There's another pause. It's loaded this time. The other man is thinking. "I'll get back to you."

"Make it quick."

"Listen to me, Max – if Zeke and Rollins are going to meet up in Shreveport, I don't give a shit if they *die* in Shreveport and Oscar never gets his hands on them. He can have their bodies and do what he likes with those, I don't care. My priority – and *yours* – is to get this operation back on track as soon as possible, and the best way for us to do that is to clean up this mess he's made. Now, some of Oscar's men are already there, and we've provided them assistance from local law enforcement, but they've proven themselves slippery so far. If they get out of there, if they get as far as Honduras, they *need* to be dealt with. Is that clear?"

"You're not telling me anything I don't already know."

"I know I'm repeating myself, but this is damned important. All right, how's this for something you don't know – I'm sending out a team to enforce you. I'm worried Oscar has already leaned on you too much."

"He might be leaning on me, but I have him where I – where *we* – want him."

"I don't care. I'm still sending out the team. And listen, these are rough guys I'm planning on sending. They've all been subjected to various disciplinaries and investigations, and they will have no qualms with what we're doing out there."

"I can't wait to meet them."

"Very droll. Get this situation under control, Max."

"As far as I'm concerned, it already is."

The voice grunts. "Get it under *my* level of control. We'll talk again soon."

23

It's early in the morning. Tom and Cindy found a different motel on the outskirts of Shreveport. Tom's car is parked behind the building, out of view of the road. Tom has remained vigilant, though. He's remained by the window, looking out. He hasn't seen anything concerning. No vehicles doubling back, checking the place out.

Cindy is sleeping on the bed behind him. She's kicked off her boots, but she's still wearing her clothes and is lying on top of the blanket, curled on her side. Tom glances back at her and finds himself watching her for a moment. Her brow furrows like she could be having a bad dream.

Tom forces himself to turn away. Back to the window. He checks his phone. When they got to the motel late last night, he saw he'd received a message from Zeke. Tom responded and told him he and Cindy are both in Shreveport, and that when Zeke is ready to join them, they'll send him their whereabouts in an encrypted message. Zeke hasn't responded yet, but it was late when Tom got back to him, and from what he said, he was potentially in a compromised situation. He may not have had a safe chance to get back on his phone.

Tom hears Cindy stirring. He looks back at her. She blinks her eyes open, squinting at him. She smiles when she sees him looking. "I hope you haven't been watching me sleep all this time."

"I heard you waking."

She pushes herself up, rubbing her eyes. She sees that it's light outside. "It's morning?"

"It's still early."

"Have you heard back from Zeke yet?"

"Not yet."

Cindy pushes herself to the edge of the bed and runs her hands down her face. She goes into the bathroom and gets washed, then joins Tom by the window. "Has there been anything worrying?"

"No, not this time."

Cindy watches the road with him. "How long are we going to do this for?"

"Until we hear from Zeke."

An hour goes by. Zeke messages. Tom holds out his phone so Cindy can read it too.

> Coming soon. Convincing team to stay put.
> Will be in touch with proof it's me before
> you send your location.

"Not long now," Tom says.

24

Only one full day has passed in the safe house, but to Naomi it feels much longer.

She spends her time checking in on the kids, making sure they're all right and trying to comfort them if they're not. She can see that they're worried and they want to go home, but they're holding up well. They're strong. They pass the time in the living room, watching cartoons. Bill usually sits with them on a chair by the window, asking them who the cartoon characters are, and who their favorites are.

Ben is the more strait-laced of the two. He moves through the house at regular intervals, checking every room and looking out the windows. When he's not making his rounds, he's usually in the kitchen, sitting at the table, reading a newspaper or something on his laptop.

Naomi finds him here. He doesn't look up at her at first, assuming she's here to get a drink or make a snack. There are groceries in the cupboards and the refrigerator, but they've mostly been living off sandwiches. Naomi is too stressed to cook, and Bill and Ben have confessed they're not much in the way of chefs.

Ben glances up at her hovering in the doorway. "Can I help you, Mrs. Greene?"

Naomi steps further into the room, leaning against the counter, arms wrapped around herself. She nods at the laptop. "I was just wondering if you'd heard anything."

Ben shakes his head. "I'm afraid not. I promise you'll be the first to know as soon as I do. In the meantime, you should make yourself comfortable. Worrying isn't going to do you any good."

"I can't get comfortable," Naomi says. "I barely slept last night."

Ben nods. "I heard you moving around in your room while it was my turn on the night shift."

"I feel like a ghost."

"We hear this a lot."

Naomi sighs. "What do you usually advise?"

"What I just told you," Ben says. "Try not to worry."

"Uh-huh. Does that ever work?"

"Honestly? No. But what else can I say? I'm not going to lie to you, Mrs. Greene, and tell you that everything is going to be all right. I can't possibly know that. All I *do* know is that worrying is not going to help, or change, the situation. It'll only make you feel sick."

"Call me Naomi," she says. "'Mrs. Greene' is too formal."

"Okay. Naomi."

She sighs again. "I assume the two of you are with the CIA, too? I forgot to ask."

Ben nods. "We are."

"Do you ever do fieldwork?"

"This *is* fieldwork."

"I mean overseas."

Ben grimaces and then shakes his head. "Not anymore."

Naomi cocks her head, sensing something unspoken in his response.

Ben regards her, considering how he's going to answer. Naomi can see the cogs moving behind his eyes. He knows she's an operative's wife. He can speak to her a little more freely than he would anyone else he was guarding.

"I used to go overseas," he says. "I broke my leg on an operation. It slowed me down. Not too much that I can't do this, but too much to be abroad."

"I'm sorry to hear that."

"It is what it is."

"Did something similar happen to Bill?"

"No," Ben says. "He had a couple of kids and decided he'd rather stay close to home."

"It doesn't surprise me he has kids," Naomi says. "He's been very good with Tre and Tamika."

"He's got three."

"How about you?"

"I'm not one of his kids." Ben has a gleam in his eye, and for the first time Naomi thinks he's showing a sense of humor.

"Hilarious," she says, grinning. "But you know what I meant."

He shakes his head. "No, I don't have any kids."

"Wife? Husband?"

"Girlfriend."

"Serious?"

"Couple of years now."

Naomi nods, then stares at the ground, at the scuffed linoleum. She glances briefly around the kitchen and wonders how many people have been hidden in this house, and for what reasons. She turns back to Ben. He's looking at her, expectant but patient. "You know what all this has made me wonder?"

"What?"

"That when Zeke has dealt with this Oscar Zavala, and he comes home and we don't have to worry about this Honduran warlord anymore – well, what I've been wondering is, how many *other* Honduran warlords are out there? How many other lunatics are out there holding a vendetta against my husband and an old work colleague?"

Ben doesn't say anything for a while. He's thinking. "The world is a dangerous place," he says finally. "There'll always be someone to worry about."

"You're very comforting."

"I'm a realist. Sarah – my girlfriend – she says it's my biggest issue. I'm *too much* of a realist, she says. It makes me sound like a pessimist or a nihilist."

Naomi grins at this. "She's not wrong. Sarah sounds like she knows what she's talking about."

"I certainly think so."

"It's a nice name – Sarah. I considered it for Tamika."

"I've been told it means 'princess.'"

"It does, in Hebrew," Naomi says. "I think that's why I liked it."

"Tamika is a very lovely name, too. Does it have any meaning?"

"It has a few – 'friendly' and 'born in spring' are a couple. But mostly, we just liked it."

"What other reason do you really need?"

Naomi smiles. She looks at Ben's laptop. "Anyway," she says. "It looks like you're busy. I'll let you get on with it."

Ben nods, but then says, "I get it, I do. You're bored, and you're sick with worry. I know how this is. I see it every time."

Naomi forces a smile, then leaves the kitchen. She goes to the living room and watches her children. She doesn't pay much attention to what's on the television, but she can hear that it's loud, and out of the corner of her eye she can see the garish colors flashing on and off on the screen. She hears Billy laughing at the jokes, and then Tre and Tamika are laughing, too. She looks into their faces, and they're smiling, their laughter is genuine, and all of their worries and their fears and their concerns are gone, if only momentarily. She feels gratitude to Billy for this, and to SpongeBob, or whoever else might be playing right now.

Naomi returns to her room. Returns to her fretting and waiting and silently praying that Zeke is all right, and that this will all be over soon. The house is on one story, and she can hear her children's laughter down the hall. The sound makes her feel better.

If only momentarily.

25

Zeke has managed to get away from his team. Tom directs him to park around the back of the motel, out of view of the road, like Tom has. They embrace as Zeke gets out of the car.

"How's Naomi?" Tom says. "The kids?"

"Safe," Zeke says. They're walking back around to the front of the motel. "I want to end this damn thing ASAP so I can see them again."

In the room, Zeke and Cindy hug, and Zeke thanks her for coming along, then they all take a seat.

"What did you tell your team?" Tom says.

"I kept it simple," Zeke says. "I told them I had personal business to deal with, and they needed to stay where they are until I get back."

"And where are they?" Cindy says.

Zeke tells them the name of the motel.

"How far is that?" Tom says.

"About a half hour away."

"Took you an hour to get here," Cindy says.

"I didn't come straight here," Zeke says. "Hasn't Tom taught you anything? I took a circuitous route and made sure there wasn't anyone following me."

"Tell us your concerns," Tom says.

Zeke tells them his worries regarding his own team and the CIA at large.

"We've been trailed by the cops," Tom says, and tells Zeke the story of how he and Cindy have been tailed and observed by police.

"Hmm," Zeke says. "They're coming at us from all sides. If someone on my team is compromised, we need to know who. We find out who it is, that gives us a step-up on the rest of them."

"You got an idea how we're going to do that?" Tom says. "Isolate them and lean on them?"

"Maybe something a little more subtle," Zeke says, turning to Cindy.

Cindy sits forward. "What are you thinking?"

"If one of them has been turned, there has to be an electronic trail somewhere. Communications, I mean."

"Or a pay-off," Tom says.

Zeke clicks his fingers. "Exactly. One or the other."

"I can do that," Cindy says. "I just need some personal details first – starting with their names."

"I can answer everything you need to know," Zeke says. "I'm not saying I know every little detail about the members of my team, but I know enough."

"I just need to get started," Cindy says. "I can find the rest." She's already reaching for her laptop.

There's a knock at the door. Everyone freezes, exchanging glances. Someone has managed to sneak up on them. Tom and Zeke pull out their handguns. They both have Berettas. Tom motions to Cindy to get behind cover. He waits until she's ducking behind the bed, then goes to the door. Zeke covers him, gun raised. Tom keeps his low, ready to swing up if needed. He peers out the spyhole. There's a woman outside. Tom doesn't recognize her. She's Latina. Tom opens the door just enough to peer out. He presses the barrel of the Beretta into the door, aiming for where she's standing.

"Help you?" Tom says.

"Maybe," she says. "I followed Zeke here. I assume he's inside."

"Selena?" Zeke says.

Tom opens the door wider so Zeke can see. The woman – Selena – raises a hand in greeting when she sees him. "Hey, chief," she says.

Zeke frowns. "Let her in, Tom," he says. "We'd better talk to her."

26

T om doesn't put his gun away, and neither does
Zeke. They're both pointing at her.

"This is a hell of a warm welcome, guys,"
Selena says. She stands before them, hands raised. She
glances toward Cindy in the corner. "So," she says, to Zeke, "I
figure this guy is the Tom Rollins you've told me about, but
who's she?"

"We'll tell you if you need to know," Tom says.

"This is all feeling very hostile, Zeke," Selena says.

Tom glances toward Zeke. He hasn't said a word since
they let Selena into the motel. His brow is furrowed. It's clear
he's thinking, gauging whether he can trust her or not.
"Why'd you follow me?" he says.

"I reckon for the same reason you were sneaking over
here," Selena says. "Because you're worried someone on the
team might be compromised, right? Because I know I am."

Tom looks to Zeke. He knows Selena best. Tom awaits his
judgment.

Zeke lowers his weapon. "We were together during the

ambush," he says. "You came back for me." He nods to Tom, and Tom lowers his gun, too. As Zeke puts it away, he asks, "How'd you manage to keep up with me? I was careful."

"I *know* you were careful," Selena says. "But I was more careful. I kept my distance – way, *way* back. You think this was my first go-around?"

"I get that you might trust her," Tom says, "but she could still be compromised. Before you say too much, we need to check her."

"I get that," Selena says. "I understand the need to be careful."

Cindy holds her laptop. "Should I get started?"

Tom nods.

"Can I at least take a seat?" Selena says.

"We're not holding you hostage," Zeke says.

"Maybe *you're* not," Selena says. "Him, I'm not so sure about." She tilts her head toward Tom.

"Tom's just intense. He always has been."

Tom moves away, stands close to Cindy. She's sitting at the desk in the corner and starting up the laptop, ready to get to work. "I need a surname," she says.

"Gutierrez," Zeke says.

Her fingers get to typing. She asks a few more questions, all answered by Zeke. Selena is silent. Tom stands with his arms folded, watching Cindy work. Starting with Selena, she'll explore the team's finances, looking for any hidden and sudden increases, anything that might indicate a pay-off. As letters and numbers flood the screen and Cindy's eyes scan over them, Tom turns away. Selena has taken a seat. Zeke is standing close to her. She's covered. Zeke might trust her, might even consider her a friend, but Tom knows he won't let her get the drop on them. If she's a traitor, Zeke will put her down himself.

Tom goes to the window and looks out the front of the motel, keeping watch. Almost as soon as he peers around the curtain, he sees a police cruiser pull slowly into the parking lot. He straightens, instantly alert. The cruiser comes to a stop. Both front doors open. The cops get out. They draw their guns.

"We might have company," Tom says.

"What is it?" Zeke says.

"Cops," Tom says. "I suppose they could be here to see someone else." The officers are looking toward the motel as he says this.

"How many?"

"Only two."

"There's more of us," Zeke says.

Two more cruisers pull into the parking lot. "There *were*," Tom says. "Two more cruisers, four more cops. All with their guns in their hands. They're looking this way. Cindy, pack it up. Everyone get ready." He turns, looks at Selena. "You tip them off?"

Selena's eyes burn through him. "No," she says, her voice steely.

"Then I guess we're just going to have to trust you for now," Tom says, though he doesn't mean it. He'll be watching her.

She nods.

"How'd they find us?" Zeke says.

"Your motel, where your team are – it's probably covered. They could have followed you or Selena."

"Or tracked them via street cameras," Cindy says, slipping her laptop back into its satchel. "Especially if there *is* a traitor on the team. They could have relayed to the cops that the two of you had gone out, and the cops could have tracked you here."

"However they got here," Tom says, "I'm not planning on sticking around to ask them."

27

Z eke climbs out the rear bathroom window first, then Selena climbs down. Tom hands Cindy down to Zeke. As he climbs out himself, he hears the cops banging on the door at the front. They don't wait long for a response. Tom drops down as they kick the door open. "Get to my car," he says.

Off to their right, at the corner of the building, a couple of cops appear, attempting to encircle them. Without hesitation, the cops open fire. Tom and Zeke fire back. Their shots aren't aimed, but they back the cops up. Tom jumps behind the steering wheel while Zeke keeps them covered. Cindy sits in the front with him, and Selena gets into the back. Tom reverses the car and stops next to Zeke so he can jump into the back, landing across Selena's legs. Tom turns left, away from the corner where the cops are. He drives over grass and ploughs through a bush to get to the main road. Glancing back, he can see the cops rushing back to their vehicles to pursue. As they put distance between themselves and the motel, Tom looks into the mirror. He sees the three cruisers pile out after them, cutting over the grass.

"They haven't put their sirens on," Cindy says, peering into the side mirror.

"This isn't official business," Tom says.

The cops are coming up fast behind them. Tom cuts to the left, a tight bend. They stick with him. Tom hears a small explosion behind them. A gunshot.

"They're shooting," Zeke says.

There are other vehicles on the road. They veer out of the way, noticing the cop on the passenger side of the leading cruiser, and the gun he's waving around.

A bullet bounces off the car's rear frame. Tom takes another tight left, bouncing over the sidewalk. "Hold on tight," he says, then veers into the oncoming lane. Cindy yelps, then braces herself as the cars scatter ahead of them, flashing their lights and blaring their horns. Tom holds his nerve, pushing hard to the left to avoid being clipped by the skidding vehicles. He needs to focus. He can't risk a glance at the mirror. "What's happening back there?"

"They're sticking with us," Zeke says.

"The shooter's ducked back inside, though," Selena says.

The oncoming traffic thins. Tom steers across lanes and takes a right turn. He can see water up ahead.

"Tom, you've put us on the I220 bridge over Cross Lake," Zeke says.

"Is that bad?" Tom says.

"Well, we're stuck on the bridge until we reach the other side of the lake," Zeke says. "And those cop cars are faster than we are."

"Shit," Tom says. He looks into the mirror. The cops weave between traffic behind them, getting closer. Up ahead is a quiet stretch, nothing else around. Tom looks left and right. There's a barrier separating them from the oncoming lanes. Tom can't cross over again and hold the cops off that way. He looks into the mirror again. The three cop cars are behind them, spread across the lanes, including the breakdown lane.

Tom glances at the speedometer. They're going over eighty mph. Looking in the mirror again, he can see a couple of the cops in the passenger seats leaning out with their guns.

"Hold on *real* tight," Tom says. "We might get hit."

Before anyone can respond, he slams his foot down on the brake and simultaneously pulls up on the handbrake. The cruiser in the center has to swerve to avoid crashing into the back of them, which causes him to smash into the side of the cruiser in the breakdown lane. They hit hard, at speed, and the cruiser in the breakdown lane is forced over the barrier and into Cross Lake below. The cruiser that hit it bounces against the barrier and flips and rolls down the road.

Tom sees the drivers further back hitting their brakes and holding back to avoid the accident. The remaining cruiser is braking up ahead, and looks like it's about to turn. Tom starts driving again. "Zeke, be ready – cripple it!"

Tom swings to a stop in front of the cruiser, and Zeke leans out his window. He fires on the cruiser, peppering its hood and grille with bullets, killing the engine. He blows out the front two tires, too, to be safe.

It all happens fast. Tom starts driving again, continuing over the bridge and to the other side of Cross Lake.

28

Tom drives a wide circle and returns to the motel so they can swap vehicles for Zeke's car. Zeke is still using the rental Ford. They leave Tom's car in some nearby woodland, covering it in branches. They made a lot of mess on the bridge, and the make, model, and plates of Tom's car were likely noted by other drivers.

They get in Zeke's car and drive in the other direction. They find a strip mall and pull in, then Tom and Zeke swap the plates on Zeke's Ford for a Mercedes with Arizona markings. They leave the strip mall, and Zeke drives them to a parking lot behind a church.

"Figure we should stay in the car while Cindy does her thing," Zeke says. "That way if we need to move again, we can do it quick."

Nobody disagrees.

Tom sits in the back with Cindy and watches as she pulls out her laptop and gets to work. Selena is in the front with Zeke. She waits for the verdict. Tom watches her. She looks out the window, staring across the lot. She's not concerned. She turns to Zeke slightly and says, "Is this your church?"

Zeke shakes his head. "It's been a long, long time since I last went to church," he says. "Though Lord knows, I've been doing a damn lot of praying these last few days."

The minutes pass by and turn into hours. Nobody rushes Cindy. They wait. Her fingers only briefly stop moving across the keys from time to time, pausing while she reads. It's dark. It's starting to get late.

"All right," Cindy says finally. Everyone sits up. "I'm pretty confident that Selena is clean."

"I wasn't worried," Selena says.

"I'm sorry we needed to do that," Zeke says.

"Don't be. I understand." She turns, looking into the backseat. "Now, if someone on our team *is* dirty, let's find out who it is."

Cindy nods. She speaks to the car. "I'll do the others now, but you all saw how long that took. This could take a while."

"Do you need anything?" Tom says. "Hungry? Thirsty?"

"Actually, now you mention it, yes, I am."

"I could eat," Selena says.

"There's a burger place not far from here," Zeke says. "Tom, Selena, two of you wanna go? I'll stay here with Cindy and the car. Anything happens, I'll swing by and grab you."

Tom and Selena exchange nods, then get out of the car. "Got it," Tom says. He squeezes Cindy's leg as he goes, a reassuring gesture to let her know she's doing good. She smiles at him gratefully, then lowers her face and gets back to work.

29

O scar stands in the bathroom. He's showered. He took his time. The water was hot. He stood beneath it, his eyes closed, and felt it loosen his muscles and clear his head. The mirrors are steamed, and he can't see himself, but he doesn't need to. The water drips from his body. He's yet to wrap himself in a towel. He looks down at his hands, and there is blood still on them. Blood under his nails. A red staining that doesn't want to wash away.

Oscar dries himself. It's getting late, and he's tired. He's had a busy couple of days, and he's particularly exhausted after the time he's spent with Mateo Blanco down in the basement. As he climbs into bed, there's a knock at his door. Oscar pauses and turns, hopeful that this might be good news. He can't imagine why anyone would come and disturb him.

Unless it's bad news.

"Come in."

It's Jorge. He notices that Oscar is naked and keeps his

eyes raised. Oscar can tell from his solemn expression that this is not news he's looking forward to relaying.

"We still don't have them, do we?" Oscar says, not giving him the chance to reveal this himself.

"No," Jorge says. "Our American assistance has failed. They haven't given up, but they've lost track of them."

"And Max Ross told you this?"

"Yes."

"I'd like to speak with Max Ross."

"I can call him back."

Oscar nods. "Go to your office. I'll pull on some trousers, and I'll meet you there."

Jorge turns and leaves Oscar to dress. Oscar isn't far behind him. He pulls on some linen trousers and a shirt and follows him. Jorge already has his phone out and is calling Max. "It's ringing," Jorge says.

Oscar holds his hand out. "Give it to me."

Jorge hands it over, and Max answers soon after.

"Jorge," he says, "miss me already?"

"This is Oscar."

"Oh," Max says. "Hello, Mr. Zavala. What can I do for you?"

"You can tell me what's happening in America."

"I've already told Jorge. I'm sure he's passed that on to you."

"He did, and now I'm asking *you*."

Max is silent. He clears his throat. "What – what do you want to know?"

"I understand a man has been placed on Zeke Greene's team," Oscar says.

Max waits for a question, but when Oscar doesn't ask one, he says, "That's right."

"And yet Zeke is still running free and not being transported to me."

"He's worried that Zeke is suspicious," Max says. "He's been gone from the rest of the team for a while, and there's another member has gone with him. So now he's worried the two of them are working together. They could know it's him."

Oscar remains calm. "Who has gone with him?"

"I doubt you're going to know them."

"I'd like a name."

Max sighs. "She's called Selena."

"Here's what I want you to do, Max – ask your mole if he thinks the rest of the team will be as loyal to Zeke as this Selena is. And if not, he should know what to do about them, yes?"

"That's –"

"If you have any protestations, Max, I don't want to hear them. If Rollins and Zeke cannot be captured in America, then it is time for them to come to *me*. It is time to bait the trap."

"How do you intend to do that?"

Oscar looks at Jorge. He's leaning forward on his desk, hands steepled, watching and listening.

"I would have thought it was self-explanatory, Max," Oscar says. "To bait a trap, we need what is most valuable to them."

"How am I supposed to know what that is?"

"I believe you already do."

"You're being vague, Oscar. Just tell me what you mean."

"We can't be sure that anything is truly valuable to Rollins, but if Zeke needs him, he will help him in any way he can."

"I don't know either of them well enough to say whether that's right or not."

"Recent events would certainly indicate this is so."

"All right, yeah. I'll give you that."

"And we know what is valuable to Zeke Greene."

Max doesn't say anything, and Oscar thinks he finally understands what he's saying, but to be clear, Oscar adds, "Zeke is a family man."

When Max speaks, his voice is cold. He understands fully what is expected of him. "I've got it," he says.

30

Naomi put the kids to bed a couple of hours ago, and they're sleeping soundly. She checked in on them before she came to bed herself, though sleep has not found her. She foresees another night of tossing and turning. For now, she lies on her back and stares at the ceiling. Her eyes are wide, and her fingers are laced across her stomach.

She's tired, but her eyes are not heavy. Sleep will not come for her. It can't. Her mind is too busy. Shapes form on the ceiling. She watches them and tries to calm her thoughts.

Last she saw, Bill and Ben were both still awake. Ben had performed his customary sweep of the house and had then retired to the kitchen. Bill was watching television – something more grown-up, not a cartoon. She hears movement, and she thinks the two of them are together now. She can hear them talking in the kitchen. She raises her head a little, as if this will help her hear better. She wonders what they're talking about.

She doesn't need to wonder long. Quick footsteps come down the hallway toward her door. There's a knock, but no waiting for a response. Ben pokes his head into the room. "You're awake," he says.

Naomi sits up. "What's happened?"

Ben opens the door and holds out his hand in a placatory gesture. "Don't panic."

"How's Zeke? Is he all right?"

"It's nothing to do with Zeke," Ben says. He steps closer, keeping his voice low. "Get dressed and wake the children. We've received a message that we need to move immediately."

Naomi pushes herself out of the bed, gathering up her clothes. "Does someone know we're here?"

"Potentially," Ben says, backing out of the room so she can dress. "We need to move. It's better to be safe than sorry." He leaves, closing the door.

Naomi dresses fast and quickly packs up what few things she has here. She hurries from the room and through to Tre and Tamika. She doesn't wake them straight away. She gathers up their clothes and packs them in their bags – the same bags they took to their grandparents' house just a few days ago. If it weren't for that visit, none of them would have had any spare clothes with them when they came here to the safe house. Zeke refused to return home to grab anything else, for fear that anyone should spot them and trail them here. Of course, if they hadn't been at Naomi's parents' house, they also would have been present when their attackers broke in.

Once the bags are packed, Naomi wakes them both. They sleep in two single beds, a narrow gap between them. Naomi kneels in this gap and shakes them both awake. She wishes she could be gentler with them, but this is an emergency.

Tre wakes first, pushing himself up and rubbing his eyes. "Is Dad back?" he says, and Naomi feels her heart break a little.

"No, sweetie, not yet. But you've got to wake up – we need to go somewhere, okay?"

"Where?" Tre says, but Naomi can't answer. Tamika groans and rolls over and covers her eyes.

"Tamika, honey, come on now," Naomi says. She coos, but then speaks firmer when it's not working. "Tamika, we need to go. Honey, you need to wake up."

"Where are my clothes?" Tre says.

"Forget your clothes for now," Naomi says. "I've got your bags. Just keep your pyjamas on, and you can get changed later. Go and put on your shoes and get ready to go. Go with Bill and Ben, they'll put you in the car."

Tre does as he's told. Tamika, however, steadfastly refuses to wake. She keeps her eyes firmly closed. Naomi gives up and lifts her from the bed, carrying her. Tamika wraps an arm around her neck and nestles her head into her shoulder. Naomi stoops to grab the two bags and then heads out of the room.

Ben is still in the house, waiting for her. He takes the bags from her, and she hurries out to the car while he locks the door. Bill is strapping Tre into the backseat of the SUV.

"You need a hand with her?"

"I'm good," Naomi says, strapping Tamika into the middle next to her brother. Tamika rolls her head and rests it on Tre's shoulder now.

Naomi climbs into the back, and Ben hands the bags to her. She puts them at her feet and then reaches her arm across Tamika so she can hold Tre's hand and keep Tamika propped up. She finds herself turning her head and looking up and down the dark street through the windows, like she might see someone emerge from the shadows. Bill and Ben climb into the front. Ben is driving. The SUV comes to life, and they reverse out of the driveway.

Naomi has a sick feeling in her stomach. So far, they've been moving so fast, but now they've settled, and her concern is growing. She has questions, and she wants to lean forward and talk to Bill and Ben, to ask them what's happening and why they've had to rush out so late at night, but she doesn't, because she doesn't want Tre to hear. She doesn't want him to realize that their lives could be in danger right now. She doesn't want him to feel the same sick knot of dread that she has in her chest, and the acidic burning at the back of her throat.

So she bites her lip and stays quiet and stares ahead at the dark road lit up by the SUV's headlights, and waits until they're safe.

———

31

Tom and Selena walk back to the church's parking lot with the food from the burger joint carried in brown paper bags. Selena is eating her burger, not waiting until they're back to the others. Zeke hasn't driven by to pick them up, so they take this as a good sign that they haven't been found. It probably also means that Cindy hasn't discovered who the traitor is, yet.

Tom and Selena haven't spoken much while they've been gone. They've mostly walked in silence, save for a few brief exchanges, mostly regarding the food. The night air is warm. Tom can hear cicadas singing in the grass running along the sidewalk. He turns his head to Selena a little, but before he can speak, she cuts him off.

"So how long have you known Zeke?"

Tom blinks, then casts his mind back. "It's been a long time now," he says. "Not quite ten years. Seven? Eight? Something like that. He might remember better. Time passes, and everything becomes a blur."

"He's talked about you before," she says. "He's told me about your old team."

"I assume he was making it clear he didn't want his new team to be anything like the people we used to work with."

Selena laughs. "Yeah, actually. For all the good it might have done – unless your girl Cindy comes back and tells us we're all clear. But anyway, I always got the impression the reason Zeke told me about those days is because wanted to tell me about *you*, too."

"He told you specifically?"

"Yeah."

"The two of you are close?"

"Don't go getting jealous, Tom." She grins.

"I get the impression he likes you," Tom says. "When we were looking into you, I could tell he was desperate for it not to be true. Speaking of, I hope there's no hard feelings for holding a gun on your earlier."

Selena waves his concerns off and seems to realize she's still holding her half-eaten burger in her hand. "Don't worry about it," she says, then takes another bite. "If the roles were reversed, and we'd done it to you, I'm sure you'd under-stand. I imagine the reason Zeke asked the two of us to go and get the food was so we could talk like this. Clear the air."

Tom nods and takes his soda out of the bag. The heat of the night is making him parched. He pops the tab and takes a drink. The church is in view at the end of the road.

"Just so we're clear," Selena says, "if Zeke trusts you, *I* trust you."

"Likewise," Tom says.

"I want you to know, whatever happens next, wherever this road takes us, I've got your back. You can count on me."

Tom looks at her. They lock eyes. They don't need to say anything else. They both understand.

As they get closer to the church, they can see Zeke's car still in the parking lot. When they get inside, Zeke and Cindy are both looking back at them, their faces solemn.

"This doesn't look promising," Selena says.

Zeke shakes his head. "Cindy thinks she's found the traitor."

"On the team?" Selena says.

Zeke nods.

"Damn," Selena says, the wind knocked out of her. She looks pained.

Cindy takes the bag of food from Tom. She's exhausted. Tom slides into the backseat next to her and puts an arm around her shoulders while she eats. She rests her head on his shoulder and chest.

Zeke glances at the bag. "I've lost my appetite."

Selena climbs into the front passenger seat. "All right," she says, bracing herself. "I'm as ready as I'm going to be. Who is it?"

"Shaun Andrews," Zeke says.

Selena grimaces. She looks like she's been slapped. "Did you check everyone?"

Tom feels Cindy nodding against him. "Yes," she says.

Selena turns to Zeke. "Are we *sure*?"

Zeke's lips are pursed. He nods. "We're sure. I checked it myself. *Double*-checked it."

"But it's *Shaun*," Selena says. "We've known him for years..."

"I know this," Zeke says. "Do you think this is what I want?" Zeke shakes his head. "Shaun has had my back, and I've had his. I know he's had yours, too."

Selena looks lost. She takes a deep breath and then turns, looking into the backseat, at Cindy. "Tell me what you found."

Cindy sits up, removing her head from Tom's chest. She swallows the fry she's eating and takes a drink. "I got into his accounts, and I found money was coming in that I couldn't find a source for. I also found that he once *owed* a lot of money, but then it was suddenly, magically paid off. I'm guessing gambling debts, but the money that paid it off wasn't won from gambling. If it were, I would have been able to find out where it was sent from a lot easier. So I had to go deeper. I worked backwards. I found a hell of a lot of different accounts, a lot of them under different aliases. When I went back even further, I found he'd received a large payment into an offshore account, which was then spread across other more accessible accounts. This was about six months ago. I could trace where the initial payment came from, but it was heavily laundered, and it'll take a while. Could be days."

"So if we don't know where the money came from," Selena says, "that could mean there's a chance he's not necessarily against us, right? That money could have come from anywhere. He could be dirty as opposed to treacherous."

Zeke is nodding. "We've considered this. It could potentially mean he's been doing off-the-books mercenary work, which isn't great, but it was one large payment. A *large* payment."

"What do we do now?" Selena says, turning back to Zeke.

"We don't have time to theorize or find the source of the laundering," Zeke says. "We're taking the direct route."

Selena tilts her head.

"We're going back to the motel," Zeke says. "And we're going to ask him directly."

32

Tamika has begun to stir. Naomi was content to leave her to sleep, but now that the rush to get out of the car and into the SUV is over, she wakes.

"What's happening?" she says, her voice sleepy.

"It's all right, honey," Naomi says, stroking the side of her face. "We just need to go somewhere else is all. You can go back to sleep if you want to."

Tamika doesn't go back to sleep. She straightens up in her seat and looks around.

Naomi watches both of her children. They look all right, just a little confused. Naomi feels the same way. She looks out the window. They're on the outskirts of Shreveport. She leans forward to speak to Bill and Ben. "How long will it take us to get where we're going?"

Bill turns in the passenger seat. "Not too long," he says. "We're about twenty minutes out."

Naomi hasn't kept track of the time, but she thinks they've been driving for a half hour already. They're putting a lot of distance between themselves and the safe house they've left behind.

"We're actually making pretty good time," Bill says. "With it being so late, there's hardly anyone else on the road."

"Bill, look at this," Ben says, getting his partner's attention.

Bill turns. Intrigued, Naomi leans to the side so she can see between them and out the windshield. There's nothing around them. No buildings. They stop next to a junction that leads to some factories further down the road in that direction. Directly down the road from where they've stopped, lighting up the sky, she can see blue-and-red lights. Cop cars. Ben slows the car. They're close enough now that Naomi can see what the cops are doing. They've closed the road. They've set a blockade across both lanes. There are two cruisers behind the blockade, and four cops stand around it. One of them is waving, motioning for the car to come closer and be checked.

Ben stops the car. Bill looks at him. Ben's shaking his head. "I don't like this," he says.

"What's the problem?" Bill says.

"It feels off," Ben says. "We're dealing with Hondurans, right? I spent some time in Honduras. Fake cop stops are a specialty down there. And I don't know, this just feels like too much of a coincidence to me. We're told we need to leave the house, then on the road we're taking to the new safe house, there's a blockade? This doesn't sit right."

"Then get us out of here," Bill says.

Ben reaches down to put the car in reverse. As he does so, Naomi spots movement out of the corner of her eye, to their right, coming from the junction they've stopped beside.

She turns to it. A dark shape is descending upon them. It's a car. Its headlights are off. The next thing she knows, it smashes into the side of the SUV, hitting the passenger side where Bill sits. It hits them *hard*. The children scream. Naomi, dazed, grabs at them, pulls them closer to her so she can cover them with her body. The sound of crumpling metal and shattering glass drowns them out. The door is almost completely caved in. Bill's body is thrown hard to the side, held in place by his seatbelt. The broken glass has cut him up. Beside him, Ben's head hits his own window so hard he puts a spiderweb crack in it. Blood runs down the side of his face. The SUV is pushed across the road into the other lane, and they tilt a little, like they might roll onto their side or the roof, but as the car that struck them backs up, they fall back down onto all four wheels.

Naomi blinks hard, trying to settle her vision. She feels like she might throw up. She becomes dimly aware of the door being thrown open beside her, and rough hands grabbing at her. She's cut from the seatbelt and dragged from the vehicle. She tries to fight back, kicking out and clawing at eyes. There are two men holding her. One of them grabs at her ankles, and she manages to kick him in the face, bloodying his nose. This angers him. He spits blood, then backhands her across the cheek. They flip her onto her stomach and press her down flat on the road, pinning her in place. She can barely move, can only lift her head enough to watch as Bill is dragged from the SUV in front of her. He's dropped to the road on his stomach, too. He doesn't have much fight in him after the crash. He tries to push himself up on weak arms, blood dripping from his lacerated face and mouth. A gun is pressed into the back of his skull and fired twice.

Naomi sees his blood and bits of his skull splash and spread across the road.

On the other side of the SUV, she can hear Ben being dragged out, too. He's dazed, but not as badly as Bill. She can hear him trying to fight back, but he's quickly overwhelmed. She hears two gunshots.

Naomi's eyes are hot. She grits her teeth, waiting to feel the barrel of a gun against her own skull, but it doesn't come. Instead, she's hauled to her feet. Her children are shoved toward her, and she grabs at them both and holds them as tight as she's able, while she's manhandled on either side, men tightly gripping her inner arms. She notices that someone is carrying the bags containing their clothes, retrieved from inside the SUV.

Down the road, she can see the police blockade. The four cops watch what is happening. None of them make a move. Closer, she sees the red Chevy Impala that crashed into the SUV. The front of it is buckled, and water and fluids are leaking out of it. Naomi is dragged to the side, and they move down the road, away from the crash. She can see headlights approaching. The men see them coming too. Naomi feels no hope for these lights. It's a van. It stops beside them, and the back doors are flung open from the inside.

From behind, Naomi feels a hood pulled over her head. She hears the kids cry out and whimper, and knows that the same has happened to them. Her arms are pulled back, and plastic ties bind her hands together, biting deep into the flesh of her wrists. She's pushed into the back of the van, then she feels the children land next to her. The rear doors slam shut, and the van starts moving.

They reach the motel where Zeke left his team. From the back, Tom can see the lights are on inside. There are a few other cars in the parking lot. Zeke doesn't park immediately outside the room. He goes to the other end of the lot.

"How do you want to do this?" Tom says.

"You stay back," Zeke says. "Keep us covered. The others, they've heard of you, but they don't *know* you. That might make them antsy. Me and Selena will go in. We'll raise the questions. If we're the ones asking them, and not a stranger, Daniel and Guy are more likely to hear things out. If it's coming from an outsider, they might try to defend their teammate. I want this to go easy."

Selena is shaking her head, though not at what Zeke is saying. "I still can't believe it," she says. "*Shaun?* I'm just praying he's got some kind of explanation."

Zeke's face is firm. Tom knows the look. He's been betrayed, and he's torn between wanting to understand and wanting to hurt someone. "He's either going to come clean, or he's going to try to get away. He shouldn't slip past us, but if he does – Tom?"

"I'll stop him," Tom says.

Zeke and Selena get out of the car and go to the motel room. Tom tells Cindy to stay inside the car, then he gets out and watches them go. He keeps his hand close to his Beretta. Zeke knocks on the motel door and calls something through. A moment passes. Zeke frowns and tries again. He and Selena look at each other, then take out their handguns. Tom does the same. He moves closer, but stays near the back of a neighboring parked car.

Zeke and Selena are not in the room for long. Selena comes out first and presses her back against the wall next to the open door. She presses a hand to her face, covering her eyes. Tom thinks she might be about to cry. She raises her face and looks at him and shakes her head a little.

Tom goes to the room. Zeke is still inside, standing in the center, looking at what has happened. It doesn't take Tom long to get the picture. There are only two men in the room, and they are both dead. The white one looks like he was killed without a struggle – a bullet straight through the back of his skull. He's still sitting in a cross-legged pose, almost as if he was meditating, but now his head is slumped forward, his chin touching his chest. Blood has soaked into the carpet beneath him.

It looks like the other dead man, Latino, put up more of a fight, likely in reaction to the death of the first. There are signs of a struggle – the television has been knocked over, and its screen is smashed, and the blanket and sheets have been torn from the bed, as if one or both men rolled over it. On the floor, the Latino man lies dead. Two bullets were fired into his stomach, then a third and fourth through his face.

"Guy," Zeke says, looking at the two men. "Daniel... That motherfucker... He's killed them..." There's a choked sound in the back of his throat, but then he swallows it and turns to Tom. "This unrepentant son of a bitch," he says. "He needs to pay. He's *going* to pay." Something comes over his face then, some kind of realization, and his eyes go wide. "The safe house! He could have found out where it is and passed that information on to Oscar!"

"Let's go," Tom says. "Give me the keys – I'll drive."

Zeke hands them over without protest. He understands why Tom asks for them. He's not thinking straight. He's worked up. He's worried. They run from the room. Selena follows them. They jump into the car. Selena gets in the back, and Zeke sits up front with Tom. Zeke gives directions. It's late, and the roads are clear. Tom puts his foot down. They make good time.

"Car's gone," Zeke says as soon as they reach the safe house. He jumps out of the car before it's completely stopped. Tom is out straight after him, following him inside.

The house is empty.

"Where's Cindy?" Zeke says.

"I'm right here, Zeke," she says from next to Selena, her voice soft.

"Get your laptop," Zeke says, stepping close to her. He's battling to keep himself under control. "Trace them. Find them. *Now.*"

Cindy hurries back to the car to get her computer.

Tom presses a hand to Zeke's shoulder, but Zeke shrugs it off. He turns to Tom, instantly apologetic, holding up his hands. Tom doesn't take it personally. He reaches out again, places his hand on Zeke's shoulder, and this time Zeke doesn't shrug it off. "We'll find them," he says, but inside he feels his stomach sink, and his chest tightens.

Cindy returns, the laptop already running. She goes through to the living room and takes a seat on the sofa. Zeke sits close to her, leaning forward, his fists balled. He doesn't rush her. He knows this won't help. But he's desperate for answers.

Tom looks through the rest of the house while she works, to see if there's anything that might give some indication whether they left or were taken. The fact that Zeke said the car was gone makes him suspect that they left of their own volition, but of course, anyone could move a vehicle. The inside of the house, however, shows no signs of battle. Nothing has been knocked over. There are no scrape marks in the carpet near the door as if someone has been dragged out. He pokes his head into all the bedrooms. There are three bedrooms. In two of them, the beds have been slept in and left unmade. The third bed has not been slept in tonight. Tom presses a hand to the mattress. It's cool.

There are no signs of any belongings. Nothing has been left behind. Tom checks for bloodstains, too. He checks walls and floors, every nook and corner. He looks the ceilings over and studies the bathroom sinks. No blood.

He returns to the living room. He doesn't have to wait long for Cindy to finish her search. "I found the SUV," she says, talking directly to Zeke, though Tom and Selena are listening just as intently. "And I traced it, but then it passed through an area where all the nearby camera feeds had been cut. After it reaches that blackout zone, it doesn't reappear. It doesn't come out the other side, and I can't pick up on it anywhere else."

"Maybe they were lured to that spot specifically," Selena says.

"Or else it was on their way to somewhere else," Tom says. "And it was intercepted by someone who knew where they were going."

"Could it have been Shaun?" Selena says.

"It could have been," Tom says. "But he would've needed backup. Provided the men guarding Zeke's family haven't also been paid off, but that seems unlikely. Their being selected for this assignment couldn't have been anticipated."

Zeke has been silent. His hands are clasped in front of his mouth, his elbows digging into his thighs. He stares silently at Cindy's laptop, but he's not really looking at it. He's thinking. He speaks up now. "What about Shaun?" he says. "Can you find *him*?"

Cindy gets back to work. "I can try."

"If he's taken my family, I'm going to tear him apart," Zeke says. "And if they're not with him at the time, I'm going to break every fucking bone in his body until he tells me where they are."

34

S haun Andrews is at the airport. This is the first time he's stopped moving since he received the message to get out of the motel. Now he's just waiting to get away before Zeke and his friends can track him down.

He feels hot, like he's sweating. He runs the back of his hand across his mouth until his lips feel raw, and swipes at his brow with the inside of his jacket sleeve. His mouth is dry despite the bottle of water he's finished in three gulps. His heart is hammering like he ran here. Shaun struggles to get his breathing under control. He finds himself looking around the airport, scanning every face he can see, making sure none of them are familiar. His paranoia is high. It needs to be.

Shaun is leaving the country. He's going to Haiti. He has family there. He'll hide out with them for a few days, then move on to somewhere else. He's not sure where to yet. He can decide that when he's in Haiti, and once he's got all the money from his various accounts in a handier, easier-to-reach location. He's thinking about the Caribbean, but he needs to consider whether this is the best idea. If Oscar Zavala *isn't* successful, and if Zeke and Rollins get to him before he gets to them, Shaun is going to spend the rest of his life looking over his shoulder. And now that Oscar has Zeke's family, Shaun isn't sure he'd have much of a life left. It would be short, filled with worry, and once they found him, very, very painful.

Shaun has to hope that Oscar is successful. It's to his benefit for Zavala to come out of this whole mess on top. Kidnapping Zeke's wife and kids, though, Shaun knew he had to get out of the country the second that line was crossed. God knows, Shaun is no saint, but that was too much for him. He wants no part in it.

He's met Naomi Greene. And Tre and Tamika. He's been to Zeke's house for a cookout when he was in Louisiana. That must have been a year and a half ago. Naomi was a beautiful woman, and Tre and Tamika were a pair of cute kids. Shaun remembers thinking Zeke was a lucky man.

He sits back in his seat, still scanning faces. Thinking of the Greene family, and what they must be going through now, turns his stomach. He wishes he had more water, or something stronger.

Shaun tries not to think of all that he has done, and what he has allowed and aided to happen. He tries especially not to think about what he has done tonight. About Guy and Daniel. At least Guy was easy. Meditating, like he always fucking is – like he always *was*. He didn't have to look Guy in the face while he killed him. Daniel, however – that prick. He had to make things difficult. When Shaun killed him, he was looking into his eyes. He sees those eyes every time he blinks.

It will pass. He knows it will pass. Everything will get

better. These thoughts will fade. The money will help. The money will make everything all right.

He remembers when he was first approached. He knew why they'd come to him. His gambling debts. He owed money. He needed the money. They knew that just as well as he did. Quarter of a million dollars, up front. Another quarter once everything was over with Zeke and Rollins.

Shaun said he'd have to think about it. Deep down, he knew what his answer was going to be. When he didn't go straight to Zeke and tell him what he'd been offered, he knew he was going to accept the money. That was six months ago. After he said yes, the money was his within a couple of days. First thing he did, he paid off his debts. After that, he knew he was locked in.

There was no going back. He was theirs. When they wanted to know where Zeke was and what he was doing, he told them. When the ambush occurred in El Salvador, he knew to stay out of the way. If the El Salvadorans weren't successful, Shaun was supposed to finish the job. Because of Selena, he never got the chance.

And now he's killed Guy and Daniel. Two members of his own team.

He was told to. He was following orders. He tells himself this, but it doesn't help. It was for the money. He did it all, did everything, for the money. Not once in his life, until these past six months, did he think he was this kind of man. That money could rule him. That he would find himself in a moral quandary, and he would betray all his beliefs.

There's a commotion going on around him. It takes Shaun a moment to realize something is happening. He looks up when he hears a collective groan go around the airport. People are throwing up their hands in frustration.

They grumble. Shaun turns and looks to the departure board. He scans it. All outgoing flights have been cancelled. He frowns, not understanding. He pulls out his phone and checks for weather alerts. There aren't any. He grabs his bags and tries to get to a ticket desk to ask what's happening, but there's already a queue. People are speaking loudly. Some are shouting. The staff don't understand what's going on, either. They don't know why all of the outgoing flights have been cancelled.

Shaun looks to the departure board again, but nothing has changed. The airport is in chaos. Shaun feels his paranoia growing. He spins around, checking faces. He can't stay here. There's no point, not if there are no flights. Remaining stationary is dangerous for him. He can't hang around. He leaves the airport, walking fast back to where he left the car he jacked to get here.

He walks across the parking lot, turning his head left and right. He can see the car at the end of the row. A vehicle he didn't expect to ever see again. He hotwired it after he hurried from the motel. The owner didn't spot him, didn't come rushing out after him. He wonders if they've noticed that it's missing yet.

He reaches the car. It's not locked. He had no way of locking it. He makes sure to look inside before he reaches for the handle. Checks to make sure the backseat is empty, that no one's in there trying to get the drop on him.

As his hand wraps around the handle, he spots movement over his shoulder in the glass. He starts to turn, to spin, but he feels a gun jabbed into his spine.

"Keep moving and I'll paralyze you," the man says.

Shaun doesn't know who he is. A white guy. A stranger. A carjacker? Before Shaun can respond, someone else emerges from the rear of the car. This person he recognizes. Zeke. He's glaring at Shaun, and Shaun feels himself wither. He understands who is behind him, with the gun pressed to his spine. Tom Rollins.

Zeke is angry. He can barely contain himself. "Let's not make a scene," he says. "Keep your mouth shut and *move*."

35

They tracked Shaun to the airport, but they couldn't know what flight he'd be on, or where he was planning on going. Cindy got into the airport's mainframe, and she grounded all of the flights. It was their only chance to catch him. After that, once they reached the airport, Cindy was able to get into the security cameras, and they watched as Shaun realized what was happening, and that he needed to get out.

They've brought Shaun to an abandoned house. "It burned down a year back," Zeke said. "It's just a husk. No one comes by here. There's no reason why anyone should suspect we're here." They have Shaun bound in the basement. Tom and Zeke are with him. Cindy and Selena are waiting upstairs, on lookout, watching the street and the road.

The basement is untouched by the fire that ravaged the house above. Tom leans against the wall, arms folded. Zeke stands directly in front of Shaun. He's gagged right now, but he won't be for much longer. They haven't started on him yet. From where he stands, Tom can see the side of Zeke's face. His jaw is tightly clenched. His unblinking eyes are blazing. He stares at Shaun. Shaun can't look back at him.

Zeke is so still. It doesn't look like he's breathing. Tom doesn't prompt him. He lets Zeke take his time. He knows that, internally, Zeke is in tumult. He wants to move fast. To find his family. While he's watching Shaun, he's thinking. Deliberating. No doubt Zeke wants nothing more than to tear Shaun limb from limb, but he can't be sure this will be effective in gaining him the information he needs. Shaun has had the same training they have. He knows how to compartmentalize. He knows how to disassociate during torture. From the glazed look in his eyes, he's already disassociating.

Zeke clears his throat. Finally, Shaun looks back at him, waiting. A little of the glaze goes out of his eyes. He swallows. "You betrayed me, Shaun. You betrayed all of us. You *killed* Guy and Daniel."

Already, Zeke has to stop talking. He grits his teeth and takes a step back, breathing deep. He runs a hand down his mouth. "They have my wife and my children, Shaun. You know my family. You've met my family. They've taken Naomi. They've taken Tre and Tamika." He steps close to Shaun, and for a moment Tom thinks he's going to hit him. Instead, he jabs a finger into his face. "I hold you responsible, Shaun. Tell me where my family is."

Shaun stares back at him. He blinks.

Zeke pulls the gag out of his mouth. "Tell me."

Shaun doesn't respond.

Zeke nods. He puts the gag back in place, then punches Shaun. Before he can topple back in the chair he's bound to, Zeke catches him by the front of his shirt and keeps him upright.

He slams the point of his elbow across the bridge of Shaun's nose, breaking it. He pulls out his Beretta and presses the barrel into Shaun's temple. He pulls the gag out of his mouth again.

"Tell me where they are!"

Shaun closes his eyes tight.

Tom knows Zeke is not going to pull the trigger. He can't. He needs Shaun alive. Without him, they don't have anything else. Zeke knows this. He cries out and pulls the barrel from Shaun's temple and pistol-whips him across the face, cutting a deep gouge in his cheek. He strikes him a few more times with the handle of the gun, bludgeoning him. Other than some pained grunts, Shaun doesn't make any noise. His face bloodies and swells. His right eye closes. Zeke presses the barrel of the gun into Shaun's knee.

"Tell me where they are!" he says. "Tell me where they are, or so help me God, I'll blow your fucking kneecaps off!"

Zeke is fraught. Tom has no doubts he'll do what he says he's going to. It's too far too soon. They need to save crippling him as a last resort. If that doesn't break him and make him talk, they have nothing left. Tom steps forward. "Zeke," he says.

Zeke's head snaps around.

"Let me talk to him," Tom says. "Take a step back."

Zeke doesn't back up straight away. He keeps the gun pressed into Shaun's leg, and his eyes locked on Tom's. Finally, he nods and steps back. Shaun is left alone. Blood drips from his face. He grimaces.

Zeke puts his gun away and backs into the corner where he can catch his breath.

Tom gives Shaun a chance to recover. He stands in front of him, his arms folded. "Look at me, Shaun."

Shaun looks up. He doesn't know Tom. He hasn't betrayed Tom as badly as he has Zeke. He's able to hold Tom's eye.

"You might know my name," Tom says, "but you don't know *me*. I haven't been CIA for a long time. I can do things to you, Shaun. Things you can't imagine. You think you can handle anything I can throw at you, but you're wrong. I can destroy you, but I can keep enough of you intact to answer my questions.

"But here's the thing, Shaun. I don't want to have to do any of that to you. I don't think it's necessary." He stares at Shaun for a long time. There's a stack of more chairs in the corner of the basement. Tom takes one of them off the pile and sits down in front of Shaun, so that they're sitting level. "I don't think you're a bad guy, Shaun. You've done bad things, but who hasn't? You got yourself in trouble, didn't you? We know about the gambling debts. You saw an opportunity for yourself to get out of that hole, and you couldn't say no to that. You never expected things to get as bad as they have. But long-term, you found that you'd just jumped from one hole into another, right? And that second hole, it just got deeper and deeper and deeper, until the next thing you know you're killing two men you know. Two men you were close with."

Shaun's eyes glisten. The muscles in his cheeks twitch.

"The two men on your team, what were their names? Guy and Daniel? Yeah, that's right, isn't it. Guy and Daniel are dead," Tom says. "You killed them, Shaun. We can't change that now. Nothing can take that back. But Naomi and Tre and Tamika, they could still be alive, Shaun. They could still be alive, and you could help us get them back. *That* is something you can fix. All you have to do is speak to us, Shaun. Just tell us where they are."

Shaun lowers his face. A tear falls from one of his eyes and lands on his lap. He sniffs hard. He starts to shake his head. "I don't know where they are," he says.

Zeke steps forward, but Tom holds up a hand. "Maybe you know something that *can* help us," Tom says. "Where's Oscar?"

Shaun shakes his head again.

"Think, Shaun," Tom says. "Take your time. Think long and hard. Think of something that could help us to get back Naomi, Tre, and Tamika."

Shaun's face remains lowered. He's silent. He breathes deep. He turns his head and spits blood. "I know... I know why Oscar is free. And I know who freed him."

"We're listening," Tom says. "Who freed him?"

"*We* did. The CIA."

Tom glances toward Zeke. Zeke freezes, processing this, likely trying to decide whether he believes it or not.

"Why did the CIA free Oscar, Shaun?" Tom says.

"To install him and his men as an elite unit in the military," Shaun says. "They've been having problems with the president. With Oscar in the military, he'll be close to the president. He can keep him under control. Get him to do what we want."

"Why Oscar?"

"He has the biggest organization in Honduras. If he's in place, there's no one who can stand against him."

"But he was in prison. In *Mexico*. It's not like he was close."

"They didn't need *him* – just his organization. I don't know all the details about this. I wasn't told everything, and not in detail. But the guy who's been running it all for Oscar while he was gone, the CIA would've been happy enough to put him at the head of the military, but he said no. He said he'd only help if we got Oscar out. So we did."

"But they knew this would happen," Zeke says, stepping forward. "They knew he'd come after us."

Shaun doesn't say anything.

"That's why they paid *you* off," Tom says. "Right? So that when it happened, and Oscar moved on us, you'd at least be nearby to make sure he took out Zeke nice and smooth."

Again, Shaun says nothing.

"*Who?*" Zeke says, stepping closer. "*Who* at the CIA is running this?"

Shaun looks up now. "You're not going to like the answer."

Zeke looks like he's been hit in the stomach. He braces himself, like this statement has told him all he needs to know. Like he knows who the answer is going to be, and he's ready for the worst. "Who?" he says, and his voice is quiet.

When Shaun speaks, the name is only vaguely familiar to Tom. He recognizes it, but he had nothing to do with this person while he was at the CIA. But Zeke closes his eyes and nods, once, dejected. Everything he feared. The name he dreaded.

William Taylor.

36

Oscar whistles as he moves through the house. He carries a Makarov pistol tucked down the back of his trousers, cold against the flesh of his lower back. He passes a couple of his men, and they step aside and nod to him. Oscar gives them a cheerful smile and salute. These men are on guard duty, carrying out a regular sweep of the house. There are others, outside, who are watching the grounds.

Downstairs, in the kitchen, the women working there visibly flinch as he enters. It's late, and there are only three of them. They stop what they're doing and stand with lowered heads, none of them wanting to meet his eye.

"Good evening, ladies," he says, pausing at the door leading down to the basement.

They mumble their responses, none of them loud enough to be heard clearly.

They're scared of him. They're terrified, in fact. Oscar can see the way the one closest to him trembles. Can see how pale they all are. Oscar is used to being feared. It doesn't mean anything to him anymore. When he was young and realized his reputation was growing and that the reason people were starting to look at him with such respect and such reverence, when they would speak to him with a waver in their voice – when he realized that this was because they were fearful being around him, it brought him a thrill. Over time, that thrill dulled. Now, this fear, it's just the way things are. The way they should be.

And the women here, who work in the kitchen, they've heard what happens in the basement. They've heard the screams and the bloodcurdling cries. They've seen Oscar emerge with blood splashed upon him, on his face, and covering his arms from the tips of his fingers to his elbows.

Oscar turns on the light and goes down to the basement. Realizing that someone is coming, Mateo Blanco begins to sob. It's the only sound he can make. He doesn't have a tongue anymore.

Oscar stops in front of him, admiring his handiwork. Both of Mateo's arms and both of his legs are badly broken. His right eye is gone, scooped out, and his left is bruised and swollen. Beneath his left eye, the skin is deep purple where his cheekbone has been fractured. A large portion of his right cheek is missing. His chipped and broken teeth can be seen through the hole. There are other wounds covering his torso and his legs. Crisscrossing cuts and whips. Dark bruising. He's missing his right nipple, and in its place is a crust of scab that struggles to heal. Oscar can hear a rasp when Mateo breathes. A deep, chest-rattling wheeze.

Mateo sobs, expecting more of the same. Oscar has not permitted him any pain medication. He has not allowed him any medical attention. "You're looking well, Mateo," he says, then chuckles to himself.

Mateo, with his one remaining eye, can't look back. His is a different, stronger kind of fear. Oscar has seen it many times before, but this fear remains sweetest to him, and he revels in it for a moment.

"Truthfully," Oscar says, "I'm surprised you're still alive. Clinging on, Mateo. You're tough. I appreciate that. Too many of my toys have broken on me long before we've ever had a chance to get to the good stuff. Not you, though. You're different. Stronger. I appreciate that, truly, I do. You've made an old man very happy these past couple of days."

Oscar takes another moment to look him over. His eyes pass over the mix of blood, piss, and shit that has pooled beneath him. It stinks down here, but Oscar doesn't notice it. He grew accustomed to it fast. He's spent enough time down here that it barely affects him at all.

"This is the last time I'll come to see you, Mateo," Oscar says. "I'm sure this isn't easy to hear, but you've been a place-holder. A warm-up. Something for me to pass the time with. You've served your purpose, Mateo. You've served it well. But now, the toys I *truly* want will be coming my way, and I need to be ready for them. I'm going to need this space. I'm sure you understand, Mateo. Goodbye."

Oscar takes the Makarov from his waistband and puts a bullet through Mateo's skull. It doesn't take a double tap. Mateo is barely clinging as it is. Oscar puts the gun away and leaves Mateo hanging. He'll get someone to come down and dispose of the body and clean the mess up.

He needs this space ready for when Rollins and Greene arrive.

37

Tom and Zeke drive in silence. They don't need to talk. They know where they're going, and what they're going to do.

This isn't a trip to William Taylor. Not yet. That comes next. After that, they're probably going to Honduras, or wherever Oscar Zavala is.

First, they need to be prepared. They need weaponry. They need more than they have on them.

Selena and Cindy have remained behind, at the house. They're watching over Shaun. He's still in the basement, still tied to the chair and gagged.

Zeke knows where they can get weapons. "I know where all the drug dealers operating in this area are," he said back at the house, in the kitchen, while the four of them stood around a charred table and deliberated their next move. "I know their corners, I know their safe houses, and I know where they hang out."

"Why do you know all this?" Cindy said.

"If there are drug dealers operating near me, you'd best *believe* I know where they all are."

Tom and Selena nodded in agreement.

Zeke turns into a run-down neighborhood. Tom can see people hanging around in their yards and sitting on their doorsteps. It's late, and any passing car draws their attention. Zeke carries on, unperturbed. He pulls up in front of a house on a corner. There's a man standing guard outside the front door. He straightens up as the car stops, and pounds on the door with the side of his fist.

Tom and Zeke get out of the car. Zeke leads the way. The guard blocks their path. "Help you?"

"We're gonna talk to the men inside," Zeke says.

The guard grins. He shows off a metal canine tooth. "Sure," he says, lifting the front of his shirt to reveal the handgun tucked down the front of his jeans. "You got an appointment?"

Tom eyes the gun. It's an FN Five-seven. "You don't have the safety on."

The guard eyes him. "What did you say?"

Tom grabs the gun, slipping his finger inside the trigger guard but leaving the gun in the man's waistband. "I *said,* if I squeeze this trigger, I'm gonna blow your dick off."

The guard's eyes go wide. He freezes.

Tom pulls the gun out and points it at his chest. "That was a stupid fucking place to keep it," he says. "Knock on the door again. Tell them we're coming in."

The guard backs up, hands raised, and does as he's told.

Inside, the air is thick with marijuana smoke. There are half a dozen men in the living room. Half of them are sitting down. The rest of them are standing. All of them turn as Tom and Zeke enter. Tom shoves the guard to one side. The six men pull out guns. They don't point them, they let them hang down by their sides, but they make it clear that they're packing. Tom keeps hold of the FN Five-seven. He doesn't point it, either.

A man with a shaved head comes from the kitchen and stands in front of Tom and Zeke. He sees the guard. "The fuck's going on here?" he says.

Zeke gets straight to the point. "Here's what's going to happen," he says. "All the heavy weaponry you have in this house – it's ours. Once I'm finished talking, you're gonna turn your ass around and go get it for us."

The leader smirks. "Is that right?" He chuckles and looks to the other men in the room. "Now why'd we wanna go and do something like that?"

"I'm going to tell you," Zeke says. "I wasn't done talking. I'm sure you're all looking at me and my friend right now, and you probably think we're cops, right? We ain't cops. We're CIA. Do you hear that? Black ops. We're not here to play, do you understand?"

"We're just supposed to take you at your word?" the leader says.

"Do you want to test us?" Zeke says. "And do you think we came here alone? This house is surrounded. So listen up. We can do this one of two ways. You go and get the hardware and hand it over without any fuss, or else we take it. It doesn't matter to you why we want them. All you need to know is that we do."

Silence falls. Zeke and the leader are locked eye to eye. Tom watches everyone else, but he snatches glances at Zeke. He's never seen him like this before. His eyes burn. His lower lip twitches. He looks ready to explode at any moment.

The leader picks up on all of this, too. He can see that Zeke is on the warpath.

"All right," he says, backing off and waving a hand toward his men. "Go and get them what they want."

The few men who are standing around leave the living room and go down the hallway to a room at the rear of the house. While they're gone, the tense, silent standoff resumes. The other men aren't gone long. They return with a sports bag, which they put down at Tom's feet. Tom gets down and opens the bag, looking inside. There's an M500 shotgun on top. Under that, there's an AAC Honey Badger, an Armalite AR-18, an AMP-69, and a couple of Heckler & Koch MP5s. There's plenty of ammo for all of them, too. Tom zips the bag back up and shoulders it.

Zeke doesn't make to leave straight away. The leader looks toward the bag. He opens his mouth, but Zeke cuts him off.

"We're going," he says. "Don't try to follow us. You won't get very far. Now listen closely – you're done here. When I get back, you don't want me to find you still here. You understand what I'm saying? You're done in this neighborhood. I ever find you again, you're done. Full stop."

The leader doesn't look happy, but he knows he shouldn't retaliate. "You didn't say when you're gonna be back."

"No," Zeke says. "I didn't." He and Tom leave the house with the guns and take them to the car. They drive away. No one tries to follow them.

Wayne Jacques lives on the outskirts of
Shreveport, on the banks of Red River, close to
the Red River National Wildlife Refuge. His
house is a small mobile home parked next to an airstrip.

Tom pulls the car to a stop next to the runway, down
from Wayne's home. There's a single light on inside. It's late.
After midnight. "Does he know we're coming?" Tom says.

Zeke shakes his head. "Figured it was best if we just turn
up. Didn't want to run the risk of any of our transmissions
being intercepted."

Selena and Cindy sit in the back. Shaun is with them,
but he's tightly bound, gagged, blindfolded, and lying on his
side in the fetal position in the trunk of the car.

Selena leans forward, eyeing the home. The guns Tom
and Zeke took from the drug dealers' house lie in the bag
between her and Cindy's feet. "You said he's a pilot?"

"That's right," Zeke says. "Planes and airboats. That's
how we met. Me and Naomi took the kids out on an airboat
on Red River. Wayne was the pilot. Since then, he's taken us

up in his plane a few times. But he's a friend, too. We keep in touch."

"And you trust him?"

"I don't see any reason why we shouldn't. He doesn't have anything to do with the CIA, and they aren't aware of his existence."

"What we're going to ask him to do," Tom says, "it's dangerous. He's going to take some persuading. What are we going to offer for his help?"

Zeke's face is grim. "Whatever we have to. I'll give him my life savings if that's what it's going to take to get my family back."

Tom and Zeke get out of the car. Cindy joins them. Selena stays behind to guard Shaun. Zeke motions for Tom and Cindy to hold back. "I know he has a shotgun in there," he says. "So stay here until I've let him know who you are."

Tom and Cindy step back and wait. Cindy folds her arms and shivers.

"You cold?" Tom says as Zeke walks toward the mobile home.

"I'm fine," she says, but she leans a little closer. She tilts her head suddenly. "Can you hear a dog?"

Tom can hear yapping coming from inside the mobile home. "Sounds like it belongs to Wayne."

Zeke reaches the mobile home. He knocks on the door, then steps back, calling out, "Wayne – it's Zeke Greene."

The door doesn't open straight away, but Tom can see how the home rocks as the man inside moves around. He hears a muffled voice call back through the door, punctuated by the dog's barking.

"Who'd you say?"

"Zeke Greene, Wayne," Zeke says, speaking louder. "And I've got some friends with me."

The door slowly opens, and a man peers out, squinting through the darkness as he looks beyond Zeke and takes in the other people in the nearby vicinity. Wayne wears a fisherman's cap pushed back on his head. His body is squat and firm, and he wears a vest that shows off the muscles of his shoulders and arms. Other than his hat and vest, all else he has on is his underwear. He looks like he's been sleeping.

He blinks down at Zeke and picks some sleep out of his eye with a fingernail. "Zeke," he says. "Little late for a boat trip."

"We need your help, Wayne."

Wayne looks surprised by this. He looks around again. The dog in the home tries to get past him, but he holds it back with his bare legs. "You all want to come in a moment?" he says. "Give me a chance to get my bearings."

Zeke goes in first. Tom and Cindy follow. Selena stays at the car, leaning against the trunk. It's cramped in the home. Zeke, Tom, and Cindy take a seat. The dog runs around their legs and jumps up at them. It sniffs at their hands.

"She's very friendly," Cindy says, scratching the dog behind the ears.

Wayne is in the kitchen area. He's rummaging through the cupboards, pulling out coffee. "Yeah," he says. "Tammy, get down. Leave them alone."

"She's okay," Cindy says, keeping the dog close to her. "What breed is she?"

Wayne shrugs. "I'm not sure. Some kind of mix. I found her at the side of the road, no collar, looking hungry and scared, so I took her in. Never been able to work out what her breeding is. You all want some coffee?"

Nobody does. Wayne makes himself a mug and then remains standing in the kitchen. "Who was that out at the car?" he says. "I assume she's with you?"

"We've got someone in the trunk," Zeke says.

"She's keeping him company," Tom says.

Wayne blinks. He drinks more coffee. He clears his throat. "What are you doing here, Zeke? You said you needed my help...?"

Zeke gives Wayne the rundown of what's happened so far, and what their plans are going forward. Wayne listens in silence. He doesn't ask any questions. He takes one final, slow drink from his mug, then puts it in the sink. As he turns back, Zeke is wrapping up. "We need a flight. Likely to Honduras. Definitely with a stop off in Virginia first."

"And they have your family?" Wayne says. "They took your children?"

Zeke nods.

"All right," Wayne says, pushing himself upright. "Let me get my jeans on, and then we'll go."

"I appreciate this, Wayne," Zeke says, getting to his feet. He holds out his hand to shake. "What do I owe you?"

Wayne frowns at the question, but he takes the proffered hand. They shake. "You don't owe me anything," he says.

"I can pay," Zeke says.

"*We* can pay," Tom says. "Whatever it takes."

Wayne shakes his head. "I'm not gonna take money to help you get your family back," he says. He grabs a pair of jeans off the back of a chair and starts pulling them on. "What kind of man would I be if I took payment for something like that?"

"It's going to be dangerous."

Wayne shrugs.

"I appreciate this, Wayne," Zeke says.

Wayne pulls on his boots. To Cindy he says, "Pick Tammy up for me, will you? My girlfriend lives near here. She'll come take care of Tammy while we're gone. I'll give her a call. It's not gonna take her long to come." He straightens up and pops his spine. He turns to Zeke and Tom. "Virginia, then Honduras? Reckon we'll take the Cessna 208. It's got the best range, but we'll have to stop off in Florida on the way down to refuel. Have to do the same on the way back, too."

"You'll know best," Zeke says.

Naomi wakes. Her head is pounding. Her mouth and throat are dry. Sunlight streams in through an uncovered window, landing full on her face. She struggles to open her eyes. The light stings them and amplifies the ache in her head.

She feels groggy and dazed. Her mind is struggling to put together where she is. The bed she's lying on is big and comfortable, but it's unfamiliar. She's not under the blanket. She's on top of it and, from the feel of it, still wearing all of her clothes, including her shoes.

Suddenly, she pushes herself upright, her stomach lurching as she does so. She almost throws up, but she swallows it down and looks around, searching for Tre and Tamika. She doesn't have to search long. They're beside her on the bed, under the blanket, both of them curled up close to each other and still deeply asleep.

Relieved, Naomi rests her head in her hands. Through squinting eyes, she looks around the room. She's never seen it before. Nearby, there's an en-suite bathroom. The door is slightly open, and she spots the toilet, and her stomach does another flip, wanting her to go to it and throw up. She turns away. The room's floor is tiled, with a rug in the center of it, leading to the window. For a moment, Naomi thinks she might be in a hotel, but that doesn't seem right. She wonders where Bill and Ben are, and then it all comes back to her.

At least, to a point. She remembers the crash. Remembers being dragged from the car. Remembers what happened to Bill and Ben. Witnessing it. Then being thrown into the back of a van.

And then?

It's a blur. Her head was covered so she couldn't see. They drove with her and the kids on the floor in the back of the van, and then – and then – and then Naomi remembers something pricking her in the arm. She felt sleepy after that.

Then there's nothing.

They must have drugged her.

She looks at Tre and Tamika again and wonders if they were drugged, too. They're still sleeping so deeply, and she thinks they might have been. She leans over to check their breathing. They're fine. She leaves them and tries to get off the bed.

Her legs are unsteady. She falls and stays on the rug on her hands and knees, feeling surprisingly breathless. The room spins. She braces herself, then shuffles closer to the wall and uses it to get to her feet. She makes her way to the door. She notices their bags are in a pile against the wall next to the door. The bags they first packed to go to her parents' house for their wedding anniversary. That feels like a lifetime ago.

By the time she reaches the door, it feels like she's run a mile. The door is locked. She thinks about banging on it, but then decides against it. Instead, she turns, and still pressing her weight to the wall to keep her upright, she goes to the window, shielding her eyes against the light with a hand. The first thing she does upon reaching the window is check if it will open. It does not. It's locked, too, and there's no sign of a key. She breathes hard, exasperated, and then looks out. In the distance, she can see the sea. She looks at the grounds below. She spots a helicopter. She blinks, wondering if she's imagining this. It stays where it is. It looks like it's military. She's sure Zeke could tell her all about it.

Away from the helicopter, the grounds are swarming with men. They're dressed like they're in the army. Some of them are running drills, and others are standing in two rows of ten and performing jumping jacks. She spots a couple of armed men who are not running drills patrolling the grounds, presumably on guard duty. The men are all Latino. Naomi had suspected, but now she's quite certain, that she and the children are no longer in America. Or, at least, North America.

Naomi breathes hard. She wonders if there's someone outside, standing guard on this room. She has to assume there is. It would be careless not to have someone covering them.

She thinks about Zeke. If they're here, then that must mean he hasn't been successful in his hunt for Oscar Zavala. And if he wasn't successful, does that mean he's dead? Naomi clenches her jaw. She can't think about something like that. She looks at her sleeping children and knows that she has to be strong. She has to believe that her husband is still alive, and that he's out there looking for them.

But how's he going to find them? If they've been taken out of the country, what is he going to do?

While Naomi thinks, the door to the bedroom is unlocked. It swings open. Two armed men step inside, and another steps between them. He has a handgun strapped to his hip, but his hands are empty. He clasps them behind his back and motions for someone behind him to enter the room. A woman does. She carries a tray with breakfast foods upon it. She lowers it to a bedside table, her eyes flickering toward the sleeping children, then she leaves the room.

The man with his hands clasped behind his back smiles at Naomi. He seems to be in charge of this small group. "I see that you're awake," he says. His accent is thick. It's clear English is not his first language. Naomi wonders if this is Oscar.

Naomi tries to talk, but her voice croaks. She noticed orange juice on the tray, and she wants to go to it and drink, to soothe her throat, but she's afraid to push herself away from the wall. She's not sure if she has the strength to hold herself up yet. The last thing she wants is to fall and show weakness in front of these men. She forces herself to swallow, then clears her throat and says, "Where are we?" Her voice is still quiet, not much more than a whisper, but the man hears her.

"This is Honduras," he says. "You've never been?"

"First time," Naomi says. "You drugged my children."

The man shrugs one shoulder. "It was necessary for the journey. We didn't want their crying to disturb the pilot. I'm sure it passed quickly and more smoothly for them." He glances at Tre and Tamika, smiling. "They look so peaceful, don't they? Like angels, I'm sure you'll agree. We expected you to still be sleeping, too, Señora Greene."

Naomi doesn't like him looking at her kids. She draws his attention back to her. "Are you Oscar?"

He laughs. "Me? No. My name is Jorge Cruz. But your husband has told you about Señor Zavala, yes?"

Naomi nods.

"I'm sure he did not mention me. I don't believe I am on his radar, but who knows? America is always surprising us, isn't it? Like when they came and took Señor Zavala away from us the first time. That was not expected."

"Why are we here?"

Jorge looks at her, like she's being either naïve or willfully stupid. "You're here to draw your husband and his friend, of course."

Naomi feels a flitter of hope in her chest at this, but she tries not to let it show. Keeps her face solemn. If they need her to bring Zeke and Tom down here, that means they're still alive. "You don't need my children," she says. "Let them go. Keep me here, but let them go. Please. *Please.*"

Jorge pulls a regretful face, though Naomi doubts its legitimacy. "I'm afraid we can't do that. A package deal, yes?"

Jorge's regrets turn into a smile. He straightens and sweeps a hand toward the tray of food. "Please, eat. And when the children awaken, encourage them to do the same. We don't want you to be uncomfortable while you're here. Oscar will want to see you all later, and he'd like for you to be well rested and settled by then."

Jorge turns and waves the armed men out of the room. He continues to smile at Naomi. "It was a pleasant surprise to find you awake, Señora Greene," he says. "I was hoping we would have a chance to meet properly, face-to-face. I know Oscar is looking forward to meeting you in the same way." He turns.

"Wait," Naomi says.

"We're done here, Señora Greene," Jorge says, pausing at the door. "I said I was hoping to meet you. I didn't say I wanted to get to know you." He leaves. The door closes, and Naomi hears a key turn in its lock.

40

Max Ross meets his new team. "How was the flight?" he says. They're outside his Honduran home. They drove here from the airstrip.

"It was fine, sir," says the man at the front. Max has seen pictures of his new team, and he knows that this is Ivor Strickland. He has a shaved head and a grizzled face, with a deep white scar on the right side of his skull. Max's eyes unwittingly go to the scar. "Skimmed by a bullet," Ivor says, knowing where his eyes have roamed to. "Bled like a motherfucker, and took a chunk out of the bone, too."

"Sounds painful," Max says.

"Would've been more painful just an inch more inward."

Max chuckles at this, but Ivor does not. Max clears his throat. "Yes, well. If it went that way, I'm sure you wouldn't be here with us now. Did you come over on the flight with Oscar's men?"

Ivor nods. "Along with the woman and the kids. They

were out. I assume they've taken them to the Zavala residence. The men gave us this car and sent us on our way."

Max shakes hands with the other two members of the team. Lance Lee, and John 'Ricky' Ricardo. "Do you prefer John or Ricky?"

The man shrugs, then snorts and turns his head to the side to spit. "I couldn't give a fuck," he says.

"We call him Ricky," Lance says. Lance Lee is tall, six feet five, and Max wonders how much of a hindrance his height is while he's running missions.

Ricky lights up a cigarette. He blows the smoke in Max's direction.

Max steps back, looking over his team. They're a charming bunch, he thinks, refusing to cough as the smoke invades his air. "I assume it's safe to say you've all been briefed on what we're doing out here," he says, "and your new role in it."

"We know why we're here," Ivor says. "We have bags in the trunk. We're going to drop them in the house, then take a look around the area."

"You don't need to do that," Max says. "I'm very familiar with the area."

"Uh-huh," Ivor says. "But we're not. So we're gonna drop our bags in the house, and then we're going to take a look around. Get ourselves acquainted. And when we get back, we'll be ready to eat."

Max frowns. "I'm not your housemaid."

"Sure," Ivor says, grinning, and his smile is a terrifying sight. "But we're your guests, and I'm sure that on our first day in this shithole, you're gonna want to make us feel welcome. Isn't that right?"

Max knows what he's trying to do. Ivor and the others are

seeing how far they can push things. They're seeing what they can get away with, and they're testing if Max is a pushover. Max is not a pushover. He's been out here, alone, for a long time, and he's still alive.

"I couldn't give a fuck whether you feel welcome or not," Max says. "This ain't a hotel. You're here to do a job, and I'm here to make sure you do that job well."

Ivor grins again. "Our job is to look out for you."

"Then you'd better plan on doing it to the best of your motherfucking abilities," Max says, taking a step closer to him. He won't back down. He can't. It's important not to with men like this. "Because my life is the most important thing to me, so if I'm placing it in your hands, you'd better be *overqualified* for the job."

Max turns away, heading back to the house. "I'm going to get a drink. Bring your bags in and then go out on your little reconnaissance, but if you want food, you're on your own." He pauses, turns back. "I could recommend a bar. They do decent tacos, but they don't take too kindly to white strangers. They know me, though. They recognize me. I'm not a stranger to them. If you ask nicely, maybe I'll take you along sometime."

"Sure," Ivor says. "Sounds like it could be a hell of a night. We'll keep it in mind."

Max turns his back again, confident that he's asserted his dominance, and heads into the house, leaving his new team to deal with their own bags, and to decide on their own lunch plans.

41

Z eke knows where William Taylor lives. Zeke has been to his house before. They usually meet up when Zeke has to come to Virginia. They've eaten dinner together.

Wayne flies them to a private airstrip belonging to another pilot he knows. "I've got friends across the country," he told them. "Friends, acquaintances, whatever you want to call them."

When Wayne got in touch with his buddy, he also asked if there'd be a vehicle they could borrow. He told them there was a truck in the hangar, and he'd leave the keys behind the sun visor. After the Cessna 208 lands, Tom, Zeke, and Cindy make a beeline to the truck. Selena and Wayne stay behind. Selena stays on guard with Shaun.

Before they left, Selena warned Shaun that she wouldn't hesitate to hurt him if he tried to escape. "I will put a bullet through your brain," she said, looking him dead in the eye. Shaun remained bound and gagged. Tom had sat next to him on the flight to Virginia, watching him, making sure he didn't try anything. "You killed Guy and Daniel," Selena said. "We're not teammates anymore. You're not our brother anymore. You're nothing to us. You're nothing to *me*. I will not hesitate to put you down, you son of a bitch."

In the truck, Tom takes the wheel. Cindy sits between him and Zeke. Cindy gets on her laptop. She searches the area near where William Taylor lives, going through footage to make sure he's at home. Tom pulls out of the hangar and gets away from the airstrip and onto the road. He asks, "What are you planning on doing with Shaun?"

"I don't know yet," Zeke says. "I want to bury the son of a bitch..." He trails off. He's silent for a moment. "I don't want to get ahead of myself. We might still need him yet. For now, I'm not thinking about what to do with him. That's for later. Right now, I'm thinking about how deep this might go within the CIA."

"Can't bury them all," Cindy says.

"We can always try," Tom says.

Zeke gives directions.

"Speaking of," Tom says. "I assume, after this, you can't go back to the CIA."

"How could I?" Zeke says, leaning forward so he can see Tom. "I should've got out when you did."

"What will you do instead?" Cindy says.

"I'm not thinking about that yet, either," Zeke says. "Right now, my priority is my family. Nothing else matters until I get them back. I can think about the future when and if it comes. Without them, there is no future."

Tom looks around. The road is lined with red maple trees. "It's been a long time since I was last in Virginia," he says.

"It's my first time," Cindy says. She still has her laptop

open. She taps the screen. "So far as I can see, William got home around eight thirty last night, and he hasn't left since."

It's early morning. The sun is coming up, its light only just beginning to stream through the trees.

"How close to his house could you see?" Tom says.

"Pretty close, as it turns out," Cindy says. "A couple of his neighbors have security cameras, and between the two of them, they cover the whole street. I was able to hack into their systems and check their footage."

"Was there anyone else on the street?" Zeke says. "Anyone who looks like they might be standing guard or watching over the place?"

"Not that I could see. I checked the parked cars, and I looked a little further afield, too."

"Keep an eye on the house," Tom says. "We want to know if he starts to leave."

Tom and Zeke are equipped with their Berettas. Tom also has the FN Five-seven he took off the guard back at the drug house. They've left the heavier weaponry back at the plane with Selena. The Berettas should be more than enough here.

They reach William's neighborhood, and Tom parks the truck at the end of the street. They can see William's house. Cindy puts her laptop away. Tom looks the houses over. It's a white-picket-fence kind of street. The gardens are well tended. Even William has blooming flowerbeds. Tom assumes a gardener is paid to maintain these, as well as keep the lawn trimmed. William should be too busy to tend to it himself, especially if he's busy plotting some kind of Central American coup, while simultaneously betraying members of his own agency.

Zeke checks the time. "If we're lucky, he should be leaving to go to the office soon."

"Is William a family man?" Tom says.

"Unmarried," Zeke says. "No kids."

They watch his house. His car is on the driveway. His curtains are not drawn. The front door begins to open.

"Let's go," Zeke says, getting out of the truck.

"Cindy, stay here," Tom says.

Tom and Zeke approach William's house. They catch up to him as he's unlocking his car. He sees them approach. They're too close for him to attempt any kind of escape.

"Zeke," he says. "Tom." He looks at them both in turn. He's not surprised to see them. He's calm. He takes a deep breath and lets out a weary sigh. He leaves his car locked and starts heading back toward the house. "I assume the two of you want to come inside?"

42

Villiam leads the way through to his study. Tom watches him, doesn't want to give him a chance to grab for any hidden weapons. Because of this, he doesn't get to take much of a look around the rest of the house. Not a close look, anyway. Mentally, he notes its interior for points of entrance and exit, as well as cover, should they need to make a quick retreat. He notices that Zeke is watching William too, but in a different way. He's staring daggers. He's staring a hole straight through him.

In the study, William takes a seat behind his desk. There's a framed American flag on the wall behind him. Atop a filing cabinet to his left, there are pictures of William with his old team, and another of him shaking hands with the president.

Tom and Zeke remain standing.

William knows why they're here. He doesn't waste any time. "I knew that if the two of you weren't caught in Shreveport, then it was just a matter of time before you made your

way to me. Especially after all contact with Shaun fell silent."
He looks thoughtful. "Is Shaun still alive?"

Tom and Zeke don't answer.

"I assume you hurt him," William says. "To get him to talk. You probably tortured him. He wouldn't have spoken easily." William looks down at himself. "Shaun is lean. He's tough. I can't say the same about myself. I've gone soft after years behind a desk."

He doesn't look soft to Tom. William looks like he keeps himself fighting fit. Still, Tom understands what he's saying. He's not talking about his body, not really. He's talking about his mind. He doesn't have the same mental strength that he used to. What he's saying is, he can't stand up to being tortured the way he might once have been able.

"I have one question, for now," Zeke says. "*Why?*"

William sighs. It takes him a while to answer. He drums his fingers on the surface of his desk. Tom notices how he keeps both of his hands in view. He keeps them flat. He's showing them he's not a danger. He's cooperating. They're safe. Tom doesn't buy it. He won't be lulled, and he knows Zeke won't, either. Tom pays attention to this detail. He watches William's face while he talks, but he keeps his hands within sight.

"We have a problem in Honduras," William says. "They have an uncooperative president. I'm sure you're asking yourselves, in what way is he uncooperative?" He looks between them both.

Tom and Zeke are silent. They stare at him. They wait.

"All right. I can see you're not going to ask. You did say you had *one* question, Zeke. I suppose I should keep that in mind."

"I want to know why," Zeke says. "I don't care about the political climate in Honduras."

"Sure, it's one question, but it's a long answer." William straightens in his seat. He draws his hands closer to himself, but they remain flat on the desk. "Did you know that Honduras plants genetically modified corn? It's illegal in the rest of Central America. But they plant it to combat food shortages, as well as rising corn prices in the outside world. Their new president, however, wants to phase them out. He's been in power about a year now. He's concerned about the environmental impact GMOs may be having, as well as the health of his people. It's commendable, sure, but there are private trade deals in place between our countries and the people in charge of those deals... Well, let's just say they have friends in high places, and they want this forthcoming problem nipped in the bud ASAP."

Zeke looks like he's growing annoyed. "I don't care about any of this."

"I said it was a long story, didn't I? Listen, outside of the government, who do you think has the most power in Honduras? And hell, it's debatable whether the government truly does. It's the Zavala Cartel. And the way their ranks have grown even since Oscar himself was locked up, if they continue on the same trajectory, they could overthrow the government by force if they want. This situation with the president and the GMOs, it offers us a chance to kill two birds with one stone. I want you to understand, both of you, I didn't want Oscar. Jorge Cruz has been running things while he was locked up, and he was doing a fine job. *He* would have done just as well for what we have planned, but he refused to cooperate unless we gave him Oscar back."

William shakes his head. "I'm not sure why he's so loyal to the man, but there you have it."

"And what is it exactly that you're trying to do down there?" Tom says. "Are you planning on installing Oscar as the new president?"

"Not quite," William says. "We're going to install him as the head of the military. From there, he can lean on the president and get him to play ball. And if that doesn't work, he can eliminate the president, and we can install our own puppet."

"And you expect *Oscar Zavala* to play ball?" Tom says.

"We've dealt with him once before," William says. "He knows this. He's not likely to forget it any time soon. He knows full well that what we give him, we can just as easily take away."

Tom shakes his head. "You don't know Oscar Zavala at all."

"I do as I'm told," William says.

"You helped them to break him out?" Zeke says.

William takes a deep breath. "We provided a location, and we provided them a decommissioned Black Hawk. After that, it was up to them."

"Don't give me that bullshit," Zeke says. "If you provide a location and a means of escape, the responsibility is entirely upon you."

William doesn't say anything. He sits back and looks to the side, at the drawers built into his desk. "I'm going to get myself a drink, okay?" he says, slowly pulling his hands back off the table. "The bottle's in the bottom drawer. Don't shoot me."

He reaches down and pulls out a bottle of scotch and a

tumbler. He pours himself a generous drink and leaves the bottle open on the desk.

"All of this," Zeke says, shaking his head, "putting our lives in danger, my family's lives in danger, all because of some fucking private trade deal involving GMOs?"

William finishes taking a drink. "Like I said, I do as I'm told. I don't make the decisions around here. You know that as well as I do, Zeke."

Tom watches him. He drains off the glass and then places his hands flat on the desk again.

"I'd offer the two of you a drink," William says, "but something tells me neither of you would accept it." He sighs. "Look, I wasn't in your orbit when all the stuff with Oscar first went down. I didn't know he would react like this when he was freed. If I'm honest, after a few years spent in solitary in Mexican prisons, I thought he'd just be grateful to be out. But now, we're too committed. We need to see this through. You both understand this. You know how it is. I'm...I'm sorry for what's transpired."

"Where is he?" Tom says.

"Honduras."

"*Where?*"

"Gracias a Dios. Do you want me to draw you a map?"

"We can make our own way," Zeke says.

William nods. He stares at the open bottle and at the empty glass. His tongue flickers out over his lips like he's remembering the taste of it.

Tom remains wary of him. He's given up the information too easily, without protest. They haven't had to hurt him or even threaten him. He's drank a glass of hard liquor despite the early hour. He knows it's unlikely he's leaving this room alive. He's bracing himself for that. The question is whether he'll go out quiet or loud. Tom watches his hands.

William looks up at Zeke. "I *am* sorry, truly. To both of you, but especially for your family." He bites his lip. "I hope you're able to get them back."

His hands move. Tom is ready. William reaches under his desk. He pulls out a gun. As soon as it flashes into view, Tom and Zeke draw on him. They're faster than he is. They pepper him with bullets. The bottle of scotch shatters and spills the liquid across the desk. William slumps in his chair, blood pulsing out of his torso, soaking his white shirt red. His head hangs to the side. He's dead.

He went out loud.

43

Tom, Zeke, and Cindy head back to the airstrip. They tell Cindy on the way, and Selena once they get back, that William basically killed himself with their bullets. It's why he was drinking hard liquor. Why he told them so much. Why he told them where Oscar was. He knew this wasn't enough, though. He couldn't be redeemed, not after Zeke's family were taken.

"He knew there was no coming back from that," Zeke says. They're close enough to Shaun and talking loud enough for him to hear.

Selena nods while they tell her. "It sounds like maybe he didn't want too much to do with what's happening in Honduras," she says. "He kept saying he did as he was told, right? A company man. Maybe he felt in over his head, and he regretted what happened."

"Regrets aren't going to give me my family back," Zeke says.

Selena holds up her hands. "I get it," she says. "I would've killed him, too. What did you do with his body?"

"Left it where it was," Tom says. "We tossed the place and took some valuables, made it look like a burglary gone wrong. Anyone else at the CIA who knows what's happening, they'll probably know it was us, but they won't be able to prove it. There's nothing they can do."

Tom also left behind the FN Five-seven, depositing it in some bushes outside, like it had been dropped during the escape from the burglary. The FN Five-seven wasn't the murder weapon, but they'd made it look like a lot of people had been in the house during the 'robbery.'

Cindy erased the footage of Tom and Zeke entering the house, or being anywhere near it, from the security cameras on the street. "I've set the footage from both cameras onto a loop, and I've left a dark spot like they've both had an electrical fault around the time of the 'robbery.'"

Wayne stands in the open doorway of his plane, leaning out to look down on them all. "When do we fly?" he says.

"Soon," Tom says. "But first we need to fill everyone in on the plan for getting down there, so everyone listen up." He glances at Shaun. "Apart from you. You can go back on the plane."

They put Shaun back on the plane and tie him to his seat, then return outside, where they can talk out of earshot.

"We already have a plan?" Selena says. "Gracias a Dios can be a lawless place. It needs to be a good plan. We have to be careful."

"Cindy's been working on it," Tom says. Cindy has been at work on her laptop in the truck since after they left William's house and they'd told her they needed to go to Gracias a Dios.

"The Zavalas have a main rival," Cindy says. "The Colón Cartel. And they're in Gracias a Dios, too. Currently they're in a truce, but from what I've read, it's tenuous. We're heading in as drug smugglers. I've been in touch with them and told them we're new dealers, looking to make a business arrangement. They supply us, we distribute it across America with our trusty Cessna. They've sent us coordinates to their own airstrip."

"And what happens when we get there?" Selena says. "We keep up the façade and take their drugs on board, or we ask them for a ride to Oscar Zavala's home and we try to manufacture our own temporary truce...or *what*?"

Tom shakes his head. "We're not doing any of those things," he says. "What we're going to do is use their rivalry with the Zavalas to our advantage."

"How are we going to do that?"

Tom grins. "They're not going to see us coming."

44

An armed man comes to retrieve Naomi and the kids. "Come," he says. "Lunch." He's monosyllabic, and Naomi thinks he doesn't speak much English. He waves his rifle to hurry them up.

The kids have been awake a couple of hours, but they've been subdued. They yawn a lot and rub their eyes. The drugs are still swimming through their systems. They haven't said much. Mechanically, they ate the breakfast foods that had been brought to them. They allowed Naomi to re-dress them in the clothes from their backpacks. Overall, they appear numb.

She holds both of their hands tightly, and they follow the armed man out of the room. There's another man outside in the hall, and he follows behind them. Naomi doesn't see any sign of Jorge. The family are led downstairs to the dining room. A man Naomi assumes to be Oscar Zavala is already sitting at the head of the table, waiting for them. He stands as they enter, smiling. He motions to the chairs at the end of the table and tells his men to hold out the chairs for them.

Once Naomi and the kids are sitting, Oscar sends the men from the room.

"The food shall be here shortly," Oscar says. He returns to his seat.

Naomi sits directly opposite him, at the other end of the table. Tre is to her left, and Tamika is to her right. They don't look numb anymore. They look frightened. They sit hunched over, making themselves small. They don't look toward Oscar. They angle their bodies toward their mother.

"So," Oscar says, resting his elbows on the table and lacing his fingers. "Shall we become acquainted while we wait?"

The dinner table seats eight. There are two empty chairs beside both Tre and Tamika. Naomi is glad of this distance, and she imagines they are, too.

"No?" Oscar says. "No one wants to talk?"

"I don't think we have anything to say to you, Mr. Zavala," Naomi says.

"Please, call me Oscar." He's smiling. It never fades. "That's a shame." He looks from Tre to Tamika, then back to Naomi. "You have very beautiful children, Señora Greene. Or do you mind if I call you Naomi?"

"I don't think it matters what I think," Naomi says. "My children are scared of you."

"Is that so? Why should you be scared, children? This is our first meeting. We haven't had a chance to get to know each other. I am friendly enough, aren't I?" He leans toward Tre and wriggles his eyebrows.

Tre manages to nod, and then Oscar turns to Tamika and does the same, and she turns away, reaching for her mother.

Naomi takes Tamika's hand and holds it. She reaches out

for Tre and takes his hand, too. She squeezes them. "Please don't talk to my children, Mr. Zavala."

"Call me Oscar."

"All right. Please don't talk to my children, Oscar."

Oscar holds out his hands. "For now," he says.

Naomi watches the man. She studies him. He's friendly, he's charming, but he's intimidating, too. There is a clear air of menace emanating from him. Naomi can feel her heart pounding in her chest. She does her best not to let any fear show on her face.

Oscar, in turn, watches her. "You are a very beautiful woman, Naomi," he says. She feels her skin crawl. "I've seen pictures of you. Only recently, since I returned home. But my friend Jorge – I believe you've met Jorge, yes? He has had people watching you and your family for the last year or so. Sorry, no, they were watching your *husband*. You and the children just happened to be there. They'd have been watching for longer, since I was first locked up, but Jorge needed to regroup our forces. He needed to stabilize. And then, of course, he needed to find where you lived. You have a wonderful family home. Stationary. You were easy enough to find and to monitor.

"Tom Rollins, on the other hand, I have been told he was far trickier to track down. He moved around a lot. No fixed address for the longest time. Would you like to know how we were able to finally find him? You're in the story. You *helped* us to find him."

Naomi doesn't answer. She knows when he's talking about.

"A little town called Hopper Creek," Oscar says. "New Mexico. Just a few months ago, wasn't it? The men who followed, they say it looked like a birthday party. Tom's birthday? How old is he, Naomi?"

"Do you really want to know?"

"I wouldn't ask otherwise."

"Thirty-three."

"Ah, that's a good age. When I was that age, my son was three years old." Oscar stares at her. He takes a deep breath. "My boy. Edwin. I will not lie to you, Naomi, or to your children – I was not a good father. I was not always present when he was younger. But I loved my son. I did. And he grew up to be a fine man. He would have been a fine heir to my empire."

Oscar checks the time. "It won't be long until lunch is brought through. I'm sure you're all hungry."

Naomi still holds the hands of her children. She strokes their knuckles with her thumbs.

"I can see that you're tense," Oscar says. "All of you, but especially you, Naomi. You're worried about why you're here, aren't you? Allow me to make some assurances. I am not going to harm any of you, Naomi. Not you, nor your children. I have no interest in that. You are only here to bring your husband and Tom Rollins to me. They are the ones I want."

Naomi doesn't believe him. He's just saying this to make them placid and complacent, but Naomi is not a fool. She believes that they may well be safe until Oscar gets what he wants, but the second her husband and Tom are dead, so are they. He's hardly going to put them on a plane and send them back home.

Naomi won't be lulled by him. She needs to stay alert. She needs to find a way out of here. To escape. To get far, far away. It's the only way they can be truly safe.

"Tre," Oscar says suddenly, "Tamika, would you like to know why you're both here?"

"I asked you not to talk to them," Naomi says.

"And I didn't," Oscar says. "For a while, at least. But now I want to." He turns his attention back to the children. "Would the two of you like to know why you are here?"

"Please don't –" Naomi begins.

Oscar holds up a hand to silence her. His eyes don't leave the children. He's still smiling, but Tre and Tamika shy from him.

"Some years ago," Oscar says, "when both of you would have been very small, your father came to my house with his friends. One of those friends was Tom Rollins, who I believe you know. There were three other men with them, but they don't matter anymore. I lived in Mexico then. It was a very beautiful house – grander even than this one. I lived there with my wife, Marie, and with our son, Edwin. I was talking about him earlier, remember? We used to call him Eddie, but he didn't like that very much, because when he was small, we would call him Little Eddie. He said being called Eddie always made him feel like a child. So we did our best to call him Edwin or Ed. He was twenty-six when your father and his friends came to our home. He will always be twenty-six."

Naomi feels sick. She doesn't want her children to hear this.

"It was dark when they came," Oscar says. "I was sleeping. There were other men who lived in our house. Just like here. They looked after us. They protected us. They came to the room I shared with Marie, and they woke us and told us we were under attack. I could hear gunfire and explosions. I went to investigate, and I was captured. Your father and Tom

Rollins, they captured me. They bound me so I could not move. And while they did that, the other three men with them went to my bedroom, and they killed my wife. They went to Edwin's room, Little Eddie, and they killed him, too."

Tamika is crying. Naomi can't tell if it's from the story or the intensity of Oscar's telling.

"You're upsetting them," Naomi says.

"We're all upset," Oscar says. "We just have different reasons for being so. You're upset that you are here, in Honduras, away from home. I am upset that your husband was complicit in the murder of my family."

"Zeke and Tom didn't have anything to do with that," Naomi says. "Those men, they were trying to stop them for years, they –"

"But they didn't," Oscar says.

"Those men are dead now because of Zeke and Tom. They were stealing drugs, running guns, and the CIA wouldn't listen when Zeke and Tom reported them. A blind eye was turned to everything they did. But Zeke and Tom, they *did* stop them eventually."

Oscar shrugs. "Too little, too late. It won't bring back Marie or Edwin." He turns to the children again. "All I want in this world, more than anything else, is to have my family back. But I can't." For a moment, he looks truly sad. His eyes glisten. His smile falters. But then he blinks and forces the smile back onto his face, and he's terrifying again. "Hurting anyone will not bring them back, I know that. It probably won't make me feel better. But what else can I do? I cannot suffer these two men to live. I'm sorry, children, but we must all share in my pain. It's unfortunate. I'm sure you think it's unfair. Life is not fair. Life is hard and bloody, and you must be prepared to do whatever it takes to get through it."

He sits back and drums his fingers on the table. "Your father will come here looking for you, children. I know he will, because I would have done the same if you were Edwin. I would have cut a bloody swathe through the world to get my family back. He will come for you. And children, I will not lie to you. I am going to kill your father."

They're both crying now. Naomi bites her lip, staring at Oscar.

There's a knock at the door. Oscar's face suddenly lights up. "Ah!" he says, raising his eyebrows. "That will be lunch! Telling my story has worked up an appetite. I hope it has done the same for you, hearing it. Come in!"

45

M ax is informed of William's death.

He's told it looks like a botched burglary, but he doesn't believe this. With everything going on, it's too convenient that such an event would occur now. Last he'd heard, all communication had been lost with Shaun Andrews. Combine these two, and it's not looking good.

No, it's more likely that Rollins and Zeke are getting closer. They're figuring things out. Chances are, with Shaun silent and William dead, they're on their way to Honduras now. They're coming for Oscar. And, since Oscar has taken Zeke's family, who knows who else they might be coming for, looking for vengeance? If they killed William, they must know about the CIA involvement.

Max calls the team William supplied him. They haven't come back since they set out on their recon this morning. Ivor answers.

"William Taylor is dead," Max says.

"Okay." Ivor doesn't care.

Max sighs. "Do you understand why that is important?"

"Rollins and Greene did him?"

"That's my guess."

"Then that must mean they know about *your* involvement in this whole FUBAR situation."

"Do you mean *me*, or the CIA in general?"

"The latter, but maybe they *do* know about you, too. I figure you're thinking the same thing. And I'm guessing that's why you've called me."

"You need to be prepared for their arrival."

"I'll get on it," Ivor says.

"Where are you right now?"

"We're observing the Colón Cartel."

"Jesus Christ, be careful out there."

"Don't worry about us."

"I'm worried about what you could *cause*. If the Colóns were to spot you, figure out who you are, that could break the truce. On top of everything else, the last thing we need right now is a narco war breaking out." Max doesn't tell them about his own dealings with the Colóns. That is his business, not theirs. He doesn't want them making a mess of how he's running things here.

"Calm down," Ivor says. "That's not going to happen. Now, let's end this call so we can get to finding Rollins and Greene."

Max is about to hang up, but he quickly adds, "Capture them, don't kill them. Bring them in alive."

"Okay. What about anyone else with them? I understand they might not be traveling alone."

"I don't give a shit what happens to anyone with them,"

Max says. "But Rollins and Greene, I want them *alive* – that's very important."

"Got it." Ivor hangs up.

Max stands by his window and looks out at the trees. Oscar and Jorge will need to be informed of what has happened, and what is happening. Max sucks air through his teeth. He needs to get ahead of things, first. He'd like to deal with Rollins and Greene himself if possible. Capture them, truss them, and serve them up to Oscar with a pretty bow.

He retreats to a chair and takes a seat, suddenly exhausted. He rests his head in his hands. Things have become so much more complicated since Oscar was freed. So much time and resources have been wasted both in getting him out and entertaining this mission of his. Again, Max thinks to himself how much easier it would all be if Jorge were in charge.

He's been playing the long game with Jorge, trying to get him onside, to see things Max's way. The way they *could* be with Jorge at the helm of this ship, and not the psychotic Oscar. How much smoother they could sail into the waters of success. Max has been patient, but it could be time to start ramping things up. Max still isn't convinced that Oscar is the right man for what they have planned, and the events of the last few days have done nothing to disabuse him of that notion.

Oscar is already a problem. Going forward, he's only going to become a bigger problem. Max loses himself in his thoughts. Rollins and Greene reaching Honduras might not be the worst thing after all. Instead of handing them over to Oscar, he could hand them to Jorge, instead. Another oppor-

tunity to get into his ear. To show him what they are capable
of doing together.

No, Max thinks, this might not be such a bad thing at all.
This could be just what he needs to bring Jorge around to his
way of thinking.

46

Their lunch with Oscar felt like it might never end, but finally Naomi and the kids are taken back to the room. Their plush prison cell.

"Get into bed and try not to think about what he said," Naomi says. She's carrying Tamika. She tucks them both under the blanket. The sun is still streaming in through the window, but she strokes their foreheads like it's late at night and she's putting them to sleep. "Just try to get some rest, okay. Forget about where we are. This will all be over soon, okay?"

The children were shaken by Oscar. By his presence and what he said to them. They barely ate anything that was served to them. Naomi hardly touched her food, either, though Oscar emptied his plate with zeal. He didn't seem to notice, or else didn't care, that they weren't eating.

Naomi leaves the children on the bed. She doesn't think they're going to sleep, but she can't sit with them indefinitely. She goes to the door and presses her ear to the wood, listening to the hall outside. She hears someone nearby clear their throat, but no conversation. Slowly, she lowers herself to the ground and looks through the small gap under the door. It's too thin to see much, but she can make out shadows. There is one pair of legs standing on duty to her right. Just one guard. She backs away and then stands again.

"Mom, what are you doing?" Tamika says.

Naomi presses a finger to her lips. "Just try to rest, baby," she says, keeping her voice low so the man outside the door can't hear. "Don't pay any attention to me."

She explores the rest of the room, starting in the bathroom and then going back to the locked window, searching for a potential escape route. She can't see any. Even if she were able to get out the window, the grounds are swarming with men.

She looks over every inch of the room. She can fit under the bed, and she crawls under it, just in case there's anything to find. There is not. She can't find anything that can be used as a weapon, either. Except, perhaps, in the bathroom. The lid of the toilet tank can be removed. She keeps this in mind. For now, it's all she has.

She lies down on the bed next to the children.

"How long do we need to stay here, Mom?" Tre says.

Naomi reaches back and strokes his cheek. "I don't know, sweetie," she says. "But I hope it's not much longer."

47

Tom watches as the Cessna 208 comes in to land on the Colón Cartel-controlled airstrip.

Members of the cartel are already there and waiting. A couple of jeeps are parked off to one side. Half a dozen men stand by the runway, waiting for the plane to taxi around closer to them. There are four other men nearby, spread out, one standing guard at each corner of the area. All of them are armed. Most of them carry M4s, and the couple who don't have handguns on their hips.

Tom is in the trees. He's alone, but he's not the only one out here, concealed. Zeke and Selena are spread out. They parachuted off the plane five miles out and continued the rest of the way on foot. Wayne circled, giving them opportunity to get into place. Cindy had told the cartel they would arrive later than they actually have, buying them plenty of time.

It's still light, and the three of them stayed off the road as they made their way here. They crossed through fields, avoiding any signs of life, steering clear of homes and farm-houses. They traveled with guns strapped to their backs. They have their Berettas, and Tom has his KA-BAR, but they also carried some of the automatic weapons Tom and Zeke took from the drug dealers. Tom has the Armalite AR-18, Selena carries the AAC Honey Badger, and Zeke is armed with one of the Heckler & Koch MP5s.

Wayne lands the Cessna on the strip. He turns it around and brings it closer to the six cartel members waiting. Tom has a view of the plane's door. He sees how the waiting men shuffle and shift in place, preparing. This is their first time meeting prospective new partners. They don't know what or who to expect. They're prepared for anything, hence the numbers and the hardware.

Nothing happens for a while. Wayne and Cindy are taking their time. They can't be sure that Tom, Zeke, and Selena are in position. They're buying every second they can.

The door begins to open. The inside of the plane is in darkness. Tom can see the cartel men trying to see inside. Tom spots movement in the dark. A figure shuffling forward, into view of the cartel. It's Shaun, empty hands bound and raised to show he's unarmed. He's gagged. His eyes are wide and terrified.

Tom has the best view, so he takes point. He opens fire from the trees, taking out the guard off to his right and then firing on the larger group. He drops and starts moving to the left through the trees before the cartel members can turn and get an idea where he is. Already, from the other side of the Cessna, he can hear Zeke and Selena opening up. They take out the rest of the guards first and then advance upon the larger group. Tom moves on them too. They're stuck in the crossfire, and it doesn't take long until they're all on the ground. Tom, Zeke, and Selena quickly move on the dead bodies and carry out the coup de grace, ensuring they're all dead. They strip them of their weapons and pile them up near the Cessna.

Wayne pokes his head out from inside the plane. He pushes Shaun back inside. "It clear? They dead?"

"You can come out," Tom says.

Wayne and Cindy leave the plane. Zeke and Selena are gathering up the bodies of the men who were standing guard and dragging them in closer. Tom swings the Armalite over his shoulder. Wayne looks around at all the dead. "Whoa boy," he says, taking off his fishing cap and running a hand back through his hair.

"Are you heading off?" Cindy says. She can see that Tom is readying himself to get moving again.

"Yeah," he says.

"Be careful."

"What're we gonna do with these bodies?" Wayne says. "Just leave them out like this?"

"Help Zeke and Selena start loading them into the backs of the jeeps," Tom says. "But not all of them. Leave a couple of them out still."

"Why?"

"You probably don't want to know. Is Shaun secured?"

"He's secured," Cindy says. "Tied him back to his seat once the shooting stopped."

"I assume the plane avoided any damage?"

"I'm gonna check it over in a moment," Wayne says. "But I think it's okay. I didn't hear or feel anything."

"All right," Tom says. He pulls the weapon's strap tight across his chest. "I'll be back soon."

Tom starts running. He heads in the direction the jeeps originally came from. He's going to track them back to their source. He's going to find out where the Colón Cartel headquarters are.

48

Jorge has asked Oscar to come to his office. Oscar does not sit. He stands by the window, looking out. He looks toward the sea. One finger is curled around his chin. He's lost in thought.

Jorge watches him. Oscar doesn't seem to notice. Jorge leans back in his chair, one arm on his desk. He's surprised that Oscar hasn't yet asked for an office of his own. He seems content to spend most of his time in his room, or else roam the house and the grounds. He spends a lot of time staring out at the sea. When Mateo Blanco was still alive, he was down in the basement a lot.

Jorge shudders at the memory of what Oscar did to Mateo's body. He swallows, feeling an acidic burn at the back of his throat. He's seen Oscar's handiwork many times before, but there seemed something different about this. A new kind of ferocity. A deeper viciousness. A sign of things to come, when Rollins and Greene finally get here. A deep well of brutality, just waiting to be tapped and fully unleashed.

Considering what is lurking just beneath the surface, Oscar presents himself in much the same way as he always has. He's well dressed. Well groomed. He's calm. Quick to smile. He doesn't give the impression of a man so close to explosion.

He's waiting. Jorge can see it in the way he's looking out the window, his finger still wrapped around his chin. He's waiting, when he stares out to sea. When he roams the grounds. He's waiting.

"Oscar?" Jorge says, trying to get his attention. "Oscar."

Oscar blinks and then takes a breath, as if he's just woken up. His hand drops from his face, and he turns to Jorge. "I was distracted."

"I could tell," Jorge says. "You looked lost in your thoughts."

Oscar grunts. "I was thinking of Naomi Greene," he says. He smirks. "She's a very attractive woman, wouldn't you agree?"

Jorge shrugs. "I suppose she is." Jorge has never taken a wife. He's never needed or wanted one. His work has always come first, and his work has kept him very busy. When he feels the urge to take a woman, he can easily call for one. But when he's at home, he prefers his own company. He doesn't want anyone around who could interrupt that.

Oscar sighs and takes a seat. "It will be a shame when I cut her throat in front of her husband. Part of me thinks about sparing her, keeping her around." He chuckles. "But she'd never forgive me for killing her children. And so, they must all go. A package deal."

Jorge clears his throat. "Perhaps we should talk of –"

"I'm going to kill them in front of him," Oscar says. "In

front of both of them. The same way my family were killed so close to me. But I am going to make them *watch*."

"I know you are, Oscar," Jorge says. He's heard this before. He knows of Oscar's grand plans. "But shall we talk of what comes *after* Rollins and Greene are out of the picture?"

Oscar laughs. "Oh, there's still some time to go before they're gone completely. I intend to keep them alive in the basement for a very long time. Far longer than Mateo Blanco. He was merely an appetizer."

"Yes, of course. But, be that as it may, we should prepare to fulfill our end of the deals made."

Oscar waves a hand. "I don't care about these deals, Jorge. I don't care about the Americans or what they want from us. I don't care about being installed as the head of the Honduran military. If I'm completely honest, do you know how that sounds to me? It sounds like a *chore*."

Jorge blinks. These words surprise him. Oscar has shown a distinct lack of interest in anything that comes beyond Rollins and Greene, in anything regarding the future, but this is the first time he has outright said as much.

Jorge clears his throat. "The future of this organization, its survival –"

Oscar leans forward. "Jorge, I don't *care*. I don't care about Max Ross or the CIA or America at large. I don't care about *our* government. I don't care about the same things I used to, Jorge. The things I used to care about were based on legacy, but what legacy do I have left to me? My family is dead. My son is dead."

"You can have more children, Oscar –"

"Edwin is dead. What kind of father am I if I cannot avenge what happened to him? This is all I care about, Jorge."

If you had children of your own, a family, you would understand. Everything else pales when they are lost."

"Okay," Jorge says, not sure where to go from here. He
and Oscar look at each other for a long time in silence.

Jorge is not sure he recognizes the man in front of him.
He knows his face, of course, but not his spirit. The Oscar
that Jorge used to know had ambitions. He had great desires.
He had plans. He had the will to see them through. The will
to accomplish all that he set his mind to. The Oscar he used
to know was *strong* and would not be deterred from his
course of action.

This Oscar seems incapable of looking five minutes into
the future.

Jorge has to clear his throat again. He sits up. "Okay," he
says again. "But when Rollins and Greene are dead –
however long that may take – what then? What do we do
then?"

Oscar strokes his mustache, smoothing it out. Jorge
thinks he can still see some of Mateo's blood under his
fingernails. The blood should be gone now. Cleaned away. It
seems like Oscar is keeping it there on purpose. "I don't
care," Oscar says eventually. "I thought I made that clear."

"You're in charge," Jorge says. "The men look to you."

"A lot of these men never saw me before a few days ago,"
Oscar says. He stands. "Jorge, I can see that you are intrigued
by what the Americans are offering us. But I have been burnt
by Americans before. I lost my family, and years of my life, to
Americans. What they want from me now holds little
interest to me. No, I'm interested in using the Americans
only to satisfy my own ends. That's all they're good for." He
steps closer to the door. "I'm going to my room. I want to rest.

I suspect I will need my energy soon." He winks at Jorge and then leaves.

Jorge stares at the space where he last stood. He feels his brow furrowing with concern. He sees the prosperous future he had envisioned slipping away through his fingers like sand. He lets out a long and tense breath, feeling how stress has tightened his muscles. He grits his teeth. Jorge believed that once Oscar had his way with Rollins and Greene, that would get his desire for revenge out of his system. He's starting to believe that this will not be the case. This worries him.

Jorge picks up his phone, and he calls Max.

It doesn't take Max long to answer. "I think we may have a problem," Jorge says. "You should come to the house. We need to talk."

49

Tom finds where the Colón Cartel came from. It's two miles north of the airstrip, a small commune of what looks to be a couple of villas and a small warehouse that may have been a factory at one time. The area is gated and heavily guarded. He doesn't need to do anything further. For now, he just needs to know where it is.

Tom begins the journey back. It's hot, and he's sweating. He's been on the move nonstop for a few hours now. He's hungry, and he's thirsty. He pushes these needs from his mind and then spots something on the ground, in the grass. It's not much. He almost missed it. Part of a footprint, compressing strands of grass. It's heading away from the commune. South.

It doesn't mean anything. Not yet. The area is guarded. This footprint could belong to anyone, likely just doing their rounds. It looks reasonably fresh, though. Tom follows it just to be sure it's nothing to be worried about. It heads out from the west, through trees, whereas Tom approached from the east.

There is one dirt road that leads to the commune. Much like Tom did when he came here, the trail stays off the road. It avoids it, stays out of view of it. Tom finds other signs. Broken branches and snapped twigs. He finds a space where someone stopped to take a piss against a tree. The smell still hangs fresh in the air.

Tom doesn't like this. He's confident now that whoever they are, they're heading toward the airstrip. It could be trouble. More men from the cartel, sent in as reinforcements in case bad things went down? He thinks it's a small group. Three or four people, he'd guess. Moving through the trees, the same way he, Zeke, and Selena have since they arrived in Honduras.

Tom keeps the Armalite on his back, but he pulls out his KA-BAR. He moves as fast as he can, but he stays careful and quiet. If they're just ahead of him, he doesn't want to stumble across them. He needs to remain alert. He listens to the woods and presses on to the airstrip.

50

Z eke and Selena have been busy while Tom has been gone. They've disfigured a few of the cartel bodies to make it look like they've been tortured. The kind of torture that Oscar Zavala would perform.

Wayne couldn't watch. "Jesus Christ," he said, covering his mouth. "Is that necessary?"

Zeke didn't answer. He didn't look up. He kept his mind on his work – flaying a strip of flesh from a man's thigh.

"It has to look authentic," Selena said. "If we want the Colón Cartel to believe that this was done by Oscar."

Wayne kept his mouth covered. He walked away.

Zeke and Selena are done with the post-mortem torture. They add these bodies to the others already bundled into the back of the two jeeps, then use bottled water to wash the blood from their hands and arms.

While they've worked, Wayne has driven the Cessna into the airstrip's hangar. There are three other planes there, all of them smaller than the Cessna 208. Wayne has parked his at the end, with the clearest run at the runway for when they're ready to go. Now, he and Cindy are sitting on some containers, waiting for whatever comes next. Their weapons – the ones taken from both the drug dealers and the cartel members – are stacked close to them. Zeke and Selena have not worn their weapons while they were working.

Shaun is near to them, sitting to the side, still bound at his wrists and ankles. He's gagged, too, and he looks miserable.

Zeke and Selena join them. Wayne and Cindy are eating beans straight from the can. Wayne passes Zeke and Selena each a can. "Figure we've got time to eat."

"You brought this with you?" Selena says, catching the can.

"When you told me the plan, I foresaw we'd have a lot of time to kill. Figured it was a good idea to bring provisions. We need to keep our strength up."

Zeke hands his can back. "I'm not hungry."

Wayne raises an eyebrow. "You should still try to eat, Zeke."

Zeke shakes his head and takes a step back. He looks at Shaun, but he can't look at him for long. The sight of him makes him too angry.

While she eats, Cindy looks out of the hangar toward the trees. She's watching for Tom. Zeke looks in the same direction. "He shouldn't be too much longer," he says, turning back.

Cindy smiles at him. "I swear, every time I'm with him, I feel like I'm losing years of my life to worry."

"Naomi says the same," Zeke says, smiling at the memories. "She says she feels like a prairie wife waiting for her husband to return from the cattle run to the city." He feels his smile fade when he realizes Shaun is watching him. Zeke looks back at him. He can feel himself sneer. It's uncontrollable. "You got something you want to say?"

Shaun nods.

"Just ignore him," Selena says.

Zeke knows he should, but he can't. He pulls the gag from Shaun's mouth. Shaun stretches his mouth and works his jaw. He looks up at Zeke. "I'm sorry," he says.

Zeke grunts. "I'm sure you are."

"I shouldn't have done what I did," Shaun says. "I never – I never thought it would get like this. I never thought things would get so out of control and – and I'd –"

"You'd kill Daniel and Guy?" Zeke says. "You'd allow my family to be taken by a Honduran warlord? Jesus Christ, Shaun, if you were having money problems, you should have spoken to us – you should have spoken to *me*. I don't care how fucking sorry you are, I don't forgive you. I never will."

"I don't expect you to forgive me," Shaun says. "I just want you to know I'm sorry."

"Uh-huh." Zeke has a bad taste in his mouth. "Would you be sorry if you'd got to wherever it was you were running to?" Zeke stares at him. "I want to know. Do you really expect me to buy this line, this sudden remorse? I don't believe it, Shaun. I don't believe a damn word that comes out of your mouth."

"Zeke, just leave him," Selena says. "Ignore him. Put the gag back in and forget about him."

"Wait," Shaun says, staring at the gag, clearly not wanting it back between his dried lips. "Just wait a second –"

Zeke hears gunshots, and Shaun's body begins to jolt with impact, blood spraying from him. Without thinking, Zeke dives to the side. "Cover! Take cover!"

Selena, Cindy, and Wayne scramble behind the containers they were sitting on. Zeke grabs at the stack of weapons. He comes up with the AMP-69. He spins, staying on one knee, and lets loose. He doesn't know where he's aiming. He fires out of the hangar, hoping to get whoever is shooting at them to scatter. Zeke doesn't wait to see if he was successful, or if he hit someone. He joins the others behind cover.

"Tag anyone?" Selena says. They're fired upon again. Bullets whizz and echo around the hangar.

Zeke shakes his head. "Anyone see them?"

"I spotted them right before they opened fire," Cindy says.

"Me too," Wayne says. "Three of them."

Cindy nods. "I saw three, too. They opened up right before they scattered."

"Cartel?" Zeke says.

"Hard to tell," Cindy says.

"All in black," Wayne says. "Wearing masks."

Zeke fires blindly over the top of the containers.

"They've hit the Cessna!" Wayne says.

"I need a weapon," Selena says. "Can anyone reach one for me?"

Zeke grits his teeth. They're pinned down. He looks around.

"They're out of reach," Cindy says, stretching her arm toward the pile of weapons. She snatches it back as a bullet pings off the ground nearby.

Zeke drags her back behind their cover. "You okay? You hurt?"

"I'm fine," Cindy says. There's a small cut on her forearm where debris has nicked her.

"Tom would never forgive me if anything happened to you," Zeke says. He looks around again.

There's a way out of the back of the hangar. Zeke could make it, then circle back and deal with their attackers. Via hand signals, he explains to Selena what he's about to do. She nods. Zeke raises himself, though remains crouched. He braces himself.

And then realizes the shooting is beginning to die down.

51

Tom gets back to the airstrip to find three men firing on the hangar. He can't see any of his friends and assumes they must be taking cover inside.

Tom can't waste any time. The three masked men are spread out. Two of them are in the trees. One has moved closer, trying to get a clearer shot. He's on the runway. Tom runs up on the closest man in the trees. He's tall, well over six feet. He conceals himself behind the trunk of a thick tree. The tall man doesn't hear Tom's approach over the sound of his own gunfire. Tom doesn't have to worry about being quiet or careful. He tackles the shooter to the ground and drives the KA-BAR through his heart.

He pushes himself up and moves on fast, heading for the next man in the trees. He pulls the Armalite from his back and swings it forward. The second shooter notices his approach out of the corner of his eye, but too late. He begins to turn, but Tom drops to a knee and opens fire. The second shooter falls. Tom checks the third shooter is still in place. He is. He hasn't noticed what's happened behind him.

Tom could shoot him. Could kill him easily from where he is. He doesn't. It's better to keep him alive. He runs up behind the third shooter. It's quieter now, with the other two men dead. The third shooter notices the silence. He notices Tom's approach. He starts to turn. Tom is upon him. He raises the Armalite and slams the barrel into his face, just above his left eye. The third shooter goes down, stunned. He's not out yet. Tom presses him. He buries the sole of his boot into the center of his face, knocking him flat on his back. He raises the Armalite again and cracks him across the jaw. The third shooter goes limp. Tom quickly disarms him and throws his weapons to the side.

"Come on out," Tom calls into the hangar. "Is anyone hurt?"

He's pleased to see that no one is. Well, no one important to him, at least. He sees Shaun's body lying on its side and the blood beneath him. Selena goes to him to make sure he's dead, but it doesn't look to Tom like anyone could survive the number of bullets he's taken, or the amount of blood he's lost.

"That was a well-timed return," Cindy says.

"I got back as quick as I could," Tom says. "I found tracks coming back here."

Zeke steps up, looking down at the still living man at Tom's feet.

"Looks like they solved a problem for us," Tom says, tilting his head toward Shaun.

Zeke grunts. "Who are they? They don't look cartel."

Tom reaches down, pulls off the mask. He doesn't recognize the face. White guy, with a scar running deep along the right side of his skull. "You know him?"

Zeke shakes his head. "Judging by his gear, I'd say the CIA sent him."

"Well, he's still alive," Tom says, nudging him with his toe. "I'm sure he'll tell us who he is soon enough."

Selena comes over, carrying the blood-soaked bonds she has removed from Shaun. "I'm sure it's no surprise to anyone that he's dead," she says. "I'll tie this guy up."

Tom moves off while Selena and Zeke bind their new prisoner. He goes to Cindy. "You okay?"

"I'm fine," she says. "But that was close."

Tom nods. "Looked it. I was tracking them back, trying to be careful, but then I heard them open up. Figured it didn't make too much difference at that point if I started running and making some noise."

"Doesn't look like it," Cindy says. "Did you find what you were looking for?"

"Yeah." He notices blood on her forearm. He holds her wrist to inspect it closer. "Are you really all right?"

"I'm fine," Cindy says. "It's just a nick. Don't make a big deal out of it."

Wayne stands off to one side, one hand on his hip and the other holding his cap and scratching his scalp at the same time. He's looking the Cessna over.

"How bad is it?" Tom says. He can see some bullet holes.

"It could have been a *lot* worse," Wayne says, turning to him and putting his cap back on. "I can repair it, though. It won't take me too long. It'll get us back in the air, but it might slow us down a little while we're up there. But if things go the way you all are planning, we shouldn't be trying to outrun anyone." He turns back to the plane. "I can get on with this once you're all on your way."

Zeke and Selena drag the prisoner over to the containers

and prop him upright. Zeke slaps him back to consciousness. The prisoner blinks at them.

"We don't have much time to waste," Zeke says. "So you can either satisfy our curiosity, or you can be cute and find out how quick it takes us to put a bullet in your head." He taps the scar. "And you'd best believe we're better shots."

The prisoner looks between them all, and he can see that they're serious. "'Cute' is my natural disposition," he says. "I'm sure you'll agree." He sees Zeke begin to raise his gun, and he hurries on. "But what is it you want to know?"

"Who you are, for a start."

"Ivor Strickland. I assume my buddies are dead."

"As doornails," Zeke says. "Your name sounds familiar. You're CIA, aren't you?"

Ivor doesn't respond, but this feels like answer enough.

Selena speaks up. "Sounds familiar to me, too. I seem to recall you have a black mark next to your name."

Ivor grins at this.

"Yeah, you look like a real piece of shit," Selena says.

"Now, now," Ivor says. "Is there any need for name-calling?"

"What are you doing here?" Zeke says.

"Why, I'm here to stop all of you, of course." He laughs. "Can't you tell it's going well?"

"Have you seen my family?" Zeke says.

"Oh, I've seen them," Ivor says. He runs his tongue over his teeth, reveling in the pause before he adds more, testing how much he can get away with. "I was brought down here on the same flight they were. They slept the whole way. Drugged. Haven't seen them since we touched down. They're probably in Zavala's house, waiting for you."

"I don't plan on keeping him waiting much longer," Zeke says.

"Your funeral," Ivor says.

"You're working with Oscar?" Tom says.

Ivor shrugs. "I guess that falls under our remit."

"But you came from the Colóns," Tom says. "I tracked you here from there."

"You don't miss a trick, huh?" Ivor says, looking up at him. "Rollins, right? I've heard of you. I've heard you've kept yourself *real* busy since you left the Company. Some impressive stories. I've always been curious to see just how impressive you are up close." He runs his tongue over his teeth again, and it's clear this is supposed to intimidate them.

Tom shrugs. "Okay," he says. "I've never heard of you, and so far, I'm *not* impressed."

Ivor blinks at this, taken off guard by how unconcerned Tom is by him. Tom rubs further salt in the wound by stifling a yawn.

"So what were you doing with the Colóns?" Zeke says. "They're already in a truce with the Zavalas."

Ivor looks reluctant to answer after being shamed by Tom, but he glances at their guns again and decides to speak. "Looking for *you*. We got word William Taylor has been killed. Sure, it looks like a botched robbery, but we can all read between the lines here, can't we? We found this airstrip controlled by the Colóns, and we asked them if they had any Americans get in touch recently. They said they were meeting with some prospective new partners. And here we all are." He looks at the guns again. "So what now?"

"Now you come with us," Zeke says. "You might prove useful."

Cindy has been listening. She waves Tom to the side so

she can talk to him privately. "If the Colóns have spoken to him, should we be worried about them coming back here to investigate?" Cindy is staying behind with Wayne when the rest move on to Oscar's house. They'll be left with weapons, but Tom can understand her concern.

"They shouldn't," Tom says. "We plan on keeping them very busy. There shouldn't be any need for them to come back here. But if they do, don't try to fight them, neither of you. Don't try to defend the plane. Just leave everything and hide in the trees. Send us a message so we know what's happening. If anything goes down with the Colóns, we can deal with that when we get back. Don't put yourselves in any danger."

Cindy nods. "I'll stand guard while Wayne repairs the plane."

"Good," Tom says. "And listen, it's going to be dark soon. If we're not back by daybreak, that means we're not coming back. You and Wayne need to leave. Do you understand?"

Cindy blanches. She swallows. She looks into his eyes, and she doesn't say anything.

"Cindy?"

She forces herself to nod. "All right," she says. "But only at daybreak. That's still a long time away."

"I certainly think so," Tom says. "I don't *want* you to leave without us." He laughs, trying to ease the tension, and Cindy joins in.

"Y'know, I remember when you first got in touch with me," Cindy says. "I didn't think back then that I'd ever end up out in the field with you. And look at us now – in Honduras, of all places."

Tom winks. "It's never boring, huh?"

"No, it never is," Cindy says. "Sometimes I wish it were.

Next time you want to hang out, let's just go for a drive or something. Listen to some music. I'm sure I can broaden your musical palate even further."

Tom grins. He looks toward Zeke and Selena. They're hauling Ivor to his feet. They're ready to go.

52

W hen Max arrives at the house, Jorge has him brought to his office. "Did Oscar see you arrive?"

Max shakes his head. "I didn't see him."

"He's probably in his room," Jorge muses. "Sometimes, I wish he would leave that fucking room, but whenever he does, I speak to him, and I wish he would go straight back into it."

"Trouble in paradise?" Max says, eyebrow arched. He lowers himself into a chair. "Is that why you asked me here?"

Jorge pauses, and then he nods solemnly.

Max looks intrigued. He straightens up in the chair and leans forward. "I want to hear more," he says. He raises a finger in the air. "But first, I need to tell you something. A team was sent down to help me out here. Listen, to make a long story short, someone important back in America was killed, likely by Rollins and Greene. Gave me the impression they now know where we all are, and they're on their way here. So I sent my team out to find them and bring them to us. Now, I won't lie, these weren't the nicest fellas. They weren't exactly the kind to check in on the regular, but when I called them, they would at least answer. Last I heard from them was about four hours ago. An hour ago, I tried to call them. Over and over and over again. Nothing."

Jorge considers this. "Rollins and Greene got the drop on them."

"That's what I'm thinking. Dead or captured; who can be sure? Probably the former. They're not coming down here to make friends."

"They're on their way."

"Yes, they are," Max says. "And we all need to be prepared."

"You should stay here," Jorge says. "We should all stay together. This is the best place for you. There are a lot of men. Rollins and Zeke will not be able to get through them regardless of how many of their friends they have brought."

"I'm not sure they have many friends," Max says. "But be that as it may, I'm happy enough to stay here. Hell, for all we know, they could turn up tonight. If I left now, they could jump me on the road."

"We don't want that," Jorge says.

"All right, now that's out of the way," Max says, "why did you ask me to come?"

"Oscar is not interested in what you want."

Max grins. "I already had that impression."

"I mean he's *very much* not interested," Jorge says. "He has no vision beyond his vengeance."

Max looks like he understands. "Oh," he says. "I see. This is a problem."

Jorge grunts his agreement. "I have tried to press him. To ask him what comes next, after he gets his vengeance, but he won't give me an answer. Do you know what he does all day? He *waits*. Nothing more. He makes no plans beyond those that have already been made. He stares out at the *sea*, Max. The *sea*. He has seen the sea before. It's not like he was locked up for a decade. It wasn't even half of a decade. The sea does not fucking change."

Jorge sees the way that Max looks at him. Max has never seen him like this before. Never heard him use such language. He sees, too, the way that Max's brain is working, thinking how he can use this to his advantage.

Jorge doesn't care anymore. "You were right, Max," he says, and Max's eyes light up at this. "You were right. I kept this organization together while he was gone. I kept it running. I *grew* it. Oscar said himself, most of the men here don't know who he is beyond his name and his reputation. *I* did all of this" – he gestures broadly, taking in the house, the grounds, the small army – "when everything else fell apart after Oscar's incarceration. *I* did it. I saved it." He takes a deep breath. "And this is my thanks? He wants to throw it all away. He wants to leave it to rot."

Jorge settles back in his chair, staring at nothing, his eyes unfocused. He tries to calm himself. This outburst is not like him, he knows, but he stands to lose so much.

Max gives him time. He waits. He *bides* his time. Max is a smart man. Jorge knows this. He knows, too, that Max is thinking how best to play him, but Jorge can no longer be played. Jorge is finally seeing the light.

Max leans closer. He rests an arm on the desk between them. Jorge blinks his vision back into focus and turns to Max. Max is already looking back at him. A long moment passes.

"So," Max says, raising his eyebrows. "What do you want to do now?"

Jorge doesn't say anything for a long time. He watches Max, sees how he tries to play it cool, but he's giddy. Max is getting what he wants. It's time for Jorge to do the same. It's time for him to get what *he* wants.

"We're going to deal with Rollins and Greene first," Jorge says. "We have no other choice in the matter. Oscar will get his vengeance, but it will not be as he's imagined it. There will be no months-long torture in the basement. We will kill Rollins and Greene and anyone else they may have brought with them, and then...then..."

He sees how Max leans in closer, waiting for him to say it.

Jorge isn't sure he can. He swallows and tries to force the words out. He can't. Not here, in this house. The house he prepared for Oscar's return. It feels wrong. It feels like anyone could be listening, like the walls have ears, and they will relay the information back to Oscar. And he'll *know*. He'll know what they're plotting.

"And then we'll deal with him," Jorge says.

The word choice clearly doesn't matter to Max. He nods, satisfied. This is what he wants. This is what he's always wanted. He never needed Oscar. *They* never needed Oscar.

Jorge should have listened to him sooner.

53

I t's dark. Tom, Zeke, Selena, and Ivor drive in one of the jeeps. The other jeep has been left behind, the dead bodies of the Colón men pulled from the back and left strewn in the grass near to the commune. The tortured corpses were strung up on trees, their meaning apparent: this is a declaration of war from the Zavalas. The truce is over.

They set the other jeep on fire to draw the attention of the Colón Cartel, and then they drove on, heading for Oscar's. They don't need to be careful with their trail anymore. They want to be followed.

There is no guarantee that the Colóns will react right away. They can only hope that this message is clear and loud, and that they will react accordingly tonight. The Colóns are a backup plan. They know Oscar's house and grounds will be swarming with men. They know they will be outnumbered. If the Colóns turn up, they will provide a distraction. A *big* distraction. If they don't, then Tom, Zeke, and Selena are going to have to move into the house very carefully and very quietly.

Having Ivor with them changed their plans for the journey to Oscar's house, but only slightly.

Selena drives the jeep. Oscar's house is a further five miles from the Colón commune. Zeke is beside her, masked. Tom is in the back, also masked, with an unmasked Ivor beside him, clearly bound and gagged. Selena is unmasked. Latina, she doesn't need one. Originally, Tom was to be the prisoner. Now, he's sitting with his Beretta jabbed into Ivor's ribs, and an iron grip on his bound wrists.

They doubt they're going to have a clear run through to Oscar's house. They're expecting barricades and checkpoints on this road. They haven't come across any yet, but they're vigilant. They watch the trees that line the sides of the road, wary of ambush.

Ahead, way down the road, they finally spot lights. "Checkpoint," Selena says.

Tom drills the Beretta into Ivor's ribs. "Be very still," Tom says.

They slow as they reach the checkpoint. It's a crude barricade spread across the road with four men manning it. They're all armed with AKMs. Three of them are behind the barricade. The one at the front stands in the middle of the road, waving for the jeep to stop.

Selena is already slowing. The man looks them all over, frowning. Tom notices how his finger hovers near the trigger of his rifle.

Selena speaks to him in rapid-fire Spanish. The guard listens, nodding. It's all too fast for Tom to understand, but he already knows what she's saying. That they've captured an American, and they think he might be of interest – or at least some kind of worth – to Oscar Zavala.

The guard takes a good look at Ivor, and Tom hopes they haven't met before. If they have, they'll have to gun these men down. It's not a problem, but it means they lose the element of surprise.

The guard speaks a little slower, and Tom understands his response: "This isn't one of the men Señor Zavala is interested in."

Tom is sure Zeke has the same reaction to this he does: It means their faces are known. They both stay cool, though. They don't betray who they are beneath their masks. The guard in the road, talking to Selena, doesn't pay either of them much attention. His eyes move between Selena and Ivor.

"Perhaps not," Selena says. "But I never said he was. He could know them. He could know where they are. I'm sure Señor Zavala could get him to talk."

The guard is hesitant. "Where did you find him?"

"In the woods," Selena says. "With a couple of friends. They're dead now."

"You're sure *they* weren't the men Señor Zavala is interested in?"

"I'm sure," Selena says. "I know what they look like, same as you."

"Who are you with? The Colóns?"

Selena snorts. "We're with the Barrio Cartel."

"You don't look the part."

"That's the point," Selena says.

The guard frowns. He stares at Selena for a long time, then he looks back to the others. Tom looks, too, but their faces are imperceptible. The guard turns back. He's deliberating. "Okay," he says finally, nodding toward the barricade. Two of the men there lift a portion of it and move it aside for the jeep to travel through.

Selena nods her thanks and then drives through. They all hold their breath as they pass close to the other guards. They know *this* could be an ambush, too. They could be heading into crossfire. Tom's grip is tight on the Beretta, ready to swing it around if necessary.

It isn't necessary. They get clear. No one opens fire on them. No one tries to stop them. The jeep gets through, and they travel down the road. They round a corner, clear of the barricade.

"A little further and we'll dump it," Zeke says.

Selena nods. In the distance, through the trees, they can see light being thrown up against the night sky, blotting out the stars.

Oscar Zavala's house.

54

Despite their slipping in and out of consciousness on the bed all day, Naomi did not have any trouble getting the children to go to sleep as soon as it grew dark. It reminds her of when they're ill, when no amount of sleep and rest seems to be enough. For now, she needs them to get as much rest as they can. If they get a chance to move, she needs them to be ready to take it.

The drugs are still in them. Their dosage was clearly overestimated, and their systems are still battling to flush it out. Naomi still has a sickly feeling in the back of her throat, but other than that, she feels entirely normal.

There is a light switch, but Naomi keeps the room in darkness. She keeps the blanket on her side of the bed peeled back, so if the guard looks in on them, she can throw herself under it and pretend to be sleeping. The guard looks in every couple of hours. Naomi has kept this in mind. All these little things, she remembers them. Anything that might help them to escape. Anything that could prove to be important.

His timing is not precise, but Naomi has grown accustomed to the noises that precede his entrances. The way his boots shuffle as he pushes himself off the wall he's leaning against. The jingle of his keys. The insertion and turning of it in the lock. While she was still awake, and it was still light outside, he would just poke his head through the door and look the room over. Since it got dark and she's been pretending to be asleep, he steps fully into the room. She feels his eyes upon them for a long time, like he knows she's faking and he's trying to catch her out. Like he suspects they could all be faking. He watches, and when he's finally satisfied nothing is afoot, he checks the window and then steps back outside.

In between, Naomi continues to search for a means to escape. She knows she can't smash the locked window, as it would draw too much attention. Instead, she's trying to find something with which she could pick the lock. Her search is coming up blank so far. The room has been cleared before they were locked inside it. There's nothing of use.

Again and again, Naomi returns to the bathroom. To the toilet tank lid. She looks inside, at the flush mechanisms there. The ballcock is no good to her. There are metal bars that run off it that she could probably bend, but they're too thick to pick the lock. She needs something small. Something like a hairclip. She doesn't have any in, and neither does Tamika.

Dejected, she sits on the edge of the bed and stares through the window. She can see that the grounds are lit up outside. She's looked down at the grounds a few times already. There aren't as many men out there as there are in the daytime, but she knows they'll still be nearby, in the smaller houses. She spots guards roaming the grounds. She's kept track of their schedules and the routes they walk, in case she needs to avoid them. That need is looking less and less likely.

She sighs. She feels her shoulders sag and her hope fading.

Outside, she hears the guard preparing to enter. Naomi lies down and pulls the blanket over her. She closes her eyes and takes long, deep, slow breaths. The guard enters the room and stands at the foot of the bed, watching them. He takes a quick stroll around the room. Naomi watches him through her eyelashes. He stands at the window and looks out. He checks the lock. He stoops down and checks it for any kind of damage. He looks back at her 'sleeping' form. Contented, he leaves the room.

This time, after he has gone, Naomi doesn't push herself out of the bed and resume her scouring of the room. There doesn't seem to be much point. She's searched every inch of it. This time, after he's gone, she stays right where she is, lying on her side, staring out the window.

55

Tom, Zeke, and Selena watch the house from afar. They're concealed in the trees, away from all the lights that are shining around the grounds. They shine up at the house and out into the darkness. Tom, Zeke, and Selena are on the edges of its glow, in the shadows.

Ivor is tied to a tree nearby, deeper into the dark. He says he doesn't know where in the house Zeke's family are being kept, and they believe him. They left the jeep back in the woods, off the road, concealing it between trees and under branches.

They've waited, giving the Colóns a chance to turn up. They can't wait much longer.

"Looks like it's just the three of us," Selena says.

Tom nods, looking toward the house. The whole while they've been here, he hasn't looked away. He's seen the Black Hawk parked on its crudely made helipad. He watches the men. The roaming guards. The windows. The doors. Watches everything. "We'll have to be careful," he says.

"We always are," Zeke says. He's staring at the house too,

grinding his jaw. He's staring at the windows, particularly. Desperate for a glimpse of his family. Desperate to know where they are.

"Plan of attack?" Selena says.

"Three of us," Tom says, "four corners of the house. I've counted twenty-seven men, and there are probably more inside the house and in those smaller houses. They look like they could've been transformed into barracks. We need to make a distraction big enough to draw them all out and away from the house. I'm thinking we start with the barracks. I'll strike there. I'll blow it up. The two of you go to the house, get inside, get Naomi and the kids out."

"Then we get back to the jeep," Zeke says, "and we get back to the plane."

"Ivor?" Selena says.

"Fuck him," Tom says. "Leave him here." Ivor is out of earshot. He can't hear them.

"All right," Zeke says. "Gear up. Let's move."

As Tom readies the Armalite, Selena taps him on the shoulder. She does the same to Zeke with her other hand. "Hold up," she says.

They stop and look at her.

"Listen," she says. "You hear that?"

Tom listens. He can hear something. It's faint. It's distant. Gunshots. A firefight.

"The checkpoint," Selena says. She looks to Tom and Zeke. She's smiling. "I think the Colóns have come."

56

J orge and Max are still together in Jorge's office when they get news of the attack. It comes from the checkpoint first, radioing through. Men come rushing to the office to inform Jorge.

"The Colóns?" Jorge says, getting to his feet. He exchanges looks with Max. "Go," he says, waving a hand at the men. "Sound the alarm – if they're coming en masse, the checkpoint doesn't stand a chance. They'll be here within minutes. Oh, and tell Oscar." He glances at Max again. "Tell him where we are."

The men hurry away.

"This is problematic," Max says. "This is the last thing we need right now."

"Mm," Jorge says, frowning. He goes to the nearest window and looks down. It doesn't take long before he sees the men rushing out, mobilizing, preparing for the incoming threat. The Colóns will come from all angles. The men – *his* men – are prepared for this. They're prepared for everything.

He's trained them well. They've run drills for just such an occurrence.

Oscar comes to the office. "Max," he says. He looks to Jorge. "I didn't realize we had company."

"He just got here," Jorge says. Oscar doesn't need to know how long Max has truly been in the house.

"Looks like I got here just ahead of the trouble," Max says. He knows to play along.

Oscar looks doubtful, but he doesn't press things. "What's happening outside?" he says. "I was told we're under attack, but I wasn't told by whom. They said you asked for me to come here."

"It's the Colóns," Jorge says.

Oscar looks thoughtful. "I understood we were in a truce?"

"We were," Jorge says.

"Why would they choose to break it now? Has something happened that I'm unaware of?"

"If it has, I'm unaware of it, too," Jorge says.

Oscar smiles suddenly. "And we're *sure* it's the Colóns?"

"That's what we were told. The men at the checkpoint would have had the best view of them. Why are you smiling?"

"Because of the timing," Oscar says. "Have you spoken to anyone who has seen our attackers directly? I assume the men at the checkpoint are dead now."

"I would assume so," Jorge says. "And no, I haven't spoken to anyone else who has seen them, but they'll be here soon enough, and we'll be able to see for ourselves."

"There's nothing to say it's truly them," Oscar says. "It could be a ruse. Misdirection."

"A ruse?" Jorge blinks. "You think it's Rollins and Greene."

"It's them," Oscar says. "I can feel it. They've come to get Zeke's family. They've come to get *me*." He laughs. "And either they've recruited the Colóns against us, or they're here in disguise. It doesn't matter. We'll be ready for them either way, isn't that right, Jorge?"

Max is looking between them both. He's waiting to see how Jorge responds.

"Of course we will," Jorge says, because he doesn't have any other option. No matter who it is that's truly out there, advancing upon the house and coming for them all, they're in a fight for their lives here. There's no alternative.

"Good," Oscar says, turning on his heel.

"Where are you going?" Jorge says. "We're safest here. Men will be here soon to guard us."

"I'm going to get Naomi and the children," Oscar says without turning.

"I can have them sent for," Jorge says.

"No need," Oscar says. "I'm more than capable of doing it myself." He leaves the room.

Jorge and Max sit and stand in silence for a moment. Jorge stares at the door. When he turns to Max, he finds that Max is already looking back at him.

"This could be the opportunity we need," Max says. "Look at that – all of our problems, all of our birds, they've lined up. Sitting nicely in a row. And we have a big stone to knock them all down."

Jorge nods. He takes a seat. Max is right. This could be perfect for them, so long as things don't get too far out of hand. Jorge has faith in his men, though. *His* men. *His* army.

He has faith in the beauty of his future. He's driven by the opportunities that lie before him once this night is over.

"Yes," he says. "We just need to survive first."

Max grins. "And when you say *we*...?"

Jorge holds his gaze. "You and I."

57

The Colóns have taken the bait. They've reached the house. Battle has erupted.

Tom, Zeke, and Selena allow the two forces to become fully engaged before they leave the safety of the trees. They stay low, running in formation with their rifles raised. Soon they will separate. They're in touch via earpieces. With the arrival of the rival cartel, they revert back to plan A. The house is now their sole focus.

The gunfire around them is fierce. There are explosions. The Colóns are coming at the house from every angle except for the sea. They emerged from the trees. Tom and the others lay low in the branches of a fallen trunk when they realized they were approaching, holding still until they were clear. Ivor had sense enough to stay still and make himself flat, allowing the men to pass without trying to get their attention. Drawing them to him wouldn't have done him any favors. They likely would have shot him and moved on.

Tom feels the familiar rush of battle. Bullets fly overhead. He feels one cut the air in front of his face. He can feel the heat of the fires now burning. Can hear the screams of falling and injured men. Two men appear in front of him. It doesn't matter who they are or who they're with. He shoots them down with the Armalite, never breaking stride. Beside him, Zeke and Selena are the same. Anyone who gets too close, they drop them.

There's an explosion nearby. The impact knocks Tom off his feet, but he rolls with it, comes up onto a knee. There's a man opposite him, looking dazed. He's trying to push himself back up after the explosion. He's missing an arm, and the stump is spurting blood. Tom shoots him.

He glances around, wondering where the explosions are coming from. At the trees, he sees men lobbing grenades. He spots a couple of RPG-7s. A chunk is blasted out of the corner of the house. Tom sees a man's skull cave in with falling brickwork. He sees jeeps and cars spilling into the grounds, and heavily armed men jumping off the back of them and rushing into battle. From the house that Tom thought could be a barracks, Zavala's men are storming out. Some of them are gunned down before they can take more than two steps. Windows smash, and chunks are torn from walls. Tom gets back to his feet and presses on.

They're getting close to the house. They start to split, heading their separate ways. They all know where they need to go.

58

N aomi wasn't sleeping. She'd given up on finding escape, but she couldn't sleep. When the shooting started, she raised her head, not sure she was hearing it right. Glancing toward the door, which remained locked, she rolled out of bed and went to the window. She thought of her husband. Looking out, she wasn't sure what she expected to see – Zeke and Tom running across the grounds, guns blazing like Rambo? Instead, she saw a battle. Bullets blazing. Bombs going off. She couldn't see her husband or Tom. She could barely see the faces of any of the men out there.

Naomi moved fast. She didn't know who was attacking, but it didn't matter. She hurried back to the bed and roused the children. They were groggy, but they became alert at the sounds from outside.

"Get under the bed," she said, whispering. "Stay low. Cover your heads." She wanted them under cover, as low as possible, away from stray bullets.

They did as she told them. Naomi straightened and

adjusted their pillows, putting them under the blanket to look like they were still lying under there, sleeping. Naomi glanced back at the door while she worked, knowing it was only a matter of time before the guard came inside.

Now, Naomi stands close to the door, the toilet lid held tight in both hands. Her back is pressed to the wall. The guard hasn't come in yet. She's surprised. She wills him to enter. Outside, the fighting sounds like it's getting worse. Something rocks the house. She sees fire rise outside the window in an explosion.

The window shatters, and bullets thud into the ceiling and the wall. Naomi lets out an involuntary shriek. The sounds of the battle are louder now through the broken window.

The door begins to open. The guard is drawn by the gunfire. Naomi doesn't hesitate. She brings the cistern lid down hard on the back of his head. It shatters. The guard collapses. There's a large split in his scalp and the back of his skull. It bleeds heavily. Naomi doesn't focus on it. She hurries to Tre and Tamika and ushers them out from under the bed, scooping them both up in her arms and covering their eyes as she steps over the fallen guard. This could be their only chance to escape. They need to take it. Whatever is out there, no matter how bad it looks, is no worse than what awaits them in this house.

She kneels down before she leaves, plucking the guard's handgun from his holster. She's fired a gun before. Zeke has taught her. He's taken her to the range. She knows to stay calm and to aim for the center of mass. She hopes she doesn't have to use it.

In the corridor, Naomi expects chaos. Instead, she can't see anyone. The chaos sounds like it's all downstairs. She can hear men shouting in Spanish. Can hear heavy footsteps running out of the house, and doors swinging open and slamming shut. She can hear gunfire and windows being smashed. She thinks they're shooting out from inside the house. She wonders if they're besieged. If the Zavala men on the grounds have been overwhelmed, and they've fallen back to the house. If this was the case, she thinks they'd be upstairs, too. They'd be firing down from the windows up here.

She hurries down the corridor with the children, still carrying them. They need to find a way out before someone happens upon them. They can't go downstairs. They'll have to go out a window.

Naomi goes to what she thinks is the back of the house. At a window, she looks down. There are men nearby, but directly below them is clear. There's nothing for them to climb down, but there are bushes below. They'll break the fall. It'll hurt them, cut them up and bloody them perhaps, but if they're lucky, they won't break any bones. She puts Tre and Tamika down and tests the window. It isn't locked. She pushes the window open as wide as it will go.

A voice comes from behind her, down the corridor. "Naomi," it says, "are you leaving so soon?"

Naomi feels her stomach clench. Her heart leaps into her throat. She doesn't need to turn to see who is talking. She knows the voice. It's Oscar.

She grabs the children and forces them out the window. She hasn't looked back at Oscar. There's no time. "Into the bushes!" she says. "Run! Find somewhere safe to hide!" She drops them into the bushes below. She can't watch how they land. Can't see if they're hurt. Oscar is already upon her, his hand in her hair almost tugging it from her scalp. He takes the handgun from her and throws it to the side. He spins her around and pushes her up against the wall, jabbing his own handgun into her side.

"You silly bitch," he says. "Your children will die out there. Is that what you want? And if they are not killed, they will be found and brought back here. Brought back to *me*."

"I'd rather they took their chances out there than be anywhere near you," Naomi says, defiant.

Oscar grins. "You know, I'm excited to see what becomes of them. Will they survive? Will they not? What a thrilling mystery. We'll discover together, won't we? For now, you are more than enough."

He pulls Naomi away from the wall, still holding her by the hair. He presses the gun into her spine and pushes her on ahead of him.

59

Selena takes the east wing of the house. Rollins will take the west, and Zeke will go in through the rear. There's too much activity at the front of the house for any of them to hope to get in there. Once any of them gets inside, they'll find Zeke's family and get out. Naomi and the kids are the priority. Oscar Zavala, however, is a close second. If attainable, putting him down once and for all is also a goal. The three are in contact all the way.

Selena reaches the corner of the house and presses her back to it before she peers out. The fighting isn't so fierce here. She spots two men reloading, and she shoots them both. At this, gunfire erupts from further back, and she ducks into cover. Chunks fly out of the wall beside her where bullets impact. Selena holds tight. She waits. The shooting eases. They don't expect her to stay in one place. There's so much going on already, the shooter has likely already moved on.

She senses movement to her left and looks that way. Two men fight hand-to-hand, rolling with each other on the ground, grabbing at each other's throats and faces. Neither of them sees her. They're too wrapped up in trying to kill the other.

An explosion nearby throws up dirt, covering her in it. She blinks it from her eyes and spits it from her lips. Her ears ring a little, but she's not deafened. She peers around the corner. The two men she killed are lying on the grass, but there's no one else. The shooter is either dead or he's moved on. Selena raises the AAC Honey Badger and presses forward, scanning the area and glancing in the windows of the house, looking for a point of entry. She checks the upstairs, too, making sure no one is hanging out and pointing a gun down at her. She reaches a smashed downstairs window, and she pauses. It's been broken from the inside. Shards of glass lie on the grass below. The barrel of an AKM pokes out of it, resting on the sill. It's not firing. She can't be sure it's even shouldered. It could be waiting for someone to appear.

She steps lightly, approaching the window and the rifle. It twitches, and she knows someone is holding it. Selena holds the Honey Badger one handed, and with her other pushes the barrel of the AKM aside, away from her. She presses it to the broken frame and looks into the room, seeing the startled face that looks back at her. She opens up with the Honey Badger. The face disappears in a burst of red mist, the body dropping to the ground, the AKM going limp and falling with it. There's another man in the room, kneeling on the ground and loading up more weapons. He jumps to his feet, swinging up another AKM, but Selena quickly deals with him.

The fighting is thinner here. The sounds of gunshots are fainter. The sea is on this side of the house, and the cartel have not come from this direction. She sweeps the room again, making sure there's no one left. As she prepares herself to climb inside through the broken window, she hears movement up ahead, and she pauses, bracing. It's coming from close to the house, to her left. The rustling of bushes.

She lowers herself and knee walks closer, gun raised, pointing towards the noise. It's not an animal. It's too big. It could be someone injured, thrashing in pain where they've fallen, but she can't take a risk on being ambushed.

Then, through the branches of the bushes, she spots a face. A familiar face.

"Tamika?" she says.

The face turns to her but then turns away, scared.

"Tamika, it's me – it's Selena. You remember me, right?" Selena has been to Zeke's house. She's met his children and his wife. They've eaten barbecue together. The whole team was there.

Shaun was there.

Tamika looks again, and now a second face comes into view. Tre.

Selena looks around, making sure the area is clear, then hurries to them, waving them out. "Come here, come here," she says. "Get out of the bushes. Are either of you hurt?" She can see small grazes and bumps on both of them, but nothing serious.

"I cut my leg," Tamika says, showing her a bloody gash on the side of her left calf. It's not deep, and it doesn't worry Selena.

"That's okay. I can clean that right up," Selena says. "Tre, what about you? Are you okay?"

"I hurt my shoulder," he says, rolling his left to show which one it is. "But I'm okay."

"How did you get out here?"

"Mom pushed us out the window and told us to hide," Tre says, pointing at the window above them.

Selena can see that it's open. "Where's your mom now?"

"She's still inside," Tre says.

"Mr. Zavala took her," Tamika says.

Selena's throat tightens at the mention of Oscar's name. She gets in touch with Zeke and Rollins. "I have the kids," she says. "Repeat – I have the kids. Naomi is still inside. Zavala has her."

"Are they okay?" Zeke says. She can hear the simultaneous relief at her having found his children, and also the panic of knowing that they are separated from their mother.

"They're fine," Selena says.

"Do they know where Naomi is?" Tom says.

"She pushed them out a window into some bushes before Oscar took her away," Selena says.

"Get them out of here," Zeke says. "Get them back to the airstrip. Use the jeep. Me and Tom will continue into the house to get Naomi. We can find our own way back. For now, just get my children out of here."

"Got it," Selena says. "Good luck." She keeps an eye on the area while she talks to the children, making sure no one can sneak up on them, and also checking to see which way is clearest out. "Tamika, can you walk?"

"I think so," Tamika says.

"Good, good, do your best. Now, I need both of you to listen to me very closely, okay?" She's kneeling in front of them, eye level with them both. She holds each of them by a shoulder. "Tamika, I need you to hold your brother's hand as *tight* as you can. Tighter than you've ever held anything before, okay? And Tre, I need you to hold onto the belt loop in the back of my trousers, and I need you to hold onto *that* tighter than you've ever held anything before. Do you both understand?"

They nod.

"Good. Now, we're going to go that way." She points to the opposite corner of the house. "The fighting is mostly concentrated at the front of the house and across the grounds, but there are still men everywhere, okay? So it's going to be very dangerous. I need both of my hands so I can use this gun if I need to. You need to do everything the same as I do. If I run, you need to run. When I stop, you stop. If I get down on the ground, you do the same."

She looks into their faces. They're scared, but they're listening. They'll do whatever she tells them to.

Selena takes a deep breath. "If anything happens to me, run for the trees. Hide there. Make sure no one sees you. Your father and Tom will find you." She knows that if Zeke and Rollins get to the jeep and it's still there, they'll understand that something bad has happened.

Selena can't allow anything bad to happen, though. Not to her, and especially not to them. If she goes down, they go down. They can't survive out here on their own, and she knows the men fighting won't think anything of gunning down a pair of lost children.

She can't go down. She can't fall. They're counting on her. Everyone is. "Hold hands," she says. "And grab my belt loop, and get ready to run."

It's the most important run of their lives.

60

Oscar forces Naomi on to a part of the house she hasn't seen before. They reach a closed door, and Oscar bangs on it with his handgun. "It's me," he says, and then pushes Naomi in ahead of him.

It's an office. There are two men in it. She recognizes Jorge, who looks back at her. The other man, though, on the other side of the desk, she doesn't know. He's white. American, probably.

"I thought you had men coming here?" Oscar says, pushing the door shut behind them.

"I did," Jorge says, and then he exchanges a look with the other man that Naomi doesn't understand, but which nonetheless makes her uncomfortable. "But I thought they would be put to better use in the battle."

Oscar picks up on the exchanged glance, too. "What was that?" he says.

Jorge plays innocent. "What was what?"

"That look. The one between the two of you."

The American raises his eyebrows condescendingly.

"You're imagining things, Oscar," he says. "It must be the heat of battle. You've become unaccustomed to all this noise. It's making you see things."

"I don't appreciate your tone, Max," Oscar says. He glares at the American.

Naomi wonders who Max is, and what he's doing here. Max ignores Oscar's glare. He's looking at Naomi. "So this must be Zeke's wife, right?"

"That's her," Jorge says, sounding tired.

"It's a pleasure to meet you," Max says.

"Who are you?" Naomi says. She has no interest in his pleasantries.

"Max Ross," he says. Then, with a wink, he adds, "CIA."

Naomi feels like she's been slapped. She looks at Jorge and then at Oscar.

Oscar laughs and pushes her to one side. "Take a seat," he says. "On the ground will do. Back to the wall – I want to be able to see you." He glances at Max and then back at her. "I'm sure this is a surprise to you, to find that your government has betrayed you. And, more than that, your husband's employer."

Naomi doesn't know what to say.

"Where are the children?" Jorge says.

"She pushed them out a window," Oscar says, shaking his head.

"They're out *there*?" Jorge says.

Oscar laughs. "They're not going to last long. I don't know why she thought it was such a good idea."

Naomi notices that Oscar is still holding his gun. He hasn't put it away since he pushed her to one side.

Jorge notices it, too. "You can put that away, Oscar," he

says. "There's no need for waving it around in here. We're all friends here."

"Are we?" Oscar says, arching an eyebrow. "I'm not so sure. You may deny it, but I saw the look you gave each other."

"Maybe you *should* tell him, Jorge," Max says, looking across the desk.

Jorge hesitates.

Naomi watches them all with interest. The air in this room is charged. She can feel it, and she knows all of them can, too. Watching the three of them staring at each other, it feels like a standoff. It's like she's watching a Western. She clenches her jaw, very aware of the gun in Oscar's hand. If he starts to shoot, she has a chance to escape. He never locked the door after they entered. She can see a key in it, though. If she's quick, she could grab the key and lock the door from the outside.

"Jorge," Max says, and then repeats more firmly, "*Jorge*."

"Yes, Jorge," Oscar says. "What is our American friend referring to? Perhaps you *should* tell me."

"Or maybe you could *show* him," Max says.

Jorge stares at Oscar. Naomi thinks he's shaking.

"Goddammit," Max says. "I'll do it my own damn self."

Max moves fast. He reaches behind himself – for a gun, most likely.

He doesn't have a chance to pull it free. Oscar shoots him first. The gunshots are deafening. Naomi covers her ears. Oscar fires four times, all of the bullets finding a home in Max's chest. He convulses in the chair and then slumps to the ground onto his face.

The shooting galvanizes Jorge into action. He pulls out a handgun of his own, and he aims it at Oscar.

Oscar is already moving. Jorge fires at him, but his bullets hit the walls. Oscar fires back. Naomi sees blood spray from Jorge and hit the wall behind him. His left arm goes limp. The bullet hit him high in the shoulder. The blood looked like it came from close to his neck – his trapezium, perhaps.

Naomi doesn't hang around to see what happens next. While the two men are distracted, she makes her move. She lunges out the door, grabs the key, and locks it from the outside. She can hear more gunshots from inside the room. One of them punctures the door close by her head.

Naomi runs.

61

Tom and Zeke find each other upstairs. Tom got into the house and made his way past the men shooting out of windows. They were too preoccupied to turn and see him. There was too much noise for them to hear him. He came across a man rushing back to the front. Tom cracked him across the jaw with the stock of the Armalite.

Downstairs was too busy. The rooms were all occupied. Tom made his way upstairs, knowing that it's unlikely Naomi or Oscar are going to be down in the thick of the action.

Tom is checking in a bedroom when he finds Zeke. "Anything in there?" Zeke says.

"No," Tom says.

"Downstairs ain't clear, but it's too busy for them to be down there," Zeke says.

"My thoughts exactly. We start up here, work our way down."

They hear gunshots from the other side of the house. They're loud. They're not firing outside, down from a window. They came from inside a room. Tom and Zeke look at each other. They both know it's worth investigating.

They make their way down the corridor, rifles raised, stepping carefully. They don't get far. They hear footsteps approaching a corner up ahead, running toward them. They both stop and wait, ready to see who appears.

It's Naomi. She skids to a stop when she sees them ahead of her, guns raised. They quickly lower them, and Naomi sees who they are. "Oh my God – Zeke!" She runs to him, into his arms. Tom keeps the area covered while they embrace.

"Where are the kids?" Naomi says. "Do you have them?"

"They're with Selena," Zeke says. "She has them, and we're in touch with her. I just spoke to her – they're in the trees, they're almost at the jeep we came here in. She's getting them out of here."

Naomi's breathing is shaky. "Thank God," she says.

"How did you get free?" Zeke says. "We heard shooting."

"Oscar and Jorge," Naomi says, shaking her head. "And some American called Max – he said he was with the CIA. I don't understand what was happening between them, but they started shooting at each other. Oscar shot Jorge, but then I got out, and I locked them in. There was a lot more shooting. They might have killed each other."

"We need to check," Zeke says, looking at Tom. "We need to be sure he's dead."

"Get Naomi out of here," Tom says. "Get back to the kids. Contact Selena and tell her you're coming. I'll deal with whoever's left."

"I can't just leave," Zeke says. "I can't just leave *you*. And I need to know that this is over."

"You'll know it's over when I say it's over," Tom says. "Getting your family out of here is what's important. Get them safe."

Zeke doesn't want to go, it's clear, but he also knows he should. He looks to Naomi and then back at Tom. "We'll wait for you in the woods."

"No," Tom says. "Just go. I can find my own way back, one way or another."

Zeke hesitates, but then he nods grimly and does as Tom says.

"Which room is it?" Tom says to Naomi before they go.

"Round the corner and down at the end," Naomi says. "Last door on the left."

Zeke takes Naomi by the hand, and they head back the way Tom and Zeke came.

Tom advances down the corridor, rifle raised again. He's careful. Naomi said Oscar and Jorge might have killed each other, but there's no guarantee of this. Tom heads down the corridor, following Naomi's directions. He can see the door up ahead. Last one on the left. The door is open, though Naomi said she locked it. When Tom gets closer, he can see that the door has been kicked open. The jamb has splintered where the lock was forced through it. There is blood on the floor. Following its trail, Tom can see that it disappears into a room opposite. The door is closed, but there are smeared fingerprints around the handle. Tom glances into the room Naomi escaped from first. He can see two bodies. One of them lies very still. The other is Oscar. He's on the ground, crawling along like he's trying to reach something. Tom goes to him first. He'll investigate the blood trail when he's done here.

Oscar hears his approach and stops crawling. Tom sees what he was trying to reach. A Makarov pistol. Oscar is covered in blood. It's on his face and on his hands, and it soaks through his clothes. Tom can see a lot of blood around the room, too, and he thinks most of it must be Oscar's.

"It's you," Oscar says, and coughs. Blood sprays and coats his teeth. "Tom Rollins. You came."

Tom shoulders the Armalite and crouches down close to Oscar. He faces the door so he can see if anyone tries to come in. He pulls out the Beretta, but he doesn't point it. He lets it dangle.

"It's been so long since I saw you last," Oscar says. "But I've never forgotten your face. Or Zeke's. Where is he?" He turns away from Tom and looks to the open door. "Naomi must have reached him, yes? And here you are, left behind to finish me off."

Tom looks at him.

"All I have done to bring you here," Oscar says, and coughs again. Blood runs down his chin. "This was all for you and for Zeke. And for my family. And now only one of you is here, and just look at me. My most trusted and loyal follower, he turned against me..." He coughs, longer this time, degenerating into a fit. When he breathes, his breath rattles in his chest. He wheezes. "You're right here in front of me, and I can't even reach my gun." He glances at the Makarov. He doesn't have the strength to reach for it.

"I understand what it's like to lose people you love," Tom says.

Oscar manages to raise his face and meet his eye.

"If I lost my family the same way you did," Tom goes on, "I might react the same way you have. But I'd like to think that one thing I'd never do is endanger a man's family. Especially his children. There's no coming back from that. There's no coming back from any of this."

Oscar says nothing for a while. He coughs. He starts to chuckle. "I wish I'd gone down to the sea."

Tom doesn't understand. "Wherever you go now," he says, "I hope your family is waiting for you."

"I hope they're not," Oscar says. "They don't deserve to be where I'm going."

"I'll see you when I get there," Tom says.

Tom raises the Beretta. Oscar doesn't look away. He doesn't close his eyes. He meets his fate head-on. Tom squeezes the trigger and puts a bullet through his forehead.

62

Tom doesn't leave the house right away. He follows the blood trail. He assumes the blood comes from Jorge. The name 'Jorge Cruz' is faintly familiar, from back when they first took Oscar down. It would seem he rose high in Oscar's absence, right up until the point he and Oscar started shooting at each other.

Tom enters the room opposite the office, still following the blood. It's a cinema room. There are four rows of seats. Tom checks down every one. The room is empty. There's no one inside, either living or dead.

Zeke gets in touch through the earpiece. "Tom, be aware that Ivor is gone," he says. "He's no longer tied up."

"Roger that," Tom says.

"If he's got any sense, he should be trying to get away," Zeke says. "Is it done?"

"Oscar is dead," Tom says.

There's a moment of silence, and then Zeke says, "Okay. Good. We're setting off now. Don't take too long, Tom."

"I'll see you soon."

Next to the cinema screen, concealed in the wall, is another door. The blood trail disappears here. There is a bloody handprint on the wall next to it. Armalite raised, Tom goes to it. He opens the door. There's a bathroom. It's very bright and white. There is more blood on the tiles. The room is cold, and Tom can hear the sounds from outside's battle clear in here. The window is open. Tom goes to it. He looks down. It's clear below, but he can see a lattice attached to the wall directly outside, vines growing up it. On the lattice, he can see blood where Jorge has climbed down.

Tom climbs out the window and down the lattice. The battle still sounds as fierce as it did when he was in the thick of it earlier. He looks around, sweeping the area. He doesn't know what Jorge looks like, but he can't see anyone nearby. No one living, anyway.

He creeps along, sticking close to the house. He peers out at the battle. It's gotten worse since he last saw it. More members of the Colón Cartel have filed in. The barracks are burning. Bullets kick up the dirt near to Tom and slam into the wall beside him. He ducks back into cover. Tom can't cross the grounds to get back to the trees. He looks around.

The Black Hawk is nearby. It's been a long, long time since Tom last rode in a Black Hawk. He doesn't know how to fly one, but he knows how to start it up, and how to use its weaponry. He can see that it's angled toward the battle. Tom runs to it and makes sure it's empty. When he sees that it is, he climbs inside. Bullets careen off of its armored hide. He looks across the battlefield. It's wild and bloody, and it's hard to see anything in detail. Zeke and the others have to be clear by now. To safety. It's been a while since he saw them last.

The Black Hawk does not need a key. Tom flips the

switches to start it up and to send power to the weapons. He sees some heads turn as the rotors begin to spin. Before anyone can react, Tom fires missiles.

The grounds explode, throwing up grass and dirt, as well as men and severed body parts. He opens up with the fixed forward .50-cal guns, while still firing the remaining missiles. The nearest corner of the house is destroyed and begins to collapse in on itself. He sees the men on the grounds mown down, most of them disappearing in a burst of red. Everyone is open game. There is no one left here who Tom cares about. Colón and Zavala alike, he can kill them all.

He fires until the helicopter is out of ammo and missiles, and then he climbs out. He swings the Armalite back out in front of him and makes his way across the devastated grounds. The fighting is mostly over. He hears a couple of distant gunshots, closer to the house and around the corner from where the weapons of the Black Hawk could reach, but nothing nearby. When he reaches the house, he checks the nearest windows. He fires into them where he sees men and movement, but there isn't much. This part of the house has been destroyed.

Tom runs across the grounds, only needing to pause once to shoot down a couple of men on his way, leaping corpses as he goes. The Zavalas and the Colóns lie devastated, bodies mixed and mingling. The area stinks of fire, blood, death, and freshly churned dirt.

Tom needs to find a vehicle. He makes his way to where the Colóns made their arrival and began their assault. There will be vehicles there.

He needs to get to the airstrip, and then they can leave this nightmare behind.

63

Z eke wants nothing more than to hold his family, but they're not finished here yet. He needs to drive.

The road is clear on the way back to the airstrip. They pass the destruction of the checkpoint they earlier had to bluff their way through, the men lying dead at the side of the road and the barricade dismantled and left burning.

Cindy sees them coming. She hurries over to meet them as they pull to a stop next to the hangar. Zeke sees the way her eyes roam over everyone in the jeep. "Where's Tom?" she says.

"It's okay," Zeke says, "he's on his way. He just had to wrap things up."

Cindy steps back, though she doesn't look reassured. "Things got very loud back there not so long ago," she says. "Did you hear it?"

Zeke didn't hear much with the wind whipping past him in the open-topped jeep. "No," he says. "What did it sound like?"

"Explosions," Cindy says. "There's been a lot of explosions tonight, but these ones were different."

Zeke glances back the way they've come as if he'll be able to see anything. He can't. He gets out of the jeep and then takes both of his children from the back, holding them tight.

"Has there been any trouble here?" Selena says to Cindy.

"No, nothing," Cindy says. "Wayne's patched the Cessna back up. He just finished about ten minutes ago."

Wayne comes out of the hangar to join them. He sees Naomi and the kids. "Ah, good," he says, "are we all ready to go?"

"Not yet," Cindy says.

"We're just waiting on Tom," Zeke says.

Selena steps aside and tries contacting him via the earpiece. "Out of range," she says.

"What are you doing here?" Naomi says to Wayne, surprised to see him.

"I came to help," Wayne says.

"We needed a flight," Zeke says. "When Wayne heard what had happened, he didn't hesitate."

"Thank you, Wayne," Naomi says, looking at all of them. "Thank all of you."

"We should get in the Cessna," Wayne says, jerking a thumb back inside the hangar. "I can pull it out onto the runway ready for when Tom gets here."

Zeke puts the children down and tells them to go with their mother and the others. "I'll wait here," he says. "Keep the area covered."

"I'll wait, too," Cindy says. She doesn't explain why, but Zeke understands. She won't be able to relax until she knows Tom is back.

The others go to the plane. Zeke and Cindy are alone.

"I'm glad you were able to get your family, Zeke," Cindy says. "What about Oscar?"

"He's dead," Zeke says. "If we want details, we'll have to ask Tom." He watches the trees. Watches the road they just drove down. He hopes that the next person he sees is Tom. If it's anyone else, they're in another firefight.

Behind them, in the hangar, the Cessna starts up. Zeke can hear it coming out onto the runway, ready to depart. Zeke doesn't look back at it, and neither does Cindy.

"I'm glad I have my family back, too," Zeke says. "And I'm glad they're still alive." His throat is tight when he says the words. All this time searching for them, he's had to believe they weren't hurt. He's *had* to. Now, acknowledging that this whole thing could have ended up with him carrying their corpses back to America, the danger they were in feels too real. He doesn't know what his children and his wife have seen while they've been down here. He doesn't know what they've all been through. When they're safe, he'll ask. They'll tell. There might be therapy involved, especially for the children. And Zeke will feel guilty. A guilt he'll never be able to shake.

Cindy reaches out and squeezes his arm. "They're safe now," she says. "You saved them."

Zeke nods. He forces himself to laugh, trying to make light, and says, "What is taking him so long? He's always got to make an entrance, doesn't he?"

Cindy purses her lips and looks to the road.

They hear the sound of an approaching engine. They both perk up and simultaneously stiffen. Zeke raises his weapon, hoping he won't have to use it.

A car comes into view. A window comes down when it

sees them both waiting, and an arm comes out to wave. It's Tom.

He stops in front of them and gets out. Cindy runs to him, and they hug.

"You good?" Zeke says.

"I'm good," Tom says.

"Cindy says it got noisy back there. That you?"

Tom nods.

"And Oscar's one hundred percent dead?"

Tom nods again.

"Good. Then let's get the hell out of here."

They head for the Cessna waiting for them on the runway. Zeke leads the way. Tom and Cindy are behind him, walking together. Tom feels tired. The last few days are catching up to him. He hasn't slept much. And since they reached Honduras, he feels like he hasn't stopped moving.

Suddenly, Cindy is no longer beside him.

Tom turns. Ivor has Cindy. His left arm is across her throat, and his right is at the back of her neck. He's prepared to snap her neck. He keeps her body close to his, using her as a shield.

"Throw down your guns," Ivor says. "Do it now! Or else I'll break her fucking neck!"

Zeke notices that Tom and Cindy have fallen behind. He turns and sees what is happening.

"Throw yours down too, Zeke!" Ivor says. "Don't think I've missed that Beretta, Rollins. Give it here. Right at my feet."

Tom does as he says. Ivor picks up the Beretta and presses it to the side of Cindy's head.

"Zeke, throw down your fucking weapons!" Ivor says.

"How the hell did you get here?" Zeke says, disarming himself.

"I was here before *you*," Ivor says. "Hell, I was free of the tree the minute the three of you advanced on that house. I saw what was happening out there. It looked bad. I'm not hanging around. We're getting on that plane, you all clear? We're getting on that plane, and we're flying back to America, and if anyone tries to stop me, I'll blow this bitch's brains out."

"Let her go, Ivor," Tom says. "Let her go right now, and we'll take you on the plane."

"Do you think I'm an idiot, Rollins? Not a chance. Let's go. Come on – *move!*"

Tom backtracks toward the Cessna, not taking his eyes off Cindy and Ivor. They reach the plane and get inside. Selena, Naomi, and the kids stare at Ivor and Cindy. Wayne senses the silence and turns in his seat.

"Everyone stay calm," Ivor says. He sees Selena. "Pass your weapons over here. We don't need to have any trouble. We're just going to go home."

Selena looks at Zeke. He nods.

"No funny business," Ivor says. "Bring them over, nice and easy, and then we get going. You hear that, Mr. Pilot? Once her guns are over here, you start flying."

Selena sets her weapons down close to Ivor. He waves her away, telling everyone to get together closer to the front of the plane. "Let's go!" Ivor says. "Everyone sit down, come on! Make yourselves comfortable." Ivor remains standing, his grip still tight on Cindy.

Wayne turns around and begins takeoff. Ivor places his back against a seat to remain upright.

Tom has remained standing. The others are seated, but

they turn to look back at Ivor, all apart from Wayne, who focuses on flying.

"Don't you want to sit, Rollins?" Ivor says, smirking.

Tom ignores him. To Cindy he says, "Just hang in there." He braces himself as they ascend, and he sees Ivor doing the same.

They get into the sky, and the Cessna levels off. Tom's eyes have never left Ivor's.

"It's going to be a long flight for you if you don't feel like sitting down," Ivor says. "This situation ain't changing. You can quit giving me the stink eye."

Tom doesn't respond. He doesn't sit. He stares.

Selena sits up suddenly. She leans closer to her window. "Shit," she says. "I think we've got company coming up."

"What is it?" Zeke says.

"Helicopter," Selena says. "Looks military. It could be the Black Hawk from Oscar's."

"They're not armed," Tom says. "I emptied out their ammo. There's no chance they've had long enough to reload."

Ivor glances nervously toward the window. "Are you fucking with me? If there's no helicopter, I swear to Christ I'll kill her."

"Look for yourself," Zeke says.

"There's a goddamn helicopter out there," Wayne calls back. "Did you say a Black Hawk?"

"Can you outrun it?" Zeke says.

Wayne is thinking. "If I recall correctly, a Black Hawk can get up to 222 mph. Ordinarily, we could push 214, but right now we're doing 180, and I'm feeling a lot of drag – those bullet holes I had to patch up are slowing us down. So no, we can't outrun it. But Tom said they're out of ammo, right?"

"The men inside won't be," Tom says. "They'll probably try to get alongside us and shoot us down that way."

"Shit," Wayne says. "Looks like I'm gonna have to do some fancy flying while the rest of you figure out how to get it off our tail." Wayne turns his attention back to his controls. Tom and Zeke look at each other. They look back at Ivor.

"You'd better do as he says," Ivor says. "And work out how to take them down before they can do it to us."

Tom tilts his chin toward the weapons Selena placed near to Ivor. "Then you're gonna have to share," he says.

64

J orge has lost a lot of blood, but he's not dead.

Oscar's bullet clipped him through his trapezium. At the time, it felt like it caught him in the neck. Jorge thought he was a dead man. It wasn't until he reached the bathroom in the cinema room that he saw where he'd been hit. It throbs, and blood pulses out of it still. It's heavily bandaged, though the dressings are soaking through. It hurts when he turns his head.

After Oscar shot him, and Jorge was unable to immediately shoot him back, Jorge threw himself back out of his chair, but he managed to keep tight hold of his gun. He knew that if he dropped it, he was as good as dead. Out of the corner of his eye, he saw Naomi making her escape, and Oscar firing on the door she escaped through. Jorge scrambled around the desk, blood pouring from him. He was half-convinced he was already dead. Throwing himself out of the corner, he fired on Oscar, filling him with bullets, determined to take him down with him.

Jorge felt like he could be sick. He stared at the hot gun

in his hand, unable to believe what he had just done. He'd shot Oscar. *Oscar.* The man whom the last few years of Jorge's life had revolved around. And for what? All the effort to keep his organization intact, and to break him out of a prison in Mexico, just so he could kill him?

Except Oscar wasn't dead. He groaned on the ground and tried to move. Jorge went to him. He pointed the handgun at his head. Oscar was on his back, looking up at him. He grinned. "I don't know if I should be disappointed or impressed," Oscar said. He laughed.

Jorge's arm shook. He wanted so badly to squeeze the trigger. To finish him off. This man he looked up to – this man he *worshipped.* This man he freed. This man he built everything for.

Jorge couldn't do it. He couldn't pull the trigger. Looking at Oscar, and the blood coming out of him, he was as good as dead anyway. Jorge left. Behind him, he could hear Oscar chuckling on the ground. Could hear him moving still, and when Jorge last looked back, he saw him crawling toward his gun. He wouldn't give up. *That* was the man Jorge knew. The man he remembered so fondly. Jorge was proud of him, but he knew their time together was at an end.

Through the cinema room and into the adjoining bathroom. In front of the mirror, Jorge checked how bad his wound was. He saw the blood splashed on the side of his neck and face, and running down his arm, soaking into his clothes. It was bad, but he didn't think it would kill him. Not so long as he found medical attention soon.

He made his escape from the house out the bathroom window, climbing down the lattice. He didn't want to risk going downstairs inside the house and running into a rival, or Rollins or Greene, or even Naomi. He didn't have the strength to defend himself. Outside, at least, he could hide.

Stumbling to the edge of the house, he saw some of his men – *his* men – in formation and firing across the grounds into the trees. There were six of them. Jorge called them to him. They surrounded him, keeping him safe. One of them applied pressure to his wound while another emptied out a med-kit and got to work patching him up.

And then everything got very loud. The Black Hawk destroyed the grounds, cutting down friend and foe alike. It destroyed the corner of the house closest to it.

When its barrage finally ended, everything seemed so much quieter. The men protecting Jorge shot at some surviving members of the Colóns, but then they carried Jorge behind the house, into cover, away from the Black Hawk. A couple of the men went to investigate, and came back reporting that it was empty, and that the battle was over.

With his weight supported, Jorge inspected the damage. He looked across the field at the dead bodies. At all of the destruction. The house looked ready to collapse in on itself. The other houses on the grounds were burning. The fighting was over. There were only brief skirmishes here and there, where the remaining Zavala men picked off the remaining Colóns.

No, Jorge thought to himself. *They're not Zavala men anymore. They never truly were. They are* Cruz *men. They are* my *men.*

Except there weren't many of them left. Jorge's eyes burned as he looked upon everything he had worked for, in ruins. The worst thing he ever did was free Oscar.

He remembered Max, lying dead in the office. He

thought of the CIA and the deal that was made with them. Everything he could have had. They wouldn't want him now. They wanted him for his power and influence, and in one night, it'd all gone away. The Americans would find someone else. They'd forget all about him. His sacrifices would have been for nothing.

He closed his fists tight, for the first time in his life feeling a burning hatred for Oscar Zavala. The single-minded, misguided son of a bitch. He cost Jorge *everything*.

"What do we do now?" one of the men said, looking to him. They were all looking to him. For instruction. For guidance.

Jorge looked at the helicopter. "Let's get out of here," he said. "There's nothing left here for us anymore."

"Where will we go?" someone asked.

"Somewhere new," Jorge said, after a pause. "Somewhere we can start over."

Jorge and the six men got into the Black Hawk. One of them knew how to fly it. He took the controls and instructed another to get in beside him and do as he was told. "Without a proper co-pilot, it might get bumpy," the pilot said. "But I'll get us away from here."

Jorge sat with the other men. He rested his head and closed his eyes, tired from the blood loss. Tired from it all. He heard the rotors come to life, cutting through the air. He felt them begin their ascent.

And then, soon after, he felt his arm being shaken. One of the men handed him a headset. The pilot was talking to him. "There's a plane not too far from here," he said. "A Cessna. It looks like it's just taken off."

Jorge sat up. "Nearby?"

"Looks like it's coming from the Colón airstrip," the pilot said.

Jorge thought. It was hard for him to think straight. He was dizzy and tired. He put it down to the blood loss. Two words stuck with him – *Colón airstrip*. Rollins and Greene needed to find a way into Honduras, and then the Colóns broke the truce and attacked the house. A coincidence? Jorge doubted it. Had they come to some kind of agreement? Jorge wasn't sure, but it didn't matter. He didn't know who was on that plane, but that didn't matter either. Whoever they were – whether they were Rollins and Greene, or members of the Colóns, it was clear they were enemies.

"Go after them," he said.

"We don't have any weapons," the pilot said. "They were used up."

"Go after them!" Jorge said. "We have rifles – work something out! I want that plane out of the sky!"

And now Jorge sits braced, watching through the front window, seeing the plane finally coming into view. They're gaining on it. It's not as fast as they are. He motions to the men in the back with him. "Pick up your weapons," he says. "Shoot it down."

65

The Cessna lurches. "They're trying to get alongside us," Wayne calls back.

"They're going to try to pull beside us and shoot us down with their rifles," Tom says. "You can't let them do that, Wayne."

"I'm working on it!"

Tom turns back to Ivor, raising an eyebrow. "You heard what they're trying to do," he says. "You need to let us use those guns. If we're not armed, we're sitting ducks. They're going to shoot us out of the sky. And then none of us are getting back to America."

Ivor deliberates.

"You can't take long on this," Tom says.

"Take the Honey Badger," Ivor says. "Only you, Rollins. Zeke, you stay right where you are. I'm not an idiot. As soon as you shoot them down, you put the gun down, right back here beside me."

Tom nods. He comes forward, reaching for the weapon.

"Uh-uh," Ivor says, tightening his hold on Cindy. "Keep it slow. No sudden movements."

Tom holds up his hands and does as he says. He moves slowly. He still has his KA-BAR. Ivor didn't notice it when he told him to hand over his weapons. Tom was in no rush to point it out to him.

Suddenly, the plane lurches. At the front, people are thrown sideways and out of their seats. Tom almost falls. He manages to steady himself on a seat just behind Ivor and Cindy. Ivor, however, has both of his hands full. He starts to topple sideways. His right arm, holding the Beretta, straightens out to steady himself on the side of the plane.

Cindy takes her chance. She throws her elbow back into Ivor's crotch. Tom sees it happen. From behind, he slams the back of his elbow into Ivor's head. He falls forward. Cindy gets out from under him. Zeke grabs her and pulls her clear.

Ivor brings the Beretta round. Tom pulls out his KA-BAR. He drives the point of it through Ivor's wrist, pinning it to the side of the plane. He screams and drops the Beretta.

"I can't keep ahead of them!" Wayne calls. "They're catching up!"

Tom looks back. Through a window, he can see the Black Hawk coming into view. "Take us up!"

Wayne does as he says, taking the Cessna higher.

"Everyone hold on!" Tom says.

Ivor looks at him, confused, but then Tom punches him across the jaw, dazing him. He pulls the KA-BAR from his wrist and drives a knee into his stomach to double him over. There's not much space to maneuver. Tom goes to the rear door. He pushes it open. He feels the wind instantly suck at him, threatening to pull him out. Tom braces his shoulder against the side of the door and with his left hand holds onto the railing above.

"What the hell!" Wayne says. "We're going down!" He looks back. "Close that fucking door!"

Tom can see the Black Hawk below. Ivor sees it, too. He struggles, fighting back. Tom sticks a thumb deep in his eye. He feels it shift as Tom takes a deep hold in the socket. Gripping Ivor's head, Tom throws him out of the plane.

Ivor flies through the air. The wind has him. Tom knew getting the aim right was next to impossible. He did his best. Now, he wills Ivor to connect with his target. A moment later, he hits the Black Hawk's rotor blades. The helicopter begins to spiral. The pilot can't regain control. It goes into a tailspin. Tom battles against the Cessna door to get it closed. As much as he'd like to, he can't stand and watch the Black Hawk's inevitable crash. The wind whips against him, trying to drag him out of the plane. Tom holds the door one-handed, still bracing himself with the other.

"Close it!" Wayne says. "Close it now!"

Tom is trying. He strains at the door with all of his strength. It's closing, but slowly.

Then Zeke is beside him, on the other side of the opening. With the right side of his body, he braces himself, and with his left hand he grabs the door. Together, they're able to pull it shut.

Tom falls back. Zeke stays beside the door, propping himself up on the plane's wall. They're both breathing hard. Cindy descends on Tom, wrapping him in her arms. "You crazy bastard!" she says, holding him tight.

"The helicopter's down," Wayne says, leaning to the side to look back out his window. "Ain't nobody survived that."

He zeros in on Tom. "That was a hell of a fucking move – you're lucky it paid off!"

Tom laughs. He *feels* lucky. He stays where he is on the floor and holds Cindy just as tight.

Zeke slides down the wall. He places a hand on Tom's shin, and he squeezes. "Take us home, Wayne," he says, looking to his family and smiling. "Take us home."

66

They get back to Shreveport late. Tom, Cindy, and Selena spend the night at Zeke and Naomi's. Cindy and Selena share the bed in the spare room. Tom takes the living room sofa.

Wayne didn't accompany them. He stayed back at the airstrip. He wanted to get his dog back. "Tammy doesn't like being separated for too long."

Zeke shook his hand. "I owe you, Wayne. Anything you need. Any time."

Wayne patted him on the arm. "I'll hold you to that," he said, winking. "And don't think I won't."

Despite how late it was when they all went to bed, Tom wakes early. He doesn't get up. He stays where he is on the sofa, ruminating on the last few days. This feels like the first time he's stopped moving. It feels like this is the first chance he's had to think.

Soon, he'll go home. Back to Hopper Creek. Back to Hayley.

Home.

Even after all this time, it feels like a strange thing to say. Tom didn't have a home for a long, long time. He had places he stayed. The road was his home. And now he has Hopper Creek and Hayley. His new home.

And when he gets back there, it will still be in ruins after the attack by Oscar's men.

He hears footsteps on the stairs. Whoever's approaching is trying to be quiet so as not to disturb him. He raises his head. It's Zeke.

"You're awake too?" he says.

"For a while now," Tom says.

Zeke comes down the rest of the way. "Everyone else is still down for the count," he says. "Tre and Tamika slept in our bed. They wouldn't go to their own rooms. You wanna come outside?"

Tom gets up, and they head out onto the porch. They each take a seat.

The sun is rising. The sky is golden and getting bluer and bluer. Tom can't see a single cloud. Neither man says anything for a while. They enjoy the peace. The early morning stillness. The rising warmth in the air. The *silence*.

It's not complete silence. There is the distant sound of vehicles rumbling on the far-off highway, and some neighbors are rising and heading out to work. In comparison to the last few days, however, it's the most peace either man could hope for. Tom knows that Zeke can feel the hum of the fight deep down inside him still, just like he can. The explosions that ring in his ears. The hard pounding of his heart and the heavy pumping of his blood.

Tom speaks first. "Do you think this ended with William, or could it have gone higher?"

Zeke sighs. "One way or another, I'll know soon enough.

My gut tells me it ended with William. There was no one waiting at the airstrip for us, there was no one here watching the place when we got back last night. There's no one watching right now. I've checked. I know you've checked. Selena has checked. No one's watching my home. There's no one on this street who shouldn't be."

"If it went higher," Tom says, "are you worried?"

"No, I'm not worried. *They* are. They know I can get the story out if I need to. And they know, same as I do, that *you're* out there somewhere. Anything bad happens to me, you're gonna be first on the scene."

"That's right," Tom says.

They fall into silence again. They listen to the birds. This time, Zeke is first to talk.

"What next?" he says, looking out across the neighborhood.

"Are you asking me that?" Tom says. "Or yourself?"

"Both, I guess." He looks back at his house. "I loved this house, Tom," he says. "It's the only home my children have ever known. And now that love is gone. This home is destroyed. We're going to have to leave." He sighs again. "We can't ever be comfortable here again."

"I'm sorry," Tom says.

"It is what it is. Occupational hazard. How's Hayley?"

"We haven't had a chance to talk in a while."

"When are you going back?"

"We're going to head out later today."

"You and Cindy?"

"Yeah."

Zeke looks back at his house. "So," he says. "When you get back to Hopper Creek, what's the plan? I can't stay in my home. I know it's the same for you. You and Hayley gonna stay in Hopper Creek, or do you think you'll go further afield?"

Tom doesn't answer.

"That's a loaded silence," Zeke says.

"I'm just thinking."

Zeke doesn't press him.

"I think there's a bigger issue at hand," Tom says.

Zeke grunts. "The CIA."

Tom nods.

Zeke sets his jaw. "Looks like I'm leaving two homes."

"You thought about what you're going to do instead?"

"I haven't had a chance yet. I don't know what else I *can* do. I'm not like you, Tom. I can't just up and leave everything else behind. I have a family. I need to take care of them."

"I know."

"I'm gonna need some time to think. I have savings. They'll keep us going for a little while. Buy me some time. And then...who knows?"

"You'll figure it out," Tom says. "Don't sell yourself short. You've got plenty of skills, and anyone would be lucky to have you."

"I'll let you know how the search goes." He falls silent. "I should have got out when you did, Tom. I feel...betrayed."

"I understand. They let you down in the biggest way imaginable. If anything had happened to Naomi and the kids..."

"I would've burned them down," Zeke says.

"I would've been right there beside you."

"I know you would, man. I know you would."

They sit in silence. They let the morning pass, and the people inside the house sleep. More cars are passing by now. There is more activity in the neighborhood.

"You're gonna take Cindy home?" Zeke says.

"Yeah."

"Naomi asked me something. I was gonna say 'last night,' but it wasn't last night when we got back. It was the early hours of this morning. But she asked me if there's something going on between the two of you."

"We're friends."

"That was a quick answer."

"It's a question I've been asked before."

"That so? Well, shit, man, what does that tell you?"

"It doesn't tell me anything. We're friends."

"I'm not pushing you, Tom. I asked Naomi why she asked, and she said she always sees you with Cindy, but rarely with Hayley. First and last time she saw Hayley was your birthday. And Cindy was there. But listen, what you do is your business. How *are* things with you and Hayley?"

"They're fine," Tom says. "But that feels like you're pushing."

Zeke holds up his hands.

Tom doesn't dwell on the questioning, or whatever anyone else might think. He keeps his mind clear.

"They're gonna be waking up soon," Zeke says.

"They're about due."

"Should we get them breakfast?"

"Yeah, we should," Tom says, pushing himself up from the chair. "When we're already up this early, it's the least we can do."

EPILOGUE

Tom has been back in Hopper Creek a couple of weeks. He's been busy. He's repaired the house. Hayley has stayed with her parents while Tom worked. She came back home a couple of nights ago. Tom told her about Zeke's plans to move out, of his discomfort at staying in the same home the Zavala men had broken into.

"This has been my home for a long time," Hayley said. "I'm not moving just because some assholes shot it up."

They haven't spoken much since Tom returned. There is a tension between them. The last two nights when they've been in bed, she's lain on her side with her back to him. The rest of the time, she's at work.

Tom has quit the bar. Hayley doesn't know this yet. He's packed his bag, too. She doesn't know this, either.

She's on a day shift. She gets back at eight in the evening. Tom is waiting for her when she comes through the door. "We need to talk," he says.

"I'm tired, Tom," she says. "Can it wait?"

Tom looks at her. She looks back at him. Tom feels an

ache in his chest. She doesn't look at him the way she used to. She's not happy to see him. She looks at him like he's a stranger in her home, and she's not sure what he's doing here.

"I don't think it can," he says.

Hayley rolls her eyes and takes a seat. Tom sits beside her. He gets straight to the point. "It's time for me to go," he says.

She's surprised by this. "To *go*? Go where?"

"To move on."

She blinks. "You're leaving?"

"It's time."

"And how have you decided that?"

"It's not safe for you with me here. Since I got here, your life has been in danger so many times. You were nearly cut up for your organs. You were nearly shot when men came here looking for me. Oscar came out of my past, and I wasn't expecting him. I've made a lot of other enemies, Hayley. What if they come looking for me? What if they come looking for me and you're caught in the middle? I can't put you at risk like that, not again."

Hayley stares at him. Her eyes are wet, but she's not crying. She sniffs. "Where are you going to go?"

"I don't know. I never do."

She takes a deep, long breath. "And this mystery destination you have in mind," she says. "Are you going there with Cindy?"

"No, I'm not," Tom says. "I'm going there alone, wherever it is."

"Don't lie to me."

"I wouldn't."

"No? Then tell me this – is there something going on between you and Cindy?"

"No, there's not."

"Uh-huh. *Could* there be?"

Tom hesitates. He's not going to lie. He doesn't answer.

"Then I think that's as much answer as I need." A tear runs down the side of Hayley's face. She wipes it away. "I loved you, Tom," she says in a small, strained voice.

"I'm sorry, Hayley," Tom says. "I thought...I thought I could make it work here. That this was what I could grow to want. A quiet life, in a quiet town. But now I don't think I can ever have that. I'm not sure if I *want* to. But I know I don't want the people I care about to get hurt because of me. I care about you. I can't put you at risk anymore."

"I'm not going to beg you to stay, Tom," she says. "But what is it you *do* want? Do you want to die out there in the wilds where no one knows you? Do you think you're, you're – some kind of Viking, looking for an honorable death, and you won't stop until you find it? You can stop, Tom. You don't have to always look for trouble, for the next fight and the next cause. You can just...*stop*."

Tom doesn't say anything for a while. "I can't stay here. I won't put you in danger."

"If that's what you need to tell yourself, Tom," Hayley says. She doesn't look at him.

Tom's bag is down the side of the sofa. He stands, picking it up. "If you ever need me –"

"I won't."

"Okay."

She glances at his bag. "Is that all you're taking?"

"It's all I need."

A silence falls. The same, tense silence that has existed

between them for the last couple of nights, but now there is less of an edge to it. Now they both know where they stand. What they have been silently expecting to happen has come to pass, and there is some relief to this.

"Goodbye, Hayley."

There's a pause, and then she says, "Goodbye, Tom."

He leaves the house. She doesn't try to stop him. Doesn't walk him to the door and wave him off. He doesn't expect her to. He goes out to his car and slings his bag onto the passenger seat. He takes one last look around the neighborhood. He takes one last look at the house. The windows are empty. The door is shut. This place was home, except it never truly felt like home. He's not sure if anywhere ever will.

Tom gets into his car, and he drives away.

ABOUT THE AUTHOR

Did you enjoy *Search and Destroy*? Please consider leaving a review on Amazon to help other readers discover the book.

Paul Heatley left school at sixteen, and since then has held a variety of jobs including mechanic, carpet fitter, and book-shop assistant, but his passion has always been for writing. He writes mostly in the genres of crime fiction and thriller, and links to his other titles can be found on his website. He lives in the north east of England.

Want to connect with Paul? Visit him at his website.

www.PaulHeatley.com

ALSO BY PAUL HEATLEY

The Tom Rollins Thriller Series

Blood Line (Book 1)

Wrong Turn (Book 2)

Hard to Kill (Book 3)

Snow Burn (Book 4)

Road Kill (Book 5)

No Quarter (Book 6)

Hard Target (Book 7)

Last Stand (Book 8)

Blood Feud (Book 9)

Search and Destroy (Book 10)

Ghost Team (Book 11)

Full Throttle (Book 12)

The Tom Rollins Box Set (Books 1 - 4)

Printed in Great Britain
by Amazon